THE STOLEN LETTER

ALSO BY PAIGE SHELTON

SCOTTISH BOOKSHOP MYSTERY SERIES

The Cracked Spine

Of Books and Bagpipes

A Christmas Tartan (a mini-mystery)

Lost Books and Old Bones

The Loch Ness Papers

COUNTRY COOKING SCHOOL MYSTERY SERIES

If Fried Chicken Could Fly

If Mashed Potatoes Could Dance

If Bread Could Rise to the Occasion

If Catfish Had Nine Lives

If Onions Could Spring Leeks

FARMER' MARKET MYSTERY SERIES

Farm Fresh Murder

Fruit of All Evil

Crops and Robbers

Red Hot Deadly Peppers (a mini-mystery)

A Killer Maize

Merry Market Murder

Bushel Full of Murder

DANGEROUS TYPE MYSTERY SERIES

To Helvetica and Back

Bookman Dead Style

Comic Sans Murder

THE STOLEN LETTER

Paige Shelton

MINOTAUR BOOKS
New York

This is a work of fiction. All of the characters, organizations, and events portrayed in this novel are either products of the author's imagination or are used fictitiously.

First published in the United States by Minotaur Books, an imprint of St. Martin's Publishing Group

www.minotaurbooks.com

Library of Congress Cataloging-in-Publication Data

Names: Shelton, Paige, author.
Title: The stolen letter / Paige Shelton.
Description: First edition. | New York : Minotaur Books, 2020. | Series: A Scottish bookshop mystery ; 5
Identifiers: LCCN 2019049216 | ISBN 9781250203878 (hardcover) | ISBN 9781250203885 (ebook)
Subjects: GSAFD: Mystery fiction.
Classification: LCC PS3619.H45345 S76 2020 | DDC 813/.6—dc23
LC record available at https://lccn.loc.gov/2019049216

First Edition: April 2020

10 9 8 7 6 5 4 3 2 1

For my sweet dad

THE STOLEN LETTER

ONE

I must really love my job. There was no other explanation for my happy, hurried footsteps. I couldn't wait to get to work.

I hadn't been inside the most wonderful bookshop in the entire world for the last two weeks. Instead, I'd been with the most perfect man on the most perfect honeymoon. We'd seen more of Europe than I ever thought I'd see when I first moved to Scotland just over a year ago. Of course, I also hadn't planned to meet Tom Shannon, Scottish pub owner, and then marry him. Sometimes, it's all about the surprises. Maybe it's always about surprises, but it takes a few big ones for us to notice. And, boy have there been some *big* surprises along the way. It's been better than I could have ever anticipated.

I leapt off the bus and set out in a quick pace. But then I skidded to a stop and took a deep breath. I'd quit having moments of staggering awe, moments when I wondered if it was all really . . . well, real, a while ago. I had accepted that it was okay to be so happy, to be grateful for all the amazing moments that had happened since I'd answered an online ad about a job in an Edinburgh bookshop. Was I up for an adventure? A secretive sort of job in a bookshop with a coveted place behind a desk that had seen the likes of kings and queens? Oh, yes, it seemed I had been. And here I was.

As I stood there in Grassmarket, I looked toward the shop, The Cracked Spine. Nothing about its façade had changed since Tom and I had had our wedding inside. The awning above was still there, and I could see a couple stacks of books on the other side of the window. I'd put those stacks there, and I'd been the one to organize them. I always did the window displays, and this one had been about a color. None of the books in the window were part of our rare or valuable collections. They were used books, some of them I'd read, some I'd never heard of; only a few of them spoke to me. I'd used books with blue covers, and from this vantage point I thought the stacks were still exactly as I'd arranged. If that was the case, none of the books had sold, and though the shop seemed never to have any financial challenges, I decided I needed to redo the display, create something that would better sell a book or two. I could do that.

The owner of the shop and my boss, Edwin MacAlister, had plenty of money. There really was no need to worry about the financial future of the Cracked Spine, but, still, we were there to sell things.

The Tudors hated to be wrong, and therefore never were.

I blinked at the bookish voice. I looked around. It was a strange comment, coming to me from some place I didn't understand.

The Tudors? The royals?

Had that really been my intuition speaking to me as it did sometimes, through the books I'd read? If so, I didn't remember the book, and I didn't have a sense that I needed to be listening to my intuition. All was well, or so I thought. Maybe someone had actually spoken to me, or I'd overheard the words.

I looked around. Nope, that didn't seem likely.

I plunked my hands on my hips and looked toward the bookshop again. I didn't know what exactly had just happened, but I didn't dwell on it long.

My eyes scanned over to the bakery, its front window fogged around the perimeter from the early morning baking. I could imagine the delicious smells, and I decided to pick up breakfast. I didn't know if everyone would be in this morning, but Rosie would be there, with Hector, the miniature Yorkie she cared for but was worshiped and waited on by all of us. A thrill zipped through me at the prospect of seeing them both.

Hamlet might have class, but he'd be in at some point, even if only for a little while. A student at the University of Edinburgh, he was a young man, and had become much like a younger brother to me now. He'd been gifted with an old soul and named appropriately. If reincarnation was a real thing, there was no doubt in my mind that Hamlet had hung out with Shakespeare himself, had probably given the old bard a run for his money, maybe even did some editing.

It was doubtful Edwin would be there. He didn't come in as much as the rest of us, and since he'd started dating a restaurant owner from Ireland, Vanessa Morgan, he'd been around even less.

I decide to see who was inside the bookshop first, and then get breakfast accordingly.

I set out again, forgetting about the strange bookish voice and enjoying the temporarily clear skies above the lively morning crowd. Old Town Edinburgh and Grassmarket drew tourists from all over the world, and this morning the square seemed busier than usual. I was back to doing fine in my fog of happy. Until I ran into someone else who'd probably been enjoying her own version of a beautiful morning.

"Lass, watch where you're goin'," she said.

"I'm so sorry," I said.

The woman had dropped the books she'd been carrying. We both got to work picking them up.

Books, lots of books. I was curious about the titles, but we had too many to retrieve to take the time to look closely. There were no dustcovers, no protection on any of them, and the old, hard bindings all seemed to have damaged spines and worn corners. In all, we gathered thirteen well-worn books. It was quite a load.

"Can I help you carry these somewhere?" I said as I balanced five of the books on my hip.

My voice fell off as I looked at her. It couldn't be possible. For an instant I wondered if I was looking at an older version of myself; had this person I was looking at traveled back through time just to give her younger self a stack of old books?

The woman might have been twenty years older than my thirty-one, but her hair was identical to mine, both the bright red color and the frizzy texture; it rained far too much in Scotland to worry about trying to tame it.

But the similarities went even further. Our blue eyes were the same tint of diluted sky, and we both had too many freckles.

"Goodness, are you seeing what I'm seeing?" she asked, her accent as light at Edwin's—or I'd just become so used to the range of accents that I no longer really noticed the lighter ones anymore. "If I'd had a daughter, I'd wonder if you were her."

I smiled. "The resemblance is . . . uncanny. I'm Delaney Nichols."

We both held too many books to shake hands.

"Mary Stewart," the woman said with a nod. "At least we don't have the same name. That would have been quite the conundrum."

"I agree."

For a few seconds, we just looked at each other. There was no denying the resemblance, but we stared long enough that it was almost weird.

"Can I help you get these somewhere?" I said.

"I'm looking for a bookshop. I was on my way to it." She looked behind her, down the longer part of the Grassmarket square, the area toward Tom's pub. The Cracked Spine was at the other end, along a shorter street.

"The Cracked Spine?" I said.

"Aye, that's the one." She smiled. "Do you know it?"

"In fact, I do. Come with me."

Mary walked next to me, and I wondered if we looked odd, the two of us, with matching flaming hair and freckled skin, both carrying books as we made our way toward the bookshop. At least I was in slacks and she was in a dress. Chances were that everyone was in their own world, but I couldn't stop glancing over at her. She kept glancing at me too. We smiled curiously at each other.

The sign on the bookshop's door had been turned to Open. I peered in through the window as I balanced the books and reached for the door handle. Rosie was at the front desk, and I was suddenly struck by two things: I was once again infused with excitement to be back, but even with only that brief look at my grandmotherly coworker, I knew something was wrong. Maybe something just wasn't as right as it needed to be, but the pinch at the corners of Rosie's eyes and mouth told me that at least something wasn't normal. She was upset, but I'd have to wait until we were alone to ask for details. I pulled the door and the bell above jingled.

"Lass!" Rosie said as she smiled big and came around the desk. "Ye're back!"

"Rosie, Hector." I placed my stack of books on the table that held the blue-book window display. I wasn't going to ignore Hector's quick approach, no matter what else was going on. I picked up the small dog and let him whine happily at me as he licked my cheek. It was so good to see them that, momentarily, tears burned behind my eyes. As I still held onto Hector, Rosie and I hugged tightly.

"Hello there," Rosie said to Mary when we disengaged. "Are ye a relative of our dear Delaney?"

"No," Mary said.

"Rosie, this is Mary Stewart," I said. "We ran into each other out in Grassmarket. She was looking for the bookshop. Mary, this is Rosie."

"Aye?" Rosie said. "Nice tae meet ye. And the two of ye ken ye look alike?"

"Aye," Mary said.

"Yes, we noticed."

"Well, that's . . . interesting." She stared at Mary a moment and then turned back to me. "How was the honeymoon? Was it . . . romantic?"

"The most romantic," I said with an exaggerated dreamy tone. But then I remembered we had a guest and cleared my throat.

"Oh, that's lovely," Rosie said.

"Congratulations!" Mary said, still holding books and smiling at the happy reunion she witnessed.

"Thank you." Reluctantly, I handed Hector back to Rosie and turned to Mary. "Here, let me take those. You were on your way here to see if we want to purchase the books?"

"I was." She handed over her stack.

I carried the books to Rosie's front desk and then retrieved the ones I'd brought in.

"You work here, and you just got married?" Mary said as she followed me.

"Yes, and yes."

"You're from America though? That's what I'm hearing in your voice."

"I am. I moved here a year ago for this job, and it looks like it all . . . stuck, I guess." I smiled as I placed the second stack next to the first one on Rosie's desk and put a hand on top. "Are you from around here?"

She hesitated a long beat before she answered. "Aye, in a way."

"Born somewhere else?"

Mary smiled and lifted her eyebrows. "Many times."

In matching perplexed, and frozen poses, Rosie and I looked at her and blinked.

Mary waved off her comment and laughed. "I was born in Scotland, but spent a lot of time in France."

"Aye," Rosie said doubtfully, still probably caught back at Mary's strange comment.

I jumped in. "Is Hamlet here?"

"No, he'll be in later today though," Rosie said.

"Okay." I turned back to Mary. "Well, tell me about the books. I'd love for Hamlet to see them too, but Rosie and I can take a look."

"That's lovely. Thank you," Mary said. She glanced at the

book on the top of the stack. "They're not overly valuable, but I think they're worth a little something. And they're all about Elizabeth I."

"Elizabeth I of England? Elizabeth *Tudor*?" I said.

"Aye," Mary replied.

I listened for the bookish voice again. It didn't speak, but I looked at the book under my hand. It was titled *His Last Letter: Elizabeth I and the Earl of Leicester*.

I would bet that the words I'd heard were inside this book. I must have read it at some point. I must have somehow seen Mary before I ran into her. My eyes could have skimmed over her and maybe even the spine of the book, so my subconscious could push it all to the surface. I *had* been in a haze of excitement and happiness, post-honeymoon bliss.

"Delaney?" Rosie said.

I looked at her and then at Mary. "Yes. Well, let's have a look."

All thirteen of the books had been published since 2000 and they were all in less than ideal shape. But there were people who might be interested in them. I had reshelved all the books in the shop, making specific sections. There were some Tudor shelves. I could easily make a subsection, a sub-shelf of books specifically about Elizabeth I. In fact, as I looked at the books Mary brought in, I wondered if I already had and just didn't remember doing it. Surely, I had seen and read at least one of these at some point—I couldn't let go of the voice. But things *had* been busy. The wedding . . . everything.

"I think we'd be interested," I said. "I'd like Hamlet to price them. Would you like to leave them here or bring them back when he's here?"

"No, no, I'll leave them. Just let me know. I'm not selling

them for the money. I just needed to clean off some shelves, make room for more, pass them onto other interested readers." Mary smiled. "Anything will be fine."

Even our smiles were similar.

"Do ye have time for a cuppa, some coffee?" Rosie asked.

She was curious about Mary. Though Rosie was generally welcoming to all our customers, it took someone special for her to offer refreshments.

"I would love some coffee," Mary said.

"I'll go," I said, meaning I would step over to the other side, the dark side, where the attached building held our dingy kitchenette, a few offices, and the warehouse. It had been Edwin's warehouse, the place he kept his assortment of collections, but it was mine now too. We shared equally when he was around, but when it was just me, it was all mine. It was the place that also held the desk that had been mentioned in the ad, the desk that had seen the likes of the kings and queens. Even on my honeymoon with the most amazing man, I'd missed that desk. I'd missed my job, my coworkers. I'd missed the warehouse.

"All right. Ta, lass," Rosie said. She eyed Mary as if she was glad she was going to have her to herself for a few minutes.

I set off up this side of the stairs, and moved through the door separating the sides, opening it and then closing it behind me. We never left it open. The warehouse was no longer the secret it had been for decades, but we didn't advertise its existence. The dark side wasn't as cared for as the light side, and we didn't want curious customers exploring on their own. It wasn't well lit, and the stairs on this side weren't swept often. The police knew about the warehouse, and my family had been given a tour. Tom and my landlords, Elias and Aggie, had seen it, but we didn't broadcast the fact that there was a big room at the back of the building containing lots of stuff, at least a smattering of which were priceless items.

I'd become so accustomed to the cooler air on the dark side, the dusty smells, that I didn't always notice them. But, today, after being gone for two weeks, they seemed obvious. I rubbed my hands over my arms and shivered once.

The bare lightbulb didn't illuminate when I flipped the switch. I stood on the landing a long moment, flipping it up and down and looking perplexed up at the bulb. It hung from the high ceiling at the bottom of the stairs. A tall ladder would be needed to change it, and I wondered how long it had been out.

With only a few lines of natural light coming in through the dirty windows in the front and the one on the back wall, my eyes took a few seconds to adjust as I made my way down the stairs.

I bypassed the kitchenette and grabbed the keyring holding the oversize blue key from my pocket. With three adept turns to the left I unlocked the heavy, ornate, red door and pushed through.

Home. The warehouse. These lights came on when I flipped the switch. My desk and a worktable took up most of the middle of the space, shelves extended up all the way to short, wide windows at the top. These windows weren't grimy and gave me great sunlight and moonlight when the clouds weren't thick, and kept me semi-aware of the time of day.

Mostly, I did research, cleaning, archiving. But strange things had happened inside the warehouse too—not often enough to worry about, but I'd lived moments of confusion and wonder inside the small, jam-packed space. And, today, I sensed . . . something wasn't right. Something was off about the whole day so far, Maybe this was just normal back-at-it anxiety.

I looked around more slowly and with some extra focus. It appeared that nothing had been disturbed in the last two weeks. The shelves were still loaded with books as well as all the items Edwin had collected over the years. My life and work had been interrupted by Nessie herself before the wedding and the two weeks away, but before all that had happened, I'd been researching the origin of three small tapestries. Edwin had thought they'd been in Queen Elizabeth I of England's bed-chambers.

The theme of the day was only continuing. I paid close attention, in case any of the bookish voices wanted to pipe up. They remained quiet.

The tapestries were on one of the shelves—I'd cleared off the shelf and placed each individual tapestry inside its own protective and chemical-free archive folder. I squinted toward them. They looked to still be there, undisturbed.

A cursory glance told me the desk and worktable were fine, and my chair seemed to be tucked in exactly as I'd left it. It took a second, slower inspection to notice what was different.

My desk wasn't ever messy, but it usually had a few books or folders atop it. I'd left two books on a corner so I would remember to show them to Edwin when I returned. They weren't valuable but were both written in the old Scottish language, Gaelic. I knew Vanessa was intrigued by everything Gaelic, and I thought she might enjoy them. A note had been placed on top of the books.

"Oh," I said aloud as I reached for it.

Delaney—When you return, remind me to tell you all about the Burgess Tickets. Hope the honeymoon was as perfect as the lovely wedding. Always—Edwin

"Burgess Tickets," I said. "Sounds good. I can't wait to hear the details."

I placed the note back on the books and looked around one more time satisfied there was nothing else out of place or noticeably wrong. I sniffed in the dusty, old smells and wished I hadn't offered to get the coffee. It was good to be back, and I just wanted to stay right where I was.

Nevertheless . . .

I flipped off the light, closed and locked the door, and hurried to the kitchenette. Thankfully, the light in there was working too.

Balancing the tray back on the light side, I veered around a half wall that separated the front of the bookshop from a back corner that held a table. This was where Hamlet did most of his work, and where we had meetings or visited with customers. The walls in the corner were lined with wood file cabinets packed with documents Edwin had purchased or collected, or customers had sold to us. Hamlet did most of the document work, but I did a little.

As I caught Rosie's eye, I remembered the last time we'd been gathered around that table. It had been at the wedding. We'd had the reception at Tom's small pub, but we'd exchanged vows and had cake in the bookshop. It had been some back and forth parading along Grassmarket, but it had been fun. And my parents and brother had been in town for the special day. They were now back in the States, and I missed them.

Rosie's expression garnered my full attention. She was sending me some sort of unspoken communication. Her eyes grew wide with what I thought might be disbelief. She didn't look at me long enough for me to understand what might be going on, but she spoke up quickly.

"Delaney, Mary here, though she spells her name S-T-E-W-A-R-T, has the same name as a woman she thinks she used tae be."

I put the tray on the table. "I don't understand."

Rosie smiled patiently at Mary as Hector sat on Rosie's lap. Even the dog's attention was firmly and curiously aimed toward our guest.

Mary looked at me. "I was just telling Rosie about . . . well, I'm certain I've lived many lives."

"Oh. That's interesting," I said as I sat too.

"Aye, and . . ." she looked at Rosie and then back at me, "well, I believe that I lived one of my lives as a Scottish queen."

The facts came together quickly in my mind, once I zeroed in on a few things.

"Mary Stewart," I muttered. "Sounds just like Mary Stuart. Mary, Queen of Scots!"

Rosie and Mary nodded.

I sat forward and leaned my arms on the table. "You think you were once Mary, Queen of Scots?"

I didn't know if she was impressed by my apparent knowledge of the once and martyred queen, or if she was just satisfied that I now knew, that she'd shared the part of her that was the most difficult part to share.

"That's correct," she said admirably. "In fact, I'm certain of it. No doubt in my mind."

I meant no disrespect, but my response was not that of a polite Kansas farm girl. It wasn't polite no matter where I'd come from. Even across land and sea, I could sense my mother's disapproval when all I did for a good long few moments was laugh.

TWO

"I am so sorry," I said, horrified by my behavior but unable to rein it in as quickly as I should. "Please consider this embarrassing reaction a nervous laugh, not a laugh-laugh."

Mary smiled. "It's okay. I'm fully aware that my circumstances are difficult to believe and understand. Imagine my own surprise when I realized I'd lived more than one life. I didn't go searching for past lives, but they found me anyway."

"And how did that happen?" Rosie asked.

I looked at Rosie. She was someone who believed in the Loch Ness Monster, had believed even before . . . well, before we found things that *might* convince even the most skeptical of doubters. With Mary, she seemed both surprised and interested in what she had to say, but perhaps disbelieving, doubtful. Maybe I wasn't reading her correctly.

"Oh, it's a long story," Mary said. "But it started with dreams. I dreamt things I knew I'd never heard or read about before, so I started studying. There came a time when I became educated enough about some particulars that I couldn't trust the dreams anymore, but my beliefs built from there. Dreams and self-education led to things I can only describe as memories." She put her fist to her chest. "It all became a certainty, but I can't pinpoint exactly when. I understand how that can be difficult for anyone who hasn't been through it to believe."

"Sometimes people can become certain of things that arenae real anyway, sometimes they've convinced themselves," Rosie said.

"Of course." She looked at Rosie. "I'm one hundred percent certain though, and I can prove it."

"Aye?" Rosie said.

The bell above the front door jingled.

"Please give me a moment," Rosie said. She stood, and with Hector in tow, they went to help a couple customers.

It was just us two doppelgängers at the table now. Mary looked at me a long moment. I had questions, plenty of them, but they weren't organized in my mind.

"Look at us," she said filling the silence before I could. "I mean, any other day, had I stopped by, you and I might not have met. Your coworkers might have made some comment about how I looked like you, asked me to come back in to meet you, but who knows?"

I sat forward. "Do you think it's fate that we met today, or maybe something to do with how you're tuned into your past life? It's more than one past life?" I said.

"I think it's more than one, but the only one I really remember is the queen's. To answer your question though, I think me coming here today is an example of how some mysteries aren't solvable, but happen all the time anyway, forcing us to pay attention to something we might have missed. I do think it was probably destined for the two of us to meet, Delaney. I've been thinking about taking the books to a used bookshop for almost two years. What if I'd brought them in before you arrived?"

"I have been here a year."

"Except for the last two weeks, or when you might have been out briefly for something else." Mary shrugged. "We ran into each other. Literally. It's a mystery that we may never quite understand. Consider this too—what if, and this is a doozy so I'm not saying I believe it but since anything is possible—what if my desire to take these books to a bookshop set the cosmos in motion to bring you here a year ago. We really do look alike. Perhaps the universe wanted us to meet, and since I was procrastinating, those universal powers sought you out?"

"Uh, that's pretty far-fetched."

"Aye, but don't you think that the notion of past lives is just as far-fetched?"

"Yes, but in a different way."

"Have you seen pictures of the queen?" Mary asked.

"Mary, Queen of Scots? I think so, but I'm not sure I've paid much attention."

Mary pulled out her phone and searched. A moment later, she held it up for me to see. "Look at her. Look at me, at you. See the similarities?"

There were similarities. The red hair, the pale skin, though I didn't notice as many freckles on the portrait Mary held up. The three of us did have somewhat pointy chins.

"Okay," I said. "But I don't have any past life memories."

"I'm not saying you also once lived as the queen, I'm just saying there must be something between the three of us. We might never understand it, but we were destined to meet, Delaney, I'm sure of it. Today, we might not understand why, but I suspect we might someday."

I smiled, my manners coming back. "Well, I think that's lovely."

"What if I could convince you that what I'm saying is real, that there is evidence that I am a reincarnation of Mary, Queen of Scots, Mary Stuart?"

"The proof you mentioned?"

"Aye."

I squinted at her. "I'm listening."

Mary laughed. "Not here. At my house. I'd like to invite you and your new husband for dinner. Rosie too. My husband and I would love to have all of you over. He's going to be just as surprised as you and I are, more maybe." She paused. "Your husband isn't tall and bald is he?"

I laughed. "Dark, curly hair. Blue eyes."

"Phew, Henry has brown eyes. Would have been even more bizarre if they'd looked alike, huh?"

I didn't know what to make of Mary. She was delightful. She was weird. But she wasn't weirdly delightful, which is a description unto itself. I was pretty good at quickly reading people, but I couldn't get a read on her. I listened for the bookish voices to come back and nudge me the right direction. Nothing. Maybe what they'd said before we'd run into each other was all they meant to tell me.

"That's very kind," I said. "I think we would enjoy that."

Rosie and Hector rejoined us after the other customers left the shop.

"We've been invited over to Mary's for dinner," I said. "She will show us her proof that she was once Mary, Queen of Scots."

"Aye? Sounds intriguing."

"How about tonight?" Mary said.

"Oh," I said as Rosie shrugged and nodded. "Well, I think that should be fine."

"Excellent. We'll continue this tonight. I look forward to meeting your husband."

Mary wrote down her address and phone number on a scrap piece of paper and gave it to me. In an oddly formal gesture, we shook hands. So did she and Rosie.

"Thanks for taking the books. I hope they sell," she said.

"I think they will," Rosie said as we all walked toward the front door.

"Rosie, please feel free to bring a plus one if you'd like."

Rosie nodded. "Ta, but it will just be me."

"I'm looking forward to the evening. Thank you again." Mary pulled open the door, and with one last smile she exited the shop.

Rosie and I looked at each other with equal uncertainty.

"She's an odd one," Rosie said.

"Yes. I'm looking forward to dinner."

"Aye, I think I am too."

"No Regg tonight?" I asked.

Regg and Rosie were an on-again, off-again couple. They were on again as of the few minutes before Tom and I left for our honeymoon.

"He'll be busy tonight." Rosie looked at me. "But, we're getting along verra well."

"Good. Okay, Tom and I will pick you up."

"Ye ken he's available?"

"If he isn't, he'll want to clear his schedule. I don't think he'll want to miss this."

"We might all be chopped up and thrown in her cooker."

I laughed, but then sobered when I saw Rosie wasn't smiling. "Really?"

"She's an odd one." Rosie repeated, but smiled now. "But I like the odd ones. I used to be one myself, I suppose."

"How's that?"

"Ah, maybe I'll share that story with ye soon." She reached down and picked up Hector.

I looked at the scrap of paper Mary had written her address on. Rosie slipped on her reading glasses and looked too.

"A lovely neighborhood." She squinted. "Look at the M in her name."

Mary had printed the words, all the letters legible and ordinary, except for the M in Mary. The two straight lines had extra lines added at their bottoms, perpendicular dash-like marks. It made the M fancier than the rest of the note.

"Hmm," Rosie said as she looked again. "321 *Leven* Court. That's interesting."

"Why?"

"Can we call up some internet information on Mary—the real Queen of Scots' version?"

"Sure." I pulled out my phone and quickly found the Wikipedia site. I handed the phone to Rosie; she scrolled and read.

"I thought I remembered that. The queen once escaped from Loch Leven castle," Rosie said.

"That's either a coincidence or she moved there on purpose," I said. "I can see forcing the similarities to prove a story."

"Lass, can ye see if there are samples of the queen's handwriting online?"

"Absolutely." It took only another second to find several examples.

Together Rosie and I inspected. The handwriting was identical, even down to the extra lines on the Ms. Not all of them, but many of the queen's Ms had those dash-like lines.

"I can't find this spooky yet," I said. "It could all be forced, on purpose. Googled," I said. "None of this is evidence."

"No."

I bit my lip and looked out the front window. There was no sign of Mary, and Grassmarket had become much less busy now that the morning rush had mellowed.

"Should we go or should we cancel?" I asked.

"Och, lass, I'm going. Some of yer adventures are simply too much for me, but I'll not miss this one. I'm intrigued."

"Sounds good." I plunked my hands on my hips. "Okay, I think it's time to either go get some breakfast or get back to work. Did I miss much? You looked deep in thought when Mary and I first came in."

"We missed ye, lass, and I'm glad ye're back. It would be verra unladylike of me tae ask any personal questions, but I do hope ye and Tom had a good time." She smiled.

"We had a great time." I winked.

"Oh, tae be young and in love." Rosie smiled and Hector barked.

Then Rosie's demeanor transformed, as if she'd lowered a curtain or turned down the lights. "But, aye, ye missed some . . . drama."

"I'm listening."

"I think we should sit down."

"Rosie?" I put my hand on her arm. "Tell me. What's up?"

We didn't sit down, but there's a chance we should have. I couldn't have been less prepared for what Rosie had to tell me.

"Lass, it seems as if . . . as if the bookshop is tae be shut down. We're going tae close."

Surely, I hadn't heard her correctly. I shook my head, once, twice. "Rosie. What?"

"Aye, t'is verra bad news."

It was almost the worst news possible.

THREE

"I don't . . . I don't understand," I said after my stomach returned from the plummet it took. "That's simply not possible. The bookshop can't close—not permanently. That can't be what you mean."

"Lass, that's preceese what I mean."

"Precesse?" I asked, hoping it was the Scots word for *not even close to.*

"Och. Precisely."

"I was afraid of that. Why?" I said. My muddled and shocked mind searched for a solution and the problem that might go with it. "I mean, if it's a matter of Edwin not wanting to work anymore, I can do whatever he needs me to do."

Rosie put her hand on my arm. "Lass, it isnae that t'all. Edwin would never choose to close the bookshop. There are apparently some issues with building codes."

"Building codes?"

Rosie frowned. "I should have let Edwin tell you. He has the details, and I'm afraid I'll tell it wrong. I'm sorry, lass, I've been thinking about it for a few days now. I should not have just dropped the news so inconsiderately." She smiled weakly. "At least I asked if you wanted tae sit down first."

"Oh, Rosie, the bookshop just can't close." I grabbed my phone. "I'm calling a meeting."

That's exactly what I did. I texted Edwin and Hamlet, requesting their presence as soon as possible—demanding it, actually. I didn't care if I interrupted important meetings or classes. I needed everyone there. I needed to understand what was going on. They greeted me with hugs and kisses on my cheek, but I didn't have time for such frivolity. I told everyone to sit at the back table, and I even turned the sign on the front door to Closed.

I began by asking what in the world was going on. In bits and pieces, they said the same thing Rosie had said, however, with more detail.

"We have structural issues, problems," Edwin said.

"Structural issues?" I said to Edwin. "What are the specific problems?"

"I'm still trying to understand," Edwin said. "I received a phone message a few days ago. It was a strange recording that said we were to be out of the building by the end of next month, that the inspector's findings regarding our building's structural integrity issues were ironclad. The final vote will set everything in motion."

"Final vote?" I asked. "Who's voting?"

Hamlet sat forward, placing his arms on the table. "The city is governed by a Lord Provost, similar, I believe, to an American mayor. Under that position is the City of Edinburgh Council. Councilors vote and make the sorts of decisions regarding building codes, et cetera. There is also a Parliament, but they are more involved with things like foreign policy and defense.

We have done some research regarding specific people and times, but don't have the answers yet. We are certain it's a council matter. The vote is scheduled to take place one week from today, next Monday."

I relaxed a little. "This can't be real. It's a scam or something. A phone scam. They happen all the time."

"We thought so too at first, but I looked online, and there *is* a final vote scheduled for one week from now," Hamlet said. "And, the agenda item lists The Cracked Spine specifically."

"What does it say?" I asked, my panic zipping back up to high alert.

"The Cracked Spine failed its building inspection and is deemed unsafe to continue operating within the city limits of Edinburgh. The vote will finalize the decision, or maybe it was formalize. Well, something like that. I can show you," Hamlet said as he began to scroll over his phone.

"Are there other buildings at risk? How many others?" I asked.

"Not that I could see."

"But, this building is fine," I said. "And Edinburgh—Scotland—is filled with older buildings, for goodness' sake!"

"Aye," Edwin said. "That's why I'm not too worried. I think we'll be fine. I am trying tae figure out the best approach tae get this taken care of. If all else fails, we'll be at the meeting, all of us."

"I can't find it right off," Hamlet said. "I will at some point."

I nodded at him and looked back at Edwin. "Do you know the Lord Provost?"

"I do, but he and I don't see eye to eye on a few things. We've not gotten along as of late."

"What's happened?"

"Some particularly old and lovely trees were taken out in Princes Street Gardens. The council voted, in the most secretive way possible to remove the trees, and they were gone soon afterward. Something to do with museum renovations not being possible without first removing the trees. I, along with many others, wasn't pleased. We've been vocal, and I'm afraid I overspoke my disapproval when I complained about the trees being removed. I used my friendship—well, acquaintanceship—with the Lord Provost to more effectively—at least in my opinion—vent my and the others' anger. I should have probably handled it better."

"Huh," I said. Edwin was all about the history of his country, his city. Trees would be just as important as buildings to him. But our building should be the most important to all of us.

"Aye," Edwin said. "Trees. They were around for hundreds of years, along the walkway to an oft-visited museum."

"By the gardens? Which museum?"

"Scottish transportation over the centuries. Fascinating."

"I haven't been there, but it does sound fascinating."

"Aye."

"Are we going to have to move the shop?" I asked, more whine to my voice that I would have liked.

Edwin and Rosie looked at each other quickly before they both looked at me again. Neither of them spoke. In fact, it seemed they pursed their lips more tightly.

"What?" I looked at Hamlet.

He said, "Delaney, this building is as important to the bookshop as the books inside it, almost as important as we are. The time, the history, the things it has been and seen. It's a whole being. This is where the bookshop was born, and this is where it will die—though, hopefully, not at the end of next month."

I got what Hamlet was saying, but I wasn't going to give up on the idea of relocation quite yet—if only to give myself *something* to hang onto. They'd had more time than me to process this information, but I wondered if they'd been as rocked at first as I felt now. I wanted to throw a temper tantrum.

Hamlet read my mind. "We're all upset, but we're trying to figure out the best approach."

"Does the council have regular meetings, something before the vote?" I asked.

"We couldnae find one scheduled earlier than the vote," Rosie said.

"That seems convenient, that they contacted you with no other chance to make our case." I shook my head. "Hang on. There was a building inspector's report? When was an inspector in here?"

"None of us remember an inspector," Edwin said.

"Then this just *can't* be real."

"We hope not," Rosie said. "We are proceeding as if it's something we need to fix though, or at least clear up."

"Of course. Me too. What should I do?"

"Delaney," Edwin said. "I left you a note in the warehouse . . ."

"Yes, I saw it. Something-tickets."

"Burgess Tickets. Aye. I wondered if you might have come across The Cracked Spine's. Historically, it was a certificate that was once used as a way of giving someone permission to do business in a burgh. It gave the holder the right to other things too; to vote, attend church service, and be an important part of the community. It's not something that's used any longer, but back when I opened the shop, I did receive one. By then it was more honorary, but nevertheless I'd like to find it."

"Will it keep us open?" I asked.

"I doubt it, but it might give me more ammunition, at least historically speaking. I'd like to have it."

"I'm not sure I would recognize something like that, but I don't think I've seen it."

"I haven't either." Hamlet looked toward his file cabinets and then back at the rest of us. "If we do have it, I think ours might be somewhere in my files, but I'm sure I haven't seen it. I've seen my fair share over the years."

"Well," Edwin said. "Everyone keep looking please. It might not trump a questionable building inspection, but it can't hurt."

"I'll look today," I said.

Edwin smiled and reached over the table to put his hand over mine. "I really do think it will be all right."

I looked at Rosie—she forced a smile. I looked at Hamlet—he frowned uncertainly.

"I hope so," I said.

What I didn't say, but what they certainly knew was that this bookshop was my life. Yes, I was now happily married to the most amazing guy ever, but my life was still *my* life. This bookshop was a big part of what made me the person I was, the person I liked the best, and it was probably the place that made me the best person I could be to everyone else around me. I loved these people. I loved Scotland. I loved this old building too. This had to be fixed.

"Lass, I do have money. If that's what it takes, I'll spend it." Edwin sat back again.

"Bribery?" I said. "That's a good idea."

"Well, I was thinking that maybe the building just needed reinforcement, some work done, but I won't rule out bribery."

"Good. Good plan."

I was willing to do anything, including spend Edwin's money.

"We will work on it," Hamlet said.

I sat back too and tried to think clearly. I wasn't there quite yet. I'd still need some time to get over the shock.

"Okay," I said. "Okay. That's good. I'm going to try to get to work, but if anyone comes up with any ideas, please let me know."

They all nodded.

"Very good. We will all work on it." Edwin pushed himself up from the chair. "I'm afraid I have to go for now though. I will be available on my mobile though."

"We'll keep looking for the ticket," Hamlet said.

"Aye," Rosie said halfheartedly.

I was the only one who seemed to notice her tone. I looked at her. She sent me a weary, quick smile that looked more like she was simply trying not to frown. I was glad I'd be with her this evening. If there was more to this that she wasn't saying in front of everybody else, I'd do my best to get it out of her.

We told Edwin we'd see him later, and the rest of us got to work.

I'd already noticed that other than Edwin's note, the warehouse didn't seem to have been disturbed while I'd been gone. Everyone who worked at the bookshop had a key, but it was a rare moment that Rosie or Hamlet visited. Rosie had been around for so many years that the walk over two flights of stairs didn't warrant the harassment to her knees unless she was also grabbing some tea or coffee from the kitchenette. Hamlet would stop by when he had a few extra minutes to chat, but those few minutes would usually grow to more; we could spend hours in discussion. Our last conversation had been speculation about space travel. It had been lively and we both decided we'd probably pass on a visit to Mars, no matter how curious we were about its inhabitants.

I did a cursory search for the Burgess Ticket, but I didn't find it, still wasn't sure what it might look like, even after I did some quick internet research. There wasn't one style, other than they all looked like official certificates, even the handwritten ones. I'd searched the file drawers in the warehouse enough times to be fairly certain there wasn't a Burgess Ticket inside one.

I was too wound up, too freaked out. I needed to channel my energy into something else for a bit, if only so I could think more clearly about our predicament.

I'd brought Mary's books over with me. I glanced at the stack and realized I was curious about her motives. All the books were, indeed, about Queen Elizabeth I, but none of them were specifically about Elizabeth's relationship with Mary, Queen of Scots. Mary *had* been the queen of Scotland, even as she lived some of her younger days in France, for twenty-five years, but Elizabeth had been the queen of England for a much longer time.

Elizabeth had been so influential that her name gave birth to an era—the Elizabethan era. It was when her sister died that Elizabeth was crowned queen. Her sister had been a "legitimate" child of Henry VIII, but because Elizabeth's mother's, Anne Boleyn's, marriage to Henry VIII had been annulled,

Elizabeth was considered illegitimate, though Elizabeth reigned anyway, for forty-four years.

Her status as illegitimate was what many held onto as the reason Mary Stuart should be the ruler of England, but, ultimately, most of the problems came down to their strong ties to their religions. One of the first things Elizabeth did as queen was to establish the English Protestant Church, dissing the old Catholic ways. Mary stuck with the Catholic church to the end. The internal and external struggles, indeed deadly battles included, because of the different religions and their ties to the rulers of the nations caused constant turmoil back then.

It was a volatile time. I shook my head as I thumbed through the last of Mary's books and skimmed the interesting fact that after Elizabeth's rule, it was Mary, Queen of Scots' son, James VI, who became the king of England. He turned out to be a well-liked king.

It was a sad, violent history, but part of what made the countries what they were today.

I set the books aside, gathered the tapestries I'd been working on pre-wedding, and brought them over to the worktable. They were small pieces, which wasn't the norm. Tapestries had served as castles' wall coverings, wallpaper, as well as insulation. Decorative in nature, they sometimes also depicted a story. The one I placed in front of me first seemed to be a story from the Bible, the story of Abraham. I knew that because Hamlet had somehow recognized the scene.

I was close to zeroing in on the approximate date it had been created. The stitches weren't even and identical, therefore, I'd determined that this one had been handmade. That determination had been as simple as looking through a magnifying glass at the stitches.

I counted the colors. Older tapestries could only be made using about twenty different colors, inks that dyed the thread being made from plant and insect dyes. With the magnifying glass again, I determined that there were only about twenty colors used on the tapestry, and some of the light blues were a little different than the other light blues. That sort of thing happened when dye ingredients weren't always consistent.

In my studies, I'd also learned that some dyes were still created using insects to this day. Most interesting to me, the cochineal, an insect that liked to live on cactus, was used to make dye that was still found today in some foods and lipsticks. The more I learned about certain things, the more I became concerned about what we consumed. I tried not to let it bother me too much.

As I now moved the magnifying glass over the top of the tapestry, two things happened at once. I thought I saw something that needed extra attention, and a bookish voice spoke.

Magesty, there is less danger in fearing too much than too little.

I stood up straight.

I had an inkling of an idea that I'd just read those words as I'd thumbed through Mary's books, but my looks had been cursory and tinged with the still overriding anxiety about the bookshop's fate. I wasn't sure I could find those words again. I blinked and wondered what the voice may be trying to tell me.

I had no idea. But I knew that I had also come upon something on the tapestry that wanted my attention.

I looked at it again and zoned in on a coat of arms. It was small. I leaned closer and put the glass over just the bottom right corner. Yellow, blue, and red, the coat of arms depicted three lions, though one looked like a dragon to me, guarding a crown. Semper Eadem adorned the bottom. *Always the same.* I ran over to my computer and googled everything to confirm that yes, this was Elizabeth I's coat of arms. Did that mean this tapestry belonged to her? Maybe. The time frame might work. Not machine made, handsewn, and simple ink. The elements were there to make me wonder enough to know I needed more research.

I put the glass down and tried to figure out what the universe, via the things and the voices, was trying to tell me.

And I had an idea of something. It was faded and far away, but the idea was filled with the news of the closing of the bookshop as well as the woman I'd met who looked so much like me and who thought she was once Mary, Queen of Scots. Were they all tied together? Working together? I was grasping for straws, *but there some something there*, I thought. I hoped.

Maybe Mary really had been onto something when she thought it was destined that she and I meet. Maybe she, the bookish voices, and the tapestries were all part of the equation to keep the bookshop open for business.

Something about the timing made me think I needed to pay close attention, put that universal equation together correctly. I would do my best.

Hopefully, dinner that evening would tell me more.

FOUR

Tom had spiffed himself up. After a day at the pub and a number of soccer (football) match crowds, their attention on the television as they cheered and sloshed their drinks incessantly, he'd come home and given me a fly-by kiss before hitting the shower.

"You clean up so nicely," I looked up from the papers I was reading as he joined me in the front room.

"Ta, my love," he said with a small head bow. "You're lovely tonight, as always."

I'd put on a dress and a little eye makeup. It was more than I usually did. "I'm probably wrinkling sitting here, but I got so interested in this article. It's about some Mary, Queen of Scots' documents found tucked away in a box in the museum. Joshua hasn't said a word about them, but, of course, he has no way of knowing about today's turn of events."

Joshua was a good friend, a young and brilliant post doc who worked at the National Museum of Scotland. We shared a love of old things and both enjoyed walking slowly through museums; really slowly.

Earlier in the day, I'd called Tom from the warehouse, and told him about meeting Mary, the strange possibility that the bookshop might be closing, and the tapestry discovery. He thought Mary and the tapestries sounded intriguing, but he'd mostly had questions and concerns about the bookshop. Along with the rest of us, he couldn't quite understand what was happening, couldn't believe it might happen while being so very afraid that it could.

"Mary, Queen of Scots' documents? About her?" Tom said.

"No, written *by* her. Journal entries, things about collecting taxes, tasks that went along with being the queen," I said.

"Aye?" he said. "In a box, in the museum cellar?"

"I don't know where the box was in the museum, but isn't it weird that it's in today's, of all days, paper?"

"Aye."

"It's astounding that any of her papers survived."

"It really is," Tom said. "How did they not disintegrate, or fall apart?"

"They weren't bothered, I guess, by humans or the environment," I said. "I'm really not sure. Maybe Joshua will let me look at them."

"You might not want to tell Mary that you know someone at the museum who could show you real Queen of Scots' papers. She might bother you to come along."

"Maybe she can tell me what they say before I even look at them," I said with a half smile.

"If she's telling the truth, maybe." He glanced at his watch. "Time to gather Rosie?"

"Let's go."

We were living in my cottage, not Tom's house as we'd expected to do. The electrical system in the old blue house by the sea had gone on the fritz, so Tom and I'd had to move out before we'd even moved in, just so the issues could be fixed. It was too cold in Edinburgh to live someplace where there wasn't heat, especially when there was a place that had plenty of heat—as long as we remembered to feed the machine on the wall that regulated the electricity with the proper amount of coins. But, that wasn't necessarily true either. My landlords and friends, Elias and Aggie, made sure the machine was always topped off. They didn't know I knew, but I knew.

We were enjoying the cottage, but it was a small space. I wondered if Tom would quickly grow impatient with the tight quarters, but he seemed fine so far.

We were newlyweds; we still hadn't quite figured out the timing of some of our routines, like getting ready for our days, cooking, cleaning, relaxing. Those things that come with time were still to be figured out some. They would be for a while, but I was enjoying every moment. It seemed Tom was too. Not once had he behaved as if the walls were closing in. Not once had I sensed that he regretted committing himself to one person.

We knew each other well, had almost lived together before we were married. But married and actually living together with that piece of paper were different, not by much, but it was sometimes noticeable. So far so good.

Elias and Aggie were thrilled we were there, no matter how temporarily. I half-wondered if maybe they'd sabotaged the blue house's electrical system just so we'd have to stick close by. They denied doing as much when I'd teased them about it, but I'd caught the quick look they'd shared: *not a bad idea*.

I hoisted myself up off the couch and smoothed my dress. I felt particularly girly.

Tom didn't hesitate but immediately pulled me close. "You are the loveliest woman I've ever seen. I can't believe how lucky I am that you're mine."

I pulled away slightly and looked up at him. "Well, this is probably all a dream and soon I'm going to wake up in my parents' house in Kansas. I'm going to be highly disappointed that none of this was real, but it's made a wonderful dream. Maybe a wizard and a tornado will be involved."

Tom smiled. "You're also adorable."

"Thank you, sir. You are not so bad yourself."

For a small moment, there was a good chance we'd miss the dinner, but we moved past it. We'd made the commitment and we'd told Rosie.

Tom sighed. "Shall we go meet the queen?"

"We shall."

Rosie lived in a flat not too far away from the bookshop. She and Hector could walk to work or jump on a bus for a quick ride. She preferred walking, but the bus was a good option for rainy days.

Tom parked in a spot directly in front of Rosie's building and joined me as we went to gather her. There were only two apartments above what was most recently a souvenir shop. From what we could discern, it looked like it was about to become a hair salon. Rosie said it had been many different things over the years, but the owner of the building, her landlord, had been very fair as rents had increased throughout the city.

Rosie had worn a lovely new dress for our wedding, but other than that day, I'd never seen her so dressed up as she was tonight.

"Och, Tom, marriage looks good on you," she said as she opened her door.

"Thank you, and you look lovely, Rosie."

"Ta. Come in, say good evening tae Hector, and then we'll be on our way." She turned and the pleated skirt of her purple dress puffed as if it wanted badly to twirl. I would have bet she had already twirled, at least once.

Rosie's flat was made just for her. A small front room, a small kitchen, two small bedrooms, and one small loo. Her fluffy furniture was covered with bright fabrics and a mish-mash of brightly colored pillows. More brightly colored throw rugs decorated the wooden floors. Edwin liked to call Rosie's flat, the most colorful place in Scotland. Though packed with stuff, it was always clean, tidy, and smelled like she'd just washed dishes—there were never any dishes in sight.

Hector was napping on his favorite pillow on the couch; a red one with gold fringe. He sat up lazily and looked perplexed at Tom and me. Once he recognized me, he jumped off the couch and ran into my outstretched hands.

"Hello," I said. "You don't see me here very often, do you?"

He seemed pleased. Once he was done greeting me with his signature cheek kisses, he looked over at Tom. Hector had become used to seeing Tom but hadn't quite accepted him into the family yet.

Tom reached over and scratched behind Hector's ears.

"Ye ken his weakness," Rosie said.

"He and I are going to be grand friends one day, but I don't think that day has come quite yet. I'm ready, but I think he's still wondering," Tom said.

"Soon," Rosie said.

I tried not to laugh at her doubtful tone as Tom and I shared quick smiles.

Once in the car, I asked her, "Rosie, is there something

more going on with the shop? I've told Tom all about it, but it seemed like you were trying to tell me something more with your eyes today."

"No, lass, there isnae anything more really, but I was trying tae tell ye something maybe." She paused a long thoughtful moment. Tom and I glanced at each other but didn't interrupt. "It's that, I dinnae think that Edwin's got the fight in him anymore. He kens how much we all love the bookshop, but he's old, lass. Maybe it's time for him to retire, at least that's what he might think. He also has Vanessa now. They seem tae be getting along verra well. I think they might want tae travel."

"We'll let them travel." I turned around in my seat and looked at Rosie. "We'll even let him retire. That bookshop can't close, Rosie, but not just because I don't want it to. I've thought about this all day, and the shop is so much more than Edwin, so much more than all of us. It's a part of the lifeblood of the city. Edwin knows that, he just might need to be reminded."

Rosie smiled a little with her mouth but fully with her eyes. "I was hoping you'd see it that way. It'll be up tae ye tae figure it out, lass. I'll help in any way I can, but ye will have tae do the legwork. Hamlet will help too, but he's so busy with school. Are ye up for the fight?"

Tom laughed once and looked at Rosie in the rearview mirror. "She's up for the fight."

"I am," I said. "I've never been up for a fight so much in my life."

And I was. *I would fight to the end,* I thought as I turned back around.

As Tom drove toward Mary's house, Rosie regaled us with a story about the "old days" with Edwin, one that she'd just remembered today for reasons she would soon illuminate. Apparently, there was a time when Edwin unknowingly befriended a bank robber. There were no cell phones in the 1970s and a storm had taken out the bookshop's phone. The "friend"—*let's call him Joe*—showed up one evening as Rosie was getting ready to close for the day because of the terrible storm and the flickering electricity.

Joe, drenched and seemingly bothered by something, hurried into the shop with a bag over his shoulder. He asked Rosie if he could keep the bag in Edwin's secret room. But, though Rosie knew Edwin and Joe were unquestionably friends, Rosie knew Edwin hadn't confirmed to him about the warehouse's existance. Back then, Edwin hadn't told anyone but Rosie about the warehouse.

When Rosie told Joe no and indicated that he had to go, he became agitated. Rosie, much younger *those years anon,* didn't have any patience for Joe and she became firm in her request that he get out of the shop immediately.

Their confrontation became physical, but even though Joe was bigger, Rosie was a "tough lass" and she punched him in the nose. He dropped the bag and ran out of the shop.

"Aye?" Tom said as he looked at Rosie in the rearview mirror.

"Aye, but the rest of the story is even better. I kept the wee bag. Well, I had Edwin put it in the warehouse."

Tom and I shared another look. "Was there money in the bag?" I asked.

"Och, aye. The bag was full of coins with Mary, Queen of Scots, on them. They're verra valuable, I would guess."

"Really?" I said. "What happened to the bag of coins?"

"Last I heard Edwin put them in the warehouse. He told Joe tae leave town, leave the country, and he wouldnae turn him in."

"Why didn't he just call the police or return them anonymously?"

Rosie shrugged. "Sometimes Edwin thinks he kens better than the law, than anyone. When he was younger, he was even surer of himself. I do remember we couldnae figure out where they'd come from, and then at some point we just quit wondering, moved onto other things."

"Do you think we could find the coins?" I asked.

"Depends on if Edwin kept them. He might have later returned them and just didnae tell me, and this is why I wanted tae tell the story. Edwin would want the coins returned, even after all these years have passed. Ye and Edwin need tae discuss it. Our visitor and our host this evening made me remember them. If they havenae been returned, Edwin would want that done, as soon as possible."

"They must be worth a fortune," I said.

"Again, that's yer job tae figure oot, lass. I've done my part," Rosie said.

I smiled. "I'm glad you remembered. And thanks for sharing."

"Ye're welcome."

Tom turned onto a dark street. "This is Leven."

I sat forward and peered out the windshield. "I can barely see the houses."

Most of the homes were set back from the road, each of them up a hill or behind a full front garden of trees and bushes.

"It should be about four or five up, on the left side," Tom said.

"Look up ahead. Do ye suppose that's it?" Rosie said.

It didn't take long to figure out which one she meant. Down a bit, along the road, there was something I hadn't ever seen in a city; torches. Fire torches stood on each side of what I guessed was a driveway.

"Those can't be real," I said.

When we were closer, Tom said, "No, they're just made to look like flames."

Inside glass cases, fanned material was lit from the bottom, giving the illusion that flames burned inside. The lights were two of the infrequent lights on the street and unquestionably marked the entrance to a driveway.

"There's the number," Rosie said. "That's the hoose."

The driveway was paved with varying sizes of smooth stones. Tom turned in and proceeded slowly.

"Careful of the moat," Rosie said.

"Moat?" Tom stopped the car.

"I wouldnae be surprised if there's one up ahead," Rosie said.

"Okay, I'll keep my eyes open." Tom continued along the driveway.

The path sloped up and toward the right, and just when I wondered if we'd taken the correct turn, the house came into view.

Correction, the castle came into view.

"Ye must be coddin," Rosie said.

My Scots translator, Hamlet, wasn't nearby, but I didn't think this one was too difficult. "Kidding?"

"Aye, something like that. That's quite the place," Rosie said.

"Wow," Tom said.

It wasn't the most beautiful castle I'd ever seen—in fact, it might not have been a castle so much as it was a replica of a castle.

"Hang on," I said. Tom had already stopped the car.

It was probably rude to remain parked there for long, but I had to know. On my phone I searched for Castle Loch Leven, and was quickly rewarded. "I thought it looked familiar. It's a replica of the castle Mary, Queen of Scots, was imprisoned in for a year or so. Well, it's smaller, but the structure seems to be the same shape."

The home before us was made with stone walls and did look like Castle Loch Leven in that it had a tall main building, rectangular with squared off corners, and lower walls surrounding what would have been the keep, if it had actually been a real castle.

"Weel, if she's not the auld, dead queen herself, she's certainly obsessed with her," Rosie said.

"Aye," Tom said.

"And look, there *is* a moat." I pointed.

A small stream of water ran along the front of the house but didn't seem to go all the way around. Technically, it was probably just a water feature, but it had been created to look like a moat.

"I'll be," Tom said. "I'm looking forward to meeting her."

"She looks just like yer new wife," Rosie said. "Only older."

"That's what Delaney said. If her husband is an older version of me, I think we'll have to wonder about more than reincarnation in the works."

"Believe it or not, she mentioned that he was bald. The thought came to her too," I said.

"Good news. Well, you know what I mean," Tom said.

We sat there way too long, but I didn't push Tom to continue up to the top. A moment later, he did though, slowly and with a few extra glances outside his side window to make sure we didn't drive over and into any "moat."

There were windows on the front of the house—small, as they would have been on the castle, but curtain sheers were on the inside over these. If I'd seen animal skins, I would have rolled my eyes, but I still wouldn't have been deterred.

Tom stopped in a paved spot that seemed to have been made specifically for visitors to park their vehicles. I didn't see a spot to tether horses, but even back in the day, the real castle might not have offered such accommodation. There were three other cars parked in the miniature parking strip.

"We might not be the only guests," I said.

"Or, all of the autos are theirs," Rosie said. "We will soon see."

Tom opened the back door for Rosie, but I was out before he could come around. Tom and I brought flowers, Rosie brought some whisky. Considering Tom owned the pub, it seemed like we should be carrying the whisky and Rosie the flowers, but it worked this way too.

"Och, I'm so excited tae see her proof," Rosie said as she led the way to the tall door, her purple pleats poofing again.

Tom and I smiled at each other and followed behind.

FIVE

"Welcome!" Mary said with an arm flourish. She wore a red gown that was tied at the waist, something a queen might wear as a robe back in the day, but of all the things I'd researched over the years, clothing hadn't been one of my strong interests.

"Thank ye for inviting us," Rosie said as she led the way inside and handed Mary the whisky. "Och, t'is a lovely place."

"Thank you," Mary said, but her eyes had stalled on Tom. "Goodness, you look *nothing* like my husband."

"Tom Shannon." Tom extended his hand. They shook and then he handed her the flowers. "Pleasure to meet you."

Mary took the flowers, all the while keeping her eyes locked on him. Lots of people stared at Tom.

"My goodness, you are . . . something," Mary said.

"And you look extremely familiar." Tom smiled at Mary and then at me, breaking Mary's locked gaze. "Delaney told me about the resemblance, but I must admit, I'm a wee bit surprised. You two could be related."

"I know," Mary said as she batted her eyelashes at him. I

didn't hold it against her. "It's uncanny! Did Delaney tell you the other part?"

"I believe she did," Tom said. "You were once someone else."

He didn't sound doubtful in the least, but I knew he was. Tom wasn't one for any sort of unexplained or unusual phenomena. I'd lived through a strange Christmas, having been visited by what my bookshop friends were sure was a ghost. Tom was still trying to find a reasonable explanation for what had happened, but he didn't like to talk about it much. I knew he didn't believe in past lives or reincarnation, but he would be a polite guest. And he was certainly intrigued by someone who claimed to have lived before.

"I *was* someone else," Mary said. "Thank you for the flowers and the whisky. How lovely."

"You're welcome," Tom and Rosie said together.

Mary set the gifts on a side table. "In fact, I have lived many lives, but only one other than this one that I remember very clearly." She winked at Tom. I thought it was interesting to see what I would look like in twenty years when I winked at my husband. Not bad.

"Mary, Queen of Scots," I said.

"Aye. We just call her *the queen* around here; it saves any confusion regarding which Mary is being discussed." She waved her hand once through the air. She moved her hands a lot, talked with them, as if they were extra punctuation. It worked for her.

I looked around the entryway, my eyes growing wider at every blink. The home was set up in a boring square, but there was nothing boring about the rest of it. The bottom floor had high ceilings and a stairway along the right wall. Other than in castles, I'd never seen a stone stairway. Stone used in buildings in Scotland was cold, and never did warm up much. A thick, red carpet moved down the middle of these stairs. Tapestries, much bigger than the ones I'd been looking at in the warehouse, filled the wall along the staircase. If the carpet and the tapestries didn't actually warm the space, they gave the illusion that they did.

The floor we stood on was also made of stone—or probably just concrete—but I didn't crouch to investigate. It was well covered in throw rugs, similar to Rosie's flat but with fewer colors. Here, there were lots of golds and reds, but not many blues or greens. A large, ornate, dark-wood secretary stood to our side next to the table where Mary had placed the flowers and whisky. A round table took up the middle space. Atop that table, a vase of fresh flowers filled the air with pleasant and surprisingly mellow scents. But it was the fireplace in the middle of the wall on the other side that was the true showpiece. Massive, with high flames inside, the heat reached all the way over to us. But I was most interested in the secretary.

"That desk is beautiful," I said as I peered at it more closely.

Made of what I thought was cherrywood, dragons had been carved onto the closed drop-section. Three drawers, with ornate, brass pulls, lined up perfectly underneath. I knew it was an old piece of furniture, but it was in mint condition.

"Thank you. My niece, Dina, gave it to me. She's an expert on such things. She's upstairs. You'll meet her in a moment."

I stood straight again and looked at the fireplace. "Is that your only source of heat in the house?"

"No," Mary said. "We have a newfangled furnace, but this just . . . felt right."

I translated in my mind: It's what she "remembered" from her days as the queen.

"Well, helloo there," a man said from the top of the stairway. He was bald and just on the verge of having a belly. Mary had already told me she was fifty-one; the man seemed around the same age. "Are you all joining the rest of us for dinner, or shall we come down there and bring some marshmallows, so we might actually do something productive with all that fire?"

He was dressed like Hugh Hefner, in a paisley robe, with a pipe in one hand. His accent was British—nothing Scottish about it, I realized; I was pleased with myself that I could tell the difference. It seemed as if he was teasing, but I wasn't sure.

"We'll be up momentarily, dear," Mary said. "My husband, Henry. Henry, this is Rosie, Delaney, and Tom. I'm sure you all are entertaining yourselves just fine up there."

From above, Henry's pleasant twinkling eyes stopped twinkling when they landed on me. He moved down the stairs and toward me so quickly that Tom sidled closer, and I thought I heard Rosie make a surprised noise.

"Good gracious me!" Henry said as he stopped in front of me. He put the pipe next to the whisky and then took hold of my arms. "Is this really you?"

"Um," I said. "Hello, I'm Delaney Nichols," I looked at Tom. We'd already talked about me keeping my name as it had always been. He hadn't protested, but I still wondered if it bothered him that I hadn't taken his.

"No, I don't think so. I think you are someone else entirely," Henry said.

"Henry," Mary said as she stepped next to him and put her hand on his arm. "You're behaving inappropriately."

"I'm . . ." Henry blinked at Mary and then looked at me,

letting go of my arms. "I'm so sorry, Ms. Nichols. That *was* inappropriate. I was struck by your resemblance to . . ."

"His wife," Mary said conclusively. She cleared her throat.

"You both look so much like the queen. Are you aware of that?" Henry asked.

"That has come to my attention," I said, finding his overbite and friendly smile very charming.

"Henry, I told you I met Delaney and Rosie today, at that wonderful bookshop. I told you Delaney and I looked alike. We discussed it, as well as our resemblance to the queen."

"Love, you didn't say the two of you looked so much alike it was uncanny. You used the word 'resemblance.'"

"All right," Mary said as she hooked her arm through his. "We do look alike. Although," she glanced around at the rest of us, "I'm afraid I've ruined poor Henry seeing the queen for what she truly might have looked like. To him, I am she. Perhaps, it's because in his eyes I *am* his only queen."

Henry was struggling. Thoughts he wasn't vocalizing were filling his eyes with something that, to me, looked like emotional pain. Was our resemblance really that bothersome to him or was something else going on?

His wife's words finally filtered through and he looked at Mary and smiled, but the odd sparkle of emotional disruption didn't leave his eyes. "That is ever so true, my dear, ever so true."

Now, a speck of sadness lined his words and I inspected his face more closely. I was probably trying too hard to understand something I might be imagining, but I couldn't ignore it.

"Well then," Henry said. "Because our house is a bit strange, we have our family room, dining room, and kitchen up on the next floor. Shall we go up?"

"We shall!" Mary said.

Mary gathered the whisky, flowers, as well as Henry's pipe and followed the rest of us up. The second level was more about comfort than castle. And it was the place where the others waited.

Four people were there, standing as if they'd been posed. That's what it felt like, as if the scene had been choreographed. One woman, probably in her sixties or so, lounged on a big-pillowed sofa. With pleasantly round features and short, gray hair cut severely at her jawline, she held a cigarette holder that didn't have a cigarette in it. Her long silk dress added to Henry's and Mary's flowing clothing, and I wondered if pajamas were the costume of the evening. But the other three changed my mind.

A man and woman who appeared to be close to my and Tom's ages sat next to each other on stools this side of a kitchen island. They turned with matching poses—their hands on their thighs—and smiled at us. They were both dressed casually in jeans and sweaters—almost matching, but not quite. The woman's red sweater also had some sort of blue design woven through, but the man's was just red. The man looked familiar to me, but I couldn't place how I knew him.

Probably in their thirties, the man's long face was topped off with a very short haircut. There was no sign of a beard over his pale skin, making his blue eyes extra-bright. The woman's brown curls fell to her shoulders, but there wasn't any frizz in sight. I wondered about her hair products and made a mental note to ask her later if the moment presented itself. Her smile and blue eyes were less electric than the man she sat next to, but they drew me in a little more.

The fourth person, a woman, also probably in her sixties,

stood closest to the landing. She inspected us, one hand on her hip, a scowl pulling her features into a deep frown. She wore jeans and a denim shirt, and might have decided not to like us. At least that's what her scrutiny felt like. Her gray hair was drawn back in a tight bun and her glasses were so thick that her eyes seemed to almost disappear behind the lenses.

"Let me introduce everyone," Mary said. She nodded toward the woman on the couch. "This is Eloise Hansen, a friend from forever." Eloise nodded and Mary turned to the woman who appeared not to like us. "And Gretchen Lovell. Gretchen and Eloise are a couple." Mary looked at us as if to gauge our reaction. It didn't seem necessary for any of us to mention that same-sex couples were or weren't novelties in our lives, so Mary continued, "Dina," she looked at the woman on the stool, "is my niece. Mikey is her husband, but there are days we like him so much more than we do Dina." She smiled at the couple, who took the teasing with their own smiles and mini eye rolls.

"It's nice tae meet all of ye," Rosie said.

Tom and I said the same, but I added, "Mikey, have we met?"

"Not that I recall, and considering how much you look like Mary, I think I would remember," Mikey said.

He reminded me a little of my friend Joshua, who worked at the history museum, but Mikey didn't wear glasses.

"The rain?" I said, somehow remembering him in a bright yellow raincoat, but unable to place where the storm had been. I was sure I'd seen those striking blue eyes before. "It was raining when we met."

"I'm sorry. I truly don't remember," Mikey said.

I decided it must be his resemblance to Joshua. Once the greetings were over, I took a better look around the cozy space.

The floor up here was once again made of cold stone or concrete, but was covered with even more throw rugs. The couch and chairs, including the dining chairs were all cushioned and inviting. The large space held all three rooms, divided by the long kitchen island. The kitchen wasn't modern, but adorned with old-fashioned appliances—not old-fashioned enough to be considered from the queen's lifetime though. In fact, I realized that the kitchen appliances weren't, in fact, old things, but new things made to look old. Retro.

I immediately loved it—the atmosphere and time-warped sense of place—but no matter the décor, it was still cool up here.

Both the temperature as well as the atmosphere. I tried to hide a shiver with a smile, but Rosie saw me. Furtively, she raised an eyebrow my direction. I nodded that I was okay. She nodded. She'd keyed in on the ambiance too. There was a distinct bump in the air, as if we'd either interrupted something we shouldn't have known about or something that was about us.

No one here really knew us, so I decided we must have interrupted a personal discussion. Maybe they didn't like new people joining their dinner parties.

Then I realized that Rosie was in her element. She wasn't one to jump in on other adventures I'd had, but this one had her full attention and she was intrigued and curious and didn't mind the icy atmosphere. I hoped it would be a fun evening for her.

"Sorry to be so abrupt, but dinner is already ready, so please take a seat, everyone. We'll eat and make merry and get to know each other over some of the best food you have ever consumed," Henry said.

With the ease of a comfortable host, Mary directed everyone where to sit. Rosie was on one end of the long table. Tom,

Mary, and I sat on one side. Henry sat at the other end, in the chair closest to the kitchen. And the other two couples filled in the other side. The table was so long that we weren't crowded, and Henry used a corner of it to set down dishes as he served. He was both the cook and the wait staff, as it were. Mary didn't offer to assist him. None of us did, though I felt like we should. Rosie picked up on that too and then shook her head once. Maybe Henry just liked to do it this way. He was in his element too.

"Soup to begin," Henry said as he carried a large pot and ladle toward the table. He ladled, and we passed the bowls down and around.

"Delaney, it is uncanny how much you look like my aunt," Dina said as she picked up her soup spoon. "I mean, you two both have the same hair even, frizz and all."

"Dina," Mary said.

"I noticed the hair too," I said hurriedly. I'd still wait to ask her about hers. Being offended by my frizz or the mention of it would make for a long life of offense. It wasn't worth the time. "It's even uncannier that we ran into each other. Well, I ran into her."

"Must have been meant to be," Mikey said.

I realized they were all staring at me. I felt my cheeks heat, but it was more just a reaction than embarrassment. I shouldn't have expected anything different. They'd get over it eventually. I smiled at each of them.

"I saw the secretary downstairs," I said to Dina. "It's beautiful."

Dina smiled. "It is, isn't it? I have an antique shop and I know my desks. The one downstairs was surely around back in the queen's day."

"Really?" I said. "That's . . ." I had much more I wanted to say to Dina, but Eloise jumped in.

"Are you sure you're not related?" she asked.

"I haven't done much genealogy, but I grew up in Kansas in America. I don't know of any connection, but I've thought about it since meeting Mary today. Is there some crossover in our family trees? I don't know," I said.

"Do you remember your past lives?" Gretchen asked. Her tone friendly, which was a contrast to the stink eye she'd been giving us.

"I don't remember any past lives," I said.

"Are you a believer?" Eloise asked, her tone also friendly.

"I'm not a nonbeliever," I said, having come up with that line after my recent run in with the Loch Ness legend. I'd become *not* a nonbeliever, but that was the best I could do.

"I see," Eloise said as she and Gretchen shared a "told you so" look.

I dipped my spoon into the soup. I didn't want to offend anyone and their beliefs, but I also didn't want someone to bring out a Ouija Board or call on some old spirits for a séance.

However, Rosie had other plans. "Och, how could ye not believe? Have ye never had a moment, a déjà vu that was so much more than a déjà vu?"

"I have had déjà vus, but they've never felt like a past life sneaking in," I said honestly. I didn't want to offend Rosie either.

"Tell us about *your* past lives," Mary said to Rosie.

Rosie swallowed a spoonful of soup. "Delicious," she said as she patted her napkin on the corners of her mouth. "I dinnae have any clear recollections anymore, but when I was a wee-un,

I would tell my dear mother, may she rest, about my time on the *Titanic*. I'm sure one of my past lives was lost during that awful tragedy."

"Really?" Henry stood and made his way back to the kitchen. He grabbed a loaf of sourdough. "Sorry, friends, I forgot the bread. Tell us more about the *Titanic*, Rosie."

I wanted to say the same, but I just looked at her, wondering if she was sharing a true story or something she'd made up to get Mary to talk more about the queen.

Rosie nodded. "As a wee-un, I would talk about things that no bairn would ken. Mother and Da never talked about the *Titanic*, so they thought it was odd. But mother was intrigued by my ramblings, and she asked me tae sketch things I remembered."

The entire table was enthralled. Rosie managed another spoonful of soup, giving dramatic pause as we waited. After she took a piece of bread from the basket, she continued.

"I sketched some dishes, and I sketched some cabin details. Back then, we lived oot in the country, my mother didnae have a way to research those details, but she kept the sketches and years later, she found pictures." Rosie shrugged. "My sketches were spot-on."

"I believe you," Gretchen said and pushed up her thick glasses.

"The *Titanic* tragedy was in the early 1900s, aye?" Tom said.

"Aye, and I drew the sketches when I was a child, and I ken what ye're going tae say—that I could have seen pictures or something. Anything is possible, but Mother was certain there was no way."

Tom nodded. He probably wondered the same thing I did; was this real?

"Aye," Gretchen said before she looked at Tom. "Anything *is* possible."

"And it's more than possible that Rosie was there, on that sinking ship," Eloise said as she smiled at my coworker.

Tom smiled and nodded too. "I would never doubt anything Rosie said. Never. I wonder though if there was a possibility that . . . well, that something happened in your life that gave you the opportunity to be . . . influenced."

"I used tae wonder about that," Rosie said. "But it was all so long ago. I remember making the sketches, but I dinnae remember their inspiration. I haven't thought aboot it for a long time. When Mary came in today, I wondered again. Some of it came back tae me. I can't tell ye, Tom. I have no idea. All I ken is what it was—a strange thing that seemed verra real at the time."

Tom smiled at Rosie. "If it was real tae you, it was real. I have no doubt."

"Aye," Rosie said.

"Henry, this honey butter!" Dina said. "It's to die for."

"Thank you," Henry said, but I saw him eye a bowl of jam he'd put on the table too.

I reached for the jam and spooned some on my bread as the others continued to talk about the *Titanic*. No one had tried the jam yet, but I could tell Henry wanted someone to.

"Delicious," I said after I took a bite.

Henry smiled knowingly and leaned toward me. "Ta, lass. I made it myself just this afternoon."

And then he smiled sadly at me. The moment stretched too long, and I even thought I saw tears come to his eyes. I smiled at him, hopefully inviting him to tell me what might be bothering him, if that's what I was picking up on. My cheeks reddened again, but I didn't break the moment. However, Henry did. He pushed his chair back from the table. He stood, but before he turned to head back to the kitchen, he looked at Mikey.

In a few brief beats I witnessed a silent exchange between the two of them. Mikey was looking at his wife's uncle with what seemed like irritation, or maybe anger. Henry stared at Mikey a long moment, but without a smile. In fact, I was surprised there were no heated words exchanged. Henry broke that stare too and hurried to the kitchen.

I blinked at the quick exchange, even more curious about what might be causing the problem but knowing it was none of my business.

I turned to Mary as a lull hit the *Titanic* conversation. "You said you have proof of your past life as Mary, Queen of Scots. I'd love to see it."

"Oh, no, Aunt Mary, you didn't say it was *proof*, did you?" Dina said.

"I did. And it is. At least I believe it is."

Henry came back to the table with the most un-Scottish pot roast, potatoes, and carrots I'd ever seen. It was just like a Kansas dinner.

"Oh, I have no doubt that it is proof," Henry said. "There's no doubt in my mind that my wife was once Mary, Queen of Scots, though. I don't need any extra proof."

"I'd love to see it," I repeated.

"Me too!" Rosie added. That was the whole reason she'd come tonight, the whole reason for the purple skirt probably.

"And I will show it to you all after dinner," Mary said.

"Ah, that's the dessert!" Rosie said with a smile.

"No, no. Dessert will be even more to die for than the honey butter," Henry said. "Mary will be the cherry on top, like she always is." He lifted his wineglass toward his wife.

The rest of us did the same as everyone chimed in with "To Mary."

"Your highness," Henry said.

And, in the most regal of ways, Mary Stewart gave us all a slightly tilted nod. I wouldn't have been surprised if she'd lifted her hand and gave a royal wave too, but she didn't.

"Oh, boy," Tom muttered so quietly that I was the only one who heard him. I hope.

SIX

Dessert was most definitely to die for. A strawberry and banana trifle, Henry had not only included a sponge cake in the delicious mix, but he'd also stirred in bits of a shortbread he'd baked himself. It was the most Scottish part of the meal, excluding the shots of whisky that were served with the trifle. Rosie's whisky.

Henry's shortbread couldn't compete with Rosie's—I secretly made sure she knew that—but the whipped cream he'd whipped himself was unlike anything I'd ever tasted.

"What is that extra flavor in there?" I asked after I'd swooned.

"I'll never tell, but it's something you wouldn't expect," Henry said. "Tell you what, think about it. If you don't come up with it by our next meeting, I will happily share the recipe."

"Goodness," Mary said. "You must be special, Delaney. Henry never tells anyone his secrets."

"I'm honored," I said.

"I think he's having a hard time telling the two of you

apart," Gretchen shook her head. "Do you two realize that you have some of the same mannerisms too? Mary moves her hands more than Delaney, but you both have the same sort of tilt to your chins. I've been trying not to stare too much, but you'll have to forgive me if I do. It's bizarre."

Mary and I looked at each other. She was probably thinking the same thing I was. Did we want to become self-conscious that way?

Mary came to the same conclusion I did. "Oh, don't point out those things, or we'll be avoiding them the rest of the evening. It will all become awkward."

"Henry, what do you do?" Tom asked.

Henry took a long moment. He seemed to chew his dessert longer than necessary as he formulated an answer. "I'm mostly retired."

"Mostly?" Tom asked.

"Yes, it's too long a story to tell, and not very interesting," he said. "I used to be in banking, but that's all so boring."

"What do you do, Tom?" Dina asked.

Tom explained he was the owner of the smallest pub in Scotland, the one located in Grassmarket. Every person there had been inside it at one time or another and seemed excited that they now knew the owner. I suspected Tom would be seeing them all again soon.

Eloise was a doctor, and Gretchen an artist, a sculptor, specializing in African wildlife. We'd been invited to tour her studio and I was excited about the prospect.

But the most interesting of the group, in my opinion, were Mikey and Dina. I finally learned that Dina's antique shop was in Cowgate, her place full of old things that she restored and sold. She and I had more in common than I would point out until we got to know each other much better. Later I would realize that we never did talk about Mikey's job, because Dina's was so interesting.

"Please visit any time," Dina said. "I love to show off my things."

"Thank you, I will. Soon," I said.

"I look forward to it." Dina smiled.

Mary volunteered. Everywhere, apparently. She'd worked at the castle on the hill, as well as a docent in several museums throughout Edinburgh. A few years earlier, she'd worked at the National Museum of Scotland, where Joshua worked. I didn't bring up knowing him. She'd recently been spending most of her time at the Writers' Museum, just off of the Royal Mile.

"I love that place. The books talk to me," she said with a laugh.

I looked at her to see if she meant it as literally as they spoke to me, but I didn't think she did.

She continued, "Museums bring back so many things from my past lives. I can't tell if they're memories or distractions. I can't work in many of the old places with old things anymore. It's just too much heartache, but I'm so drawn to museums. The Writers' Museum is safe for me, not much about the queen inside."

"Oh, are you volunteering there again?" Dina asked Mary.

Mary blinked at her. "Aye, Dina, I am. They welcomed me."

"Good to hear," Dina said.

"Seems sensible," Rosie added, filling the uncomfortable and heavy silence that came after their cryptic words. "I mean, sensible that you like being at that museum."

From the beginning of the dinner to the end, my sense of Mary had changed some, but I knew that was only because of my own interpretation. I'd first thought she'd be interesting, but she was more than that; she was consumed by her "past life." *It was both interesting and,* I thought, *somewhat sad.*

"Did you see the article about the Mary, Queen of Scots' papers that have recently been found?" I said, still not sharing my friendship with the young post doc who worked at the museum.

Everyone had read the article though, and couldn't wait to see the papers exhibited.

"Do ye feel any ties tae such things?" Rosie asked Mary.

"Not at this point," Mary said. "When I see them, I might, but I have no sense of them at the moment."

Rosie nodded.

"Come along," Henry said. "Everyone's finished. Let's move over to the comfortable chairs and I'll have coffee or more adult beverages ready momentarily. I know you're here to see Mary's proof."

We all moved to the other side of the space, the living room. Tom, Rosie, and I all sat on the couch. My senses were tuned to high alert, both because we were about to see Mary's proof and because I couldn't let go of the silent exchange I'd seen between Henry and Mikey. As furtively as possible, I tried to watch them both. Mikey fed my curiosity, but this time it was with a look between him and his wife.

And I was sure I saw fear. Mikey looked at Dina with stern eyes and pursed lips. Dina's eyes got wide before she looked away from his and pasted on a fake smile. I was sure I was the only one who noticed it, but I'd ask Rosie and Tom later.

"Oh, I look forward to showing you the Writers' Museum," Mary said to me. "And, frankly, I look forward to showing you to the people I work with. Everyone will be very surprised to see there are two of us." She quirked a half smile. "Or three of us, if you will. They all know who I used to be."

"Do they all believe ye?" Rosie asked.

"Oh, yes." Mary laughed. "Well, they say they do. Anyway, you're here for proof." She plunked her hands on her hips.

"In fact, it has been a lovely evening," Tom said. "Please don't feel obligated to show us any proof. It has been fun to get to know you all."

I looked at him. His graciousness was poorly timed, and I held back the urge to nudge him with my elbow. He looked at me and smiled.

"Although, I might be speaking out of turn." He laughed. "I think my lovely bride would be disappointed if we left without knowing . . ."

"Aye," Rosie added as she sent Tom a frown. "Aye."

Mary smiled. "Very well." She turned and spoke back over her shoulder. "You might want to come closer for a look."

Mary reached back and to the neckline of her dress. She pulled the material over about two inches, exposing a mark.

"Oh, that's not a tattoo," I said. "That's a birthmark."

"Aye," she said. "In the shape of a crown. The queen herself had one identical. That's how I knew. Like Rosie, the memories were stronger when I was a little girl. I sketched faces of people I knew and could give them first names. Some of the sketches matched some of the pictures of those people that we now have access to, though all of that is iffy I know. However, this birthmark confirmed it for me."

I didn't remember knowing anything about a birthmark on the queen. It seemed hokey, frankly, but the mark on Mary's back *did* look like a small crown.

"I don't remember reading anything aboot a birthmark," Rosie said.

Mary released the fabric and then turned around to face us again.

"It's a rare known fact, but she did have one, I'm sure," she said.

"There's documentation?" Tom asked, but then he cleared his throat. "I don't mean to be rude."

Mary smiled at him. "I understand your doubts. It is documented. In my memory. Since a girl, I have had a clear memory of having the mark, and having it in another setting, castles and other places too. Mirrors weren't common in that time, but I remember a reflection in a stream. Though over the years, the memories of the people, the faces, have faded, the memories of the mark have not. I am sure of it."

A part of me wanted to confirm with her that this was really the "proof" she'd been talking about sharing with us, because as proof went, this was pretty shaky. But I didn't express my doubts. Tom wasn't the only one who knew how to be gracious.

"That's completely fascinating," I said.

"I believe you totally," Rosie said. "I can relate tae what ye're saying. I ken those sorts of memories. I don't remember them much now, but I remember remembering them those first times. They are real."

Mary smiled at Rosie and then at me. I knew she could see my doubt, but she couldn't possibly have known that at that moment, more than all the other moments, I was looking at something else—our differences. We did look alike, but there was something in the set of her mouth, the corners of her eyes that were different than mine.

Then, everything changed again, her mouth and those eyes

were, in fact, very similar to mine—when I wasn't telling the whole truth, when I was lying.

She and I were very much alike.

The queen wasn't mentioned the rest of the evening. We learned that Eloise had been Mary's doctor for twenty years, that they'd met in Glasgow, at a clothing shop that was no longer there. Gretchen and Eloise had met at university thirty years earlier and had been together ever since. Dina and Mikey had also met at university, but only ten years earlier.

As the enjoyable evening continued, I got no sense that Mikey was angry with anyone, and Dina didn't seem afraid of him. I realized I'd probably jumped to conclusions that weren't real. I'd been rattled by the news about the bookshop, so I knew I wasn't quite in my normal headspace. We didn't mention the bad news to our new friends. I wasn't sure if that was because we didn't know them well enough yet, or if we didn't want to say the news out loud again, making it that much more real.

I thought Tom might see Henry at the pub very soon. They talked football in that way that only true fans could. Henry liked the idea of catching a match on the telly at the pub.

As we said goodbye, Mary grabbed my hands. "Oh, Delaney, it is so lovely to know you. Please, let's not be strangers. It would be a shame, and possibly an affront to the universe if we don't become friends. I will visit you at the bookshop but come see me at the museum too. Please."

"I will. I look forward to seeing you again," I said.

"Me too!"

Truth be told though, and for reasons I didn't quite understand, I couldn't wait to see her again.

SEVEN

"Well, that's disappointing," Hamlet said. "A birthmark? I've heard of such legends, fictional only, but I don't know anything about such a mark on the real Mary, Queen of Scots."

"Me either," I said.

"I still believe her," Rosie said as she walked by the back table where Hamlet and I had settled.

"I don't disbelieve her," I said. "It was an . . . interesting evening."

In fact, Rosie had been quiet on the way home the night before, lost either in the queen's world, or maybe the *Titanic*'s. Both Tom and I had tried to start conversations, but she hadn't been interested. We'd walked her to her door, given her hugs, gave some love to Hector, and then told them goodnight.

I'd been thinking about both the bookshop and Rosie all night, worried mostly about my worker. So had Tom. I'd texted him first thing this morning when she'd come in and seemed fine, if maybe still somewhat distracted.

Hamlet watched Rosie make her way to a bookshelf against the far wall. "Why are you so sure?" he asked her.

Hamlet hadn't heard the *Titanic* story.

"Here," I stood as the bell above the door jingled, "tell Hamlet about your past life. I'll help the customers."

Rosie joined Hamlet as I walked toward the front of the shop.

Life can only be understood backwards, but it must be lived forwards.

Hello, Kierkegard, I said in my head. Though a philosopher who was more interested in talking about religion, it seemed only reasonable that the bookish voice was talking about the past life experiences of the last couple of days. I didn't take the bookish voice for more than just an extra voice to reinforce that things were off kilter.

The woman who came into the shop didn't need anything specific, so I didn't hover as she browsed. Instead, I grabbed Hector as he trotted toward me. We found a spot in the middle of the other side of the shop, not far from where Rosie had been pretending to look for something herself.

"How about you, have you had other lives?" I said quietly.

Hector looked at me like he wanted to answer correctly.

"Good dog," I said as he kissed my cheek.

All of a sudden and in a stretched out beat of time, everything changed. In the blink of an eye, a boom sounded somewhere in the distance. There was a pop in the noise, but I wouldn't remember if it came at the beginning or the end of the deep bass rumble mixed with a tinny percussion. It didn't seem close enough to cause damage, but, nevertheless, my instinct was to put my arm up to protect my head. The glass in the windows rattled, Hector barked, and a solitary book fell from a shelf. When the noise stopped—I couldn't be sure how long it lasted because every time I thought about it, it expanded, Rosie and Hamlet hurried to the front. The customer froze in place, supporting herself by placing a hand on a shelf. With wide eyes, we all looked at each other, wondering if what we all thought had happened, had actually just happened.

It had.

EIGHT

A bomb—something homemade according to the first reports—had exploded a car. It was made clear that it hadn't been what we typically called a car bomb, something made to murder a large number of people when a car with an explosive device was driven into a populated location, but something with the power that would surely kill or maim the person or people only inside the car. There was one fatality, a man in his early fifties. But that was all the information the newscasters shared yesterday.

We'd spent the rest of the day walking around in a confused daze with emotions that ran the gamut. Rosie closed the bookshop and Hamlet found an old, small television in one of the offices. He'd brought it and some old-fashioned rabbit ears up to the front of the shop. I didn't even know it was possible to view television that way anymore, but that's what we did, watching the repeating, vague news over and over again.

Because the explosion took place at the bottom of the Royal Mile, it was discussed that perhaps a political figure had been targeted. With not many facts, the newspeople speculated that maybe the explosion, something the police immediately labeled a murder, had something to do with a recent scandal, one I hadn't heard about, but that sounded uncomfortably relevant when I learned some of the facts.

As I'd heard from Edwin, Burgess Tickets were once granted to merchants giving them the right to do business in a specific burgh, or geographical area, as well as offering the recipients community perks. Back in the day, the tickets were delivered in miniature coffin-like containers called Freedom Caskets. The Freedom Caskets were sometimes silver or gold and ornately decorated. When the newscasters ran out of new information to share with the public, they talked about the tickets, the caskets, and their recent revival. Granting the tickets was an old tradition and one that the Lord Provost wanted to bring back, just because it was something nostalgic and gave a nod to Scottish history. The idea had gone over poorly—as something antiquated and "coffins are weird," but it had given life to something else.

Some citizens thought that all the old Burgess Tickets should at least be tracked down. If a business didn't have one, they should have to apply for one, or at least go through the same sort of motions businesses used to have to go through, and in doing so only be allowed to continue to do business if they were able to earn one. None of the newspeople seemed to know what all the specific requirements or qualifications used to be.

However, some of the citizens of Edinburgh wanted the standards raised to a point that included the potential for lots and lots of remodeling. The circumstances sounded eerily similar to what was going on with the bookshop, but Edwin assured me that Burgess Tickets had never once been brought up in the phone message he'd received the previous week, that it had been solely his idea to try to find The Cracked Spine's. He also claimed not to have heard about the recent idea of bringing the tickets back with even higher standards, though he didn't rule out that he might not have paid close attention to the news. Perhaps something had seeped into his subconscious; he just couldn't be sure.

And because of the murder, of course we all felt some confusion.

As we all came back to work the next morning, Edwin kept the bookshop closed and Hamlet again switched on the old television. It was as if the newscasters were still in repeat mode.

"Och," Rosie said when the Burgess Tickets were brought up again. "They have no idea who was kil't. They are making things up just tae fill time now."

"I think so too," Hamlet said. "But what if the bomber was someone who wouldn't meet the new ticket standards, if those standards ever came into effect? Maybe that's what they're thinking."

"We need more information," Edwin said. "Aye, the newspeople just want something to talk about."

What we did know was that it was a miracle that only one person had been killed. The explosion had taken place in a populated area. It seemed that there was no damage to any other buildings in the area and the only other injury was an elderly man who'd been so surprised by the noise that he'd fallen and hurt his knees. I wondered how there was so little other damage and yet we'd heard and felt the explosion as if it was right next to us.

Tom had run down to the bookshop from his pub seconds after the noise. Once we knew each other was okay, we called everyone else. Edwin and my landlords, Elias and Aggie, were fine. In fact, they were far enough away from the explosion that they hadn't heard or felt it. Tom's father, Artair, was also fine, though he'd felt the explosion from his office inside the University of Edinburgh's library, which was even farther from the bombing location than we were.

Then we called my family in Kansas to let them know all was well if they heard news of the explosion. They were happy to know we were okay.

Tom had headed back to the pub. He'd left it unattended, trusting a well-known customer to make sure no one robbed the place, either of the liquor or the money in the till. He'd dropped me off at the bookshop again this morning before heading back to work. He could have remained closed like Edwin had chosen to do, but Tom thought some of his regulars might miss their routine.

Once again, the newscaster began to say that the name of the victim hadn't been released yet, but she stopped speaking suddenly and held her hand to her ear. She continued, "We've just received word. The name of the victim has now been released. We have confirmed that he was a councilor to the Lord Provost. At one time the victim had been in banking, but he was retired from that profession, devoting all his time to helping govern our fair and beautiful city. The name of the victim is Henry Stewart."

And then a picture popped up on the screen. Even in grainy black and white, the man on the screen was familiar, too familiar.

I didn't hear the next few sentences because my ears had closed as my mind swirled. What the hell?

I looked at Rosie. She put her fist to her chest and sat down hard in a chair. Oh, no.

Suddenly, nothing was as important as my friend and coworker. With my ears still closed and my mind still swirling, I jumped up and ran to her.

Edwin, Hamlet, and Hector joined me just as she went down.

NINE

Rosie was okay. It took a few minutes for her to come back from the faint, but she did. Hamlet made it to her first and, with quick thinking, he managed to get a hand under her head before it hit the hard floor. Once she was lucid, she was able to move all parts and the color came back to her face.

"Och, I'm so sorry," she said.

"No need to apologize," Edwin said as he reached across the table for her hand. "We're glad you're all right."

"Aye." She squeezed Edwin's hand. "I'm fine, but, Edwin, we just met that poor man two nights anon. He cooked us dinner."

Edwin looked at me. It hadn't even occurred to any of us to tell Edwin about the dinner. I nodded.

"Oh dear," he said when I gave him a quick summary. "I'm so sorry."

Rosie shook her head and then looked at me. "Do ye think one of the people from the dinner kil't him? Do you think we were in the same hoose as the killer?"

I had no idea. "No, no, Rosie, he worked for the government. It's something political, I'm sure."

I wasn't sure about anything, of course, and more questions were filling my head. Was there something else going on, or was meeting Mary and attending the dinner all a coincidence?

After dropping off Rosie that night, Tom and I had discussed the party. I told him what I'd noticed about Mikey and Henry and Mikey and Dina. He hadn't seen any of that and then I'd quickly forgotten about it. Mostly, we'd both just been intrigued by the birthmark and its label of "proof."

"I dinnae ken," Rosie said. "There was tension in the air. I couldnae understand why, and it felt like none of my business anyway, but there was strain there. Did ye sense it?"

"I did, but I couldn't figure it out either. We were the strangers though. They all knew each other. Who knows what's going on in their lives?"

"And now that lovely man is dead." More tears came to Rosie's eyes, but she didn't swoon.

"Hang on," Hamlet said suddenly.

We all looked at him.

"Oh, no," he said, but he'd fallen into his own thoughts. He looked up a moment later. "Rosie, I don't want to upset you further, but something just occurred to me."

"It's all right, lad. G'on."

"The queen. Mary, Queen of Scots. Her second husband was killed—in an explosion. His name was Henry Stuart. I believe his title was Lord Darnley."

"Oh, my," Rosie said. "That's . . . unbelievable."

"His name was Henry?" I said.

"Aye," Hamlet said. "I think so."

"Gracious. Wait, wasn't it alleged that the queen's lover killed him?" Edwin said.

"It was," Hamlet said. "I think . . . well, I haven't read about Mary Stuart in quite a few years,"

As Hamlet reached for a laptop he kept perched on a back shelf, I had another thought.

"Rosie, do you think we should call Inspector Winters and tell him about the dinner party?" I said.

"I do, lass. I dinnae ken if it will do any good, but I think we should talk tae the police."

"I'll call him right now."

I found my phone and pulled up the favorites screen. I kept thinking a day might come when I wouldn't need to keep the police inspector toward the top of my call list. However, that day wasn't today.

TEN

Unfortunately, I ran into an immediate roadblock. I'd called Inspector Winters's personal number, because that was the one he'd given me. It seemed he was on holiday. As his greeting continued, stating that he'd be away for a week or so, I debated whether or not to leave a message. Ultimately, I decided not to.

"Ye didnae leave a message," Rosie said when I disconnected the call.

"He's on vacation," I said. "I didn't want to bother him."

For a moment Rosie looked bothered, but shortly she nodded. "Aye, I understand. Should we call another officer, perhaps just the police's number?"

"Should we?" I said.

The four of us sat and thought about it a moment. Did we want to tell the police that we'd gotten weird vibes at a dinner Henry had cooked for us the night before he was killed? Also, Henry was a councilor and it seemed feasible that there might be a councilor or two out to make sure the bookshop was shut down, though none of us were sure who those particular councilors were. Our unspoken, but surely shared insights and concerns, suddenly seemed threadbare and potentially shone a suspicious light on all of us.

"Maybe not yet," Rosie said. "We have no proof of anything. I might be jumping to conclusions."

"We should let the police do their jobs," Edwin said.

"Aye," Hamlet added.

"I agree," I said.

For now.

I stood and made my way to the front of the store. I needed to gather my thoughts, calm down, something. I turned and looked back toward my friends. They had each fallen into their own thoughts, but they were going to be okay.

It had been a tragic couple of days, not just for Henry and his loved ones, but for the city of Edinburgh too. A bomb set off in a public place left sadness, anger, and fear behind. I'd always been one not to let fear rule my behavior, but as I looked out the window, I was grateful for the sense of security I felt inside the shop. It was all an illusion, I knew that. Anything can happen at any time. Bad things happened all the time, and usually when you least expected them. But I refused to live my life being worried about those sorts of things.

Nevertheless, I didn't push away the sadness and anger. Someone was messing with my bookshop, and now with my adopted city.

A shiver ran up my spine. Perhaps I was experiencing some sort of shock or coping mechanism. Or maybe the dreary rain outside made me cold. There were no bookish voices speaking—in fact, as I listened for them, I sensed they were too sad to speak.

Maybe I didn't want to focus on the fact that a man who had cooked me dinner two nights ago was now dead, brutally murdered. I grabbed an umbrella from the shelf and turned around. "I'm going out for a bit. I'll be back."

Edwin, Rosie, and Hamlet all looked at me with questioning eyes.

"Of course," Edwin said. "Take whatever time you need."

"Be safe," Rosie said.

"Do you want company?" Hamlet asked, but he knew the answer. He was just being polite.

I shook my head. "No. I'll be back."

I pushed through the door as I slid open the umbrella. It *was* cold and I hadn't grabbed my jacket. At least I'd worn a sweater, and I sensed I would warm up quickly.

The Royal Mile had been blocked off until just a couple hours earlier. The newscasters had announced that other than a small area, foot and vehicle traffic was being allowed back in.

I could have walked up Victoria Street and then down to the bottom of the Royal Mile; that route would have taken me past Tom's pub. Instead, I glanced toward it briefly before I hurried over the market square to where I knew a bus would be coming shortly. My timing was good and I didn't have to wait even a full minute before I boarded the bus that would at least get me up to the top of the Royal Mile.

"Hello," a voice said from behind me as I sat down. "Delaney, is it?"

I turned quickly. "Oh. Hello!"

"Fancy meeting you here," Eloise said.

I nodded and frowned. "I'm . . ."

"Going to look at where it happened?" She said without much of a question to her tone. "Me too. Mary called me a couple hours ago with the news that Henry had been identified. I'm gutted."

I nodded again. "I'm so sorry."

"I canceled patients. I've never done that. I had to get some air. It's so awful."

"May I join you?"

"Certainly."

I moved to the seat next to her. If we knew each other even just a tiny bit better I would have put my arm around her or hugged her once quickly.

Instead, Eloise nodded at me once sadly as the bus made it to the top of Victoria and waited to turn onto the Royal Mile.

"Is Mary okay?" I asked.

"Oh, no, not at all. I stopped by her house first and gave her something to calm her down. She's not one for medication but she's distraught. She's probably still sleeping."

"I'm sure it's terrible for her."

"It's so very bizarre and unreal."

"He was a lovely man," I said, mostly because I couldn't think of anything else to say. I had a million questions about Henry Stewart, but this wasn't the time or the way to ask them.

"He was," she said. She grimaced and hit her thigh with her fist. "He's made enemies though. I kept telling him to quit wanting to change so many things."

"Do you mean in his position as councilor?"

"Aye. He kept wanting to make the city a better place, at least better in his eyes. He was so used to running the show. Used to spend his days at the bank telling everyone else what to do, and they had to listen to him there. He never learned how to tread lightly because he didn't have to. Gracious, he angered some people."

I waited a good long few beats with the hopes that she'd continue. She didn't.

"Like who?" I finally asked.

"So many! That strange thing with the Burgess Tickets. What in the world was he doing, trying to bring back that old antiquated idea? And trees! He spearheaded cutting down some old trees to make a walking path easier. He knew how to work the system and the vote on those trees was sneaky, I tell you. I told him too."

Over the last couple of days, Edwin had mentioned both of the contentious items Eloise was talking about. Henry had been shaking things up. I'd been in a wedding haze and then on a honeymoon. Maybe all of this had come to a head while I was gone. I didn't quite understand the timing of everything, and I wasn't ready to tell her about the bookshop's predicament.

"Eloise, how long had he been a councilor?"

"He was starting his second year."

"What were his political aspirations?"

"Nothing beyond what he was doing. He didn't want to be Lord Provost. He didn't want a higher position. He knew he could get things done at his level."

"Sounds like it."

"Well, he certainly must have gotten under someone's skin," she said. Her fist clenched again, but she didn't pound it this time.

"Did you talk to the police?" I asked.

"Did I? No. Mary has, of course, but there's no reason I should."

I shrugged. "I don't know. Maybe you can remember something that might help them with a lead, if they don't have one, or some, already."

"Hmm. You might be right." She sat up straighter. "Here's our stop."

We exited the bus together. I was glad I was there—I was glad she was there.

Though there was no vehicle or body in the vicinity, the crime scene was buzzing. Officials were walking around in their white coveralls, some taking pictures, some taking measurements, some just looking at the destruction. The road and a streetlight had been damaged but it seemed the surrounding buildings were intact. Traffic was getting through, but slowly and as a police officer directed. We weren't far from Inspector Winters's police station and I thought again about leaving him a message.

Despite what had already been removed, the destruction and disruption at the scene was still shocking.

"Oh, my," I said quietly to myself.

"It's terrible," Eloise said. "I'm glad the auto is gone, but it's so . . ."

"Unreal," I said.

"Aye, and traumatic."

From behind a widely cordoned off area and for a long few minutes, we silently watched the police and the technicians work.

"Maybe it had something to do with Mary," Eloise said, breaking the silence.

"Mary? Why?"

She looked at me. "People either love or hate her, Delaney. She's sure she's a reincarnation of the queen. She doesn't keep it a secret. And then she goes around telling people she has proof and it's no more than a silly birthmark. People find her strange."

I shook my head. "Why would anyone care about any of that enough to kill Henry?"

"I don't know. Maybe this was to get back at her. The queen's second husband was killed in an explosion, did you know that?"

"Yes."

"Maybe this was some sort of sick act from someone who thinks Mary deserved it. *If she's the queen, she should experience the same tragedies* and such."

I blinked at Eloise. So far, she'd mentioned that both Mary and Henry had enemies. It seemed the suspect list could be long. "Well, her husband being killed in an explosion is only one of her many tragedies. I hope you're not onto something."

"Aye, it would be a terrible tragedy to see Mary beheaded."

I blinked at her again.

Eloise put her fist to her mouth. "I honestly can't believe I just said such a thing. Please forgive me."

"Of course," I said.

But it would have been impossible for me not to hear a thin thread of sarcasm in her voice. No, I would have to just let that go. She hadn't meant it.

"Wasn't it the queen's next husband, her third, the person ultimately accused of killing her second husband?"

"Something like that. Conspiring to and such."

"Is there someone out there who might fit the role as our Mary's next husband?"

"Is she having an affair? I don't think so," Eloise said. "I really and truly don't think so."

Of course, Mary, Queen of Scots, also denied an affair.

I caught the eye of someone looking at us. She was very tall and dressed in the white crime-scene coveralls, and even though her head was hooded and she was a good distance away, I could see the scrutiny in her gaze.

"I think I'm done here," Eloise said. "I should get back to my patients."

"Do you want me to go with you?"

Eloise smiled at me and suddenly her severe haircut didn't seem so severe. "You're lovely, Delaney, but no, I think I can handle it. I'm pleased we ran into each other on the bus though."

"Me too."

"I suspect we'll be in touch. Once you've befriended Mary, you've befriended all her circle. Don't fight it, that's just the way it is."

"I hope so."

"Me too. Goodbye, dear."

I watched her walk up the hill a half block before she caught another bus. I turned back around to look for the tall woman in the coveralls, but she wasn't in the same spot.

I only stayed another few minutes as I thought about the strange royal history and my new friends. Other than martyr, I didn't think I'd heard any word about the queen mentioned as much as "tragedy." There had been so much of it for her. But it had been a tragic, violent time. What the queen experienced went with the territory, I supposed.

The rain stopped and I decided to walk back to work, maybe stop by the pub for a moment on the way.

I wasn't sure why I had needed to see where the car had exploded, but Eloise hadn't asked for an explanation. I was glad, and I understood her curiosity too. It had been an unreal sequence of events, but even though Henry's car was no longer there, seeing where the explosion had occurred hadn't left me with any doubts. I wished it hadn't happened, but if it had, I needed to make sure it was real. It was.

On the way back to the bookshop, a twinge of curiosity about the tall woman came to mind, but only briefly. I forgot all about her by the time I made it down Victoria.

ELEVEN

"She mentioned the beheading and everything?" Tom said.

"Yes, but she apologized for bringing it up."

"These sorts of tragedies can cause stress." Tom was working hard at being sympathetic, but the circumstances of me running into Eloise bothered him.

There was a murder, after all.

"I chalked it up to stress."

We sat on the couch of our small cottage. It was a rare evening that Tom wasn't at the pub. He'd come home early because of the upsetting days, leaving his employee Rodger in charge. Rodger, a sworn bachelor, had demanded that Tom go and spend time with me. It hadn't taken much convincing.

"One of my customers follows the council votes closely. He mentioned that he liked Henry, admired him, but he had been pushing hard to bring back the Burgess Tickets and that the old-fashioned notion was creating some strife within the ranks, but it wasn't anything that should have led to murder."

"Eloise brought those up too. She said he's been pushing for many things, in maybe a too-pushy way. Do you think he's the one who wanted the bookshop closed? And why would he?"

"No idea. He didn't seem pushy in the least at the dinner."

"He seemed the opposite of that. Tom, do you think it was all some setup? I mean, did Mary come to the shop and invite us to the dinner on purpose? Though I can't figure out why in the world she would do that."

"It's a possibility, but she couldn't manipulate the fact that you two look so much alike. That's just the way it is."

"I thought about that too."

"Delaney." Tom frowned. "I hate to even bring this up, but now maybe the vote regarding the bookshop will be delayed. There might be more time to figure things out."

"Well, I'm sorry to say that we all thought about that too. Before the bombing, Edwin had finally put in a call to the Lord Provost, but hadn't heard back. Who knows if he will, and we all feel bad enough about Henry that we feel guilty about worrying about the bookshop's fate, but we can't help it. We also feel like we should be talking to other councilors or something."

"That sounds like a big project."

"I know." I fell back into thought. "Maybe the fact that Mary and I look alike is totally random, just a bizarre coincidence."

Tom squinted at me. "Honestly, lass, I don't think so. I don't understand what's going on, but her timing of her first visit to the bookshop *is* curious. I'd like not to think so, but I can't help it."

"I love it when you talk all Scottish to me."

He smiled. "I said, 'lass.' I can do even better than that. Och, 'tis a bunchie of blashie we're speaking, perhaps."

"You just sounded so much like Elias."

Tom's smile turned back into a frown as he reached up and tucked my hair behind my ear. "You love this cottage, don't you?"

I blinked at the change of subject. "I do, but I will love the house too."

"Are you sure?"

"Yes. Why?"

"I see you looking around this place. We haven't left yet and you're already missing it."

"Tom, I will love wherever we are together."

Tom nodded. "Me too."

My phone buzzed in my pocket. I wrestled it free.

"Hey, Rosie, everything okay?"

"Aye," she said. "I just got a call from our new friend. She called my personal mobile. I was surprised."

"Who?"

"Mary Stewart. She wants to talk to you, Delaney. She said you're the only one who can understand what she's going through, that you're soul sisters of a sort. I said I would talk tae ye tomorrow, so ye dinnae need tae call her tonight. But here's her mobile. I gave her mine at dinner, but she said she neglected tae ask for yours."

At least there was a pen close by, but with no paper I wrote the number on my arm. "How was she?"

"Awful. A mess really. I tried tae console her, but I dinnae think I did much good. I feel bad for the wee lass, but I dinnae really know her, Delaney. Neither do ye. Don't feel obligated."

"I won't." I already did.

I disconnected the call and looked at the number on my arm.

"Want to call her tonight?" Tom asked, easily overhearing the call.

I punched in the number, but something stopped me from hitting Send.

"What?" Tom asked.

"I don't know. Her husband was killed and she wants to talk to someone she just met. I mean, I felt a connection too, but . . . something tells me not to call her just yet. Is that cruel?"

"No. Rosie was correct, you don't need to feel obligated. Listen to your gut," he said.

"I might call her tomorrow, but I'm not sure." I stopped looking at my arm and gave my attention to the cobalt eyes looking back at me. "Tonight is just for you and me."

He smiled and his eyes brightened. "Aye?"

"Oh, yes, aye."

TWELVE

By the time I headed into work the next day, I still hadn't called Mary, and someone was at the bookshop to further divert my attention. Considering she'd been wearing some of the crime-scene coveralls when I first saw her, it might have been surprising that I recognized her. But I did. Immediately.

She was tall, over six feet by a couple inches, and her eyes held the same scrutiny I'd noticed on the Royal Mile. In fact, when I first walked into the bookshop and saw her talking to Rosie, I had an urge to wave when she turned toward me, as though we'd shared more than brief eye contact.

"Delaney?" she said.

"Yes, you're with the police?" I said as I approached.

She hesitated a beat. "I am. Inspector Buchanan. You look so much like . . ."

"Mary Stewart. Yes, I know."

She frowned, for some reason not pleased with the resemblance. A scenario suddenly played through my mind. Was there video of someone somewhere doing something they shouldn't have been doing—like maybe planting a bomb? Did the person look like Mary and me, and was this going to be a problem? In fact, my mind had gone there a couple of times already. It was probably too paranoid a notion as well as part of the reason I hadn't called Mary back yet.

I continued, "I just met Mary a few days ago. It was a surprise for both of us."

Inspector Buchanan nodded and plunked her hands on her hips. "That was you I saw at the crime scene yesterday. I wondered when Mary said it hadn't been her and told me about the resemblance between the two of you. Why were you there?"

For a moment, I felt truly terrible. Maybe that's why Mary was trying to get ahold of me, to warn me the police might be coming to see me. I felt like a fool.

Inspector Buchanan hadn't even asked for a private place to talk. Behind the inspector's back, Rosie sent me some high eyebrows. Hector, not liking attitude thrown at any of his people, trotted around the desk and to me. He sat at my feet protectively and faced the inspector. We all looked down at him as he panted displeasingly at the tall woman. She shook her head once and then looked back at me.

"Well?" she said.

"I'm not exactly sure. The news about Henry was tough to take and I needed some air. I boarded the bus and I realized I needed to see where . . . where it happened. It was shocking that there weren't more injuries."

She blinked at me, once, twice, and then pursed her lips. "You just met Henry recently?"

"Three nights ago. He cooked us dinner." My voice cracked. Hector moved closer. I wanted to pick him up but that seemed too frivolous.

"I see. Can you please tell me about the dinner? Who was there? What occurred?"

"Excuse me," Rosie said. "Please, won't the two of ye take a seat in the back, or perhaps in one of the offices next door? Ye're sure tae scare away any potential customers."

Without a word, Inspector Buchanan glanced toward the table and then made her way to it. I picked up Hector and joined her, sitting down and ignoring her critical expression when she looked at the dog on my lap.

Rosie didn't offer to grab coffee or tea, which of course was Rosie code for "let's not keep her here too long."

"Your coworker," Inspector Buchanan nodded toward Rosie, who was now back at the front desk, "told me her version of the events at the dinner. I'd like to hear about it from your perspective."

I told her the details, but just their barest of bones. I didn't mention what'd I'd seen Mikey do, the expressions he'd shared with Henry and Dina. I would have told Inspector Winters, but I wasn't ready to trust Inspector Buchanan. I could see that she was suspicious of me too, but not enough to question me in any official capacity. For the time being at least.

"Who was the woman you were with at the scene yesterday?"

"Eloise. She's a doctor, but I'm afraid I never caught her last name. She was introduced to us only as Eloise."

"Introduced? At the dinner?"

"Yes."

Inspector Buchanan hadn't taken any notes, until that moment. She reached into her jacket pocket for a notebook and a pen. "Her name again?"

"Eloise is all I got."

She frowned deeply as if she was highly perturbed that I

didn't know more about the doctor. I held back the shrug that made its way to my shoulders. I didn't tell her I knew Eloise was Mary's doctor.

"But she was at the dinner?" Inspector Buchanan asked.

Hadn't I said that? "Yes. Along with her partner, Gretchen. As well as Mary's niece, Dina, and Dina's husband, Mikey."

"Right." She tapped her pencil on the paper. "What do you think of Mary's claim of reincarnation? Do you believe it?"

I wanted to ask her the relevance of such a question, and then I remembered my attorney. It hadn't occurred to me to tell the police I wouldn't talk to them without my attorney present. Inspector Buchanan had made it seem so casual that I'd done what all those people on TV do, just kept talking. As I watched them, I'd roll my eyes and exclaim that "that would never happen to me."

"I didn't *not* believe, but I wasn't convinced. Why?" I crossed my arms in front of myself. Hector whined.

"It's a curious thing, is all. A very curious thing. All right then. Well, your account of those attending the party is the same as your coworker's. I guess I just have one more thing." She looked over at Rosie who was looking at us. The inspector waved her to us.

Rosie frowned but came over to the table.

Inspector Buchanan seemed to like the audience. She gave a proper dramatic pause before she continued.

"At any time that evening, did Henry, the victim, mention that he was working to shut down this place? This bookshop was going to be closed down because it was something he set in motion?"

There it was. We'd all wondered, and it now seemed so devastatingly real. Nevertheless, I tried to keep a stiff upper lip.

"No," I said.

"No," Rosie said.

At least we both kept it simple.

"I see. I just wondered if that was something that came up during the dinner Henry cooked for you. That's all," Inspector Buchanan said.

I did not like her.

"It most certainly did not." Rosie stood up straight and held her chin defiantly.

"No, it didn't. Everyone was very friendly, welcoming," I said, sadness filling my chest. The question came to me again—had that entire dinner been some sort of setup for something? It wasn't clear what end result they were looking for, but Tom was correct, something wasn't right.

"Is that really the truth? Henry the councilor was trying to close the bookshop?" I asked.

"It seems he had proposed a vote, scheduled to take place next week, as to whether or not the council would agree to an inspector's findings that this building should be torn down, that it was beyond repair." Inspector Buchanan looked around with an odd twinkle in her eyes. Schadenfreude came to mind. Was she enjoying our misfortune?

"There's been no inspector to visit us," I said.

"No," Rosie added. "We've had no inspector."

Inspector Buchanan looked back and forth between us. She was either perplexed or thought we were lying, and was determined to figure out which it was.

"Well, that's certainly most interesting," the inspector said. "Are you sure?"

"Of course we're sure," Rosie said.

Hector decided Rosie might need him more so he hopped

off my lap and moved to sit at her feet. Inspector Buchanan rolled her eyes at the dog.

"Well, I'll have to look at that more closely," she said.

"In fact," I smiled, but it probably seemed faked and forced, "we would very much like it if someone would. If there hasn't been an inspection, there can't be a vote, right?"

"Well, I don't know about that. Signals have been crossed, that's apparent. I'll get to the bottom of it."

She stood and smoothed her slacks over her thighs, pulled once at the hem of her jacket. I realized she wasn't dressed in a uniform. I'd talked to her, done as she'd wanted me to do, and she didn't even look official. I was now one of those people on TV.

"Thank you for your time," she said. She looked around. "I heard this place was dangerous, not a safe place to be at all, that no repairs would be possible. You all might want to consider shutting it down anyway."

"Does it look dangerous?" I asked.

"No. It looks old though and that might be the same thing."

I stood. "You've seen the report?"

She didn't like my question, but she couldn't lie either. "Well, no, but I heard about it. I've spoken to some other council members."

"Please, Inspector Buchanan, if you see it, may we see it too?" I asked.

"I will follow protocol, whatever that might be. But you all should consider that you're in denial here."

I opened my mouth but she turned and marched away. Rosie put her hand on my arm and shook her head. I closed my mouth.

Inspector Buchanan didn't even look back as she opened the door and went through. She was gone, but she'd left a hell of a wake behind.

THIRTEEN

"Oh dear," Edwin said after Rosie and I gave him and Hamlet the news.

Rosie had sent them both a 999 text, not bothering to ask me to do the honors as she usually did when it came to mobile technology.

However, she'd looked at her phone seriously before she'd sent it.

"It's okay," I said. "It's a real emergency. At least we have more information."

She'd nodded and hit Send.

I was by far the most riled up of all of us. Rosie had been upset briefly but Edwin had remained cool. Hamlet was bothered by the police inspector's methods and wanted to tell her as much. I bit down on my anger when Edwin's demeanor wasn't as heated as I thought it should be.

I was ready for a fight. I didn't know who I was supposed to fight, but I wanted the rest of my coworkers to feel the same.

"What should we do?" I asked.

Edwin sat up straighter and nodded. He heard my desperation. "I haven't heard from the Lord Provost, but I know others in his office. I will call them too, see if I can get more information. Surely, the vote will be postponed."

"Wait, can we go see the Lord Provost? Just stop by his office? Maybe he'd see us." I shrugged.

"No, probably not." Edwin fell into thought and looked up an instant later. "However, we *can* visit someone else, I think. Someone who works for the city. Would you like to try?"

"Yes!" I said. Hell to the yes. "Let's go."

Edwin stood. "We can walk there."

"Oh, good. I'll grab the umbrellas."

The business licensing division for the city of Edinburgh was located on the Royal Mile, another bus ride or, as we'd chosen today, a quick walk past Tom's pub (we stuck our heads in and said hello), up Victoria Street, and then not far down the Royal Mile, the street that led to the sea, the street that had seen the terrible recent tragedy of Henry's murder as well as so many other tragedies over the centuries. It was once the whole city, the place where all of Edinburgh used to work and live back in the days when people were far too crowded together and things like the Black Plague could easily have its way with the population.

Today, clouds above threatened rain, but no raindrops fell. I figured that was because I'd made sure we were well prepared with the umbrellas. If I'd forgotten them, as I frequently did, it would have surely rained. And that was an official observation.

Along the walk, we talked about Edwin's lady love and the new menu she was incorporating into her restaurant. Until he'd dated a restaurant owner, Edwin hadn't been interested in food. Now it was one of his main topics of conversation. We'd probably had more conversations about spices and food preparation techniques than we'd had books over the last little while.

I was pleased to have something to talk about other than all the horrible things we'd talked about at the bookshop.

"Here we are," Edwin soon said.

The business licensing division was housed in another beautiful, old, historical building, on its bottom floor, adorned only with a calligraphed sign in the window announcing the office's hours. Edwin pulled the door open and waited as I went through.

The inside was contemporary. The office was just like any other government office I'd been inside in the States—gray and brown and generic. If it was a busy place, we managed to hit a lull in the traffic. Only one person stood on this side of the counter as three others looked up at us from behind it.

"Help you?" A young man said as he moved toward his side of the counter.

"Aye," Edwin said. "Is Lyle in?"

"Um, well, I'll have a look. May I tell him who's inquiring?"

"Edwin MacAlister."

"One moment."

I watched the man disappear through a doorway and down a hall. Like Mikey, he also reminded me of my friend at the museum, Joshua. Tall, thin, topped off with glasses with big, black frames. I sensed I needed to pay Joshua a visit.

"Lyle doesn't get much company?" I quietly asked Edwin. "That guy seemed surprised you asked for him."

"He likes to remain hidden. You'd be surprised by the level of vitriol some people can have regarding their business licenses."

I blinked at him. "No, Edwin, I don't think I would be."

Edwin's mouth made a straight line as he nodded. "Fair enough."

"Come through, Mr. MacAlister," the clerk said as he reappeared from the hallway.

Edwin and I looked at each other. *That was easy.*

We were led down the hallway to the last office on the left. I was always surprised when something in an Edinburgh building was so normal. Even now, after I'd been in the country long enough to see both spectacular architecture and boring, normal buildings, I pushed away some disappointment at the plain walls and common linoleum floor.

The clerk pushed open the door and then stood back out of our way.

"Edwin, what a lovely surprise!" The man, Lyle, I presumed, stood from behind the desk and extended his hand.

It wasn't a tiny office, but it wasn't roomy either. If he was the head of business licensing of the entire city, the position didn't come with a luxurious office.

"Lyle. Pleasure's all mine." They shook. "This is Delaney Nichols. She's a good friend and an employee at the bookshop. Delaney, this is Lyle Mercado."

Lyle wasn't as old or as distinguished at Edwin. Maybe in his sixties, he was rough around the edges, scruffy beard and wrinkled clothes, and above a friendly smile his eyes glinted with disapproval or discomfort. His accent was lighter than Edwin's, similar to Tom's, but, again, I knew I didn't hear them the same way anymore. Before long, I might actually speak some Scots.

"Nice to meet you, Delaney." We shook, and his tight smile melted as he looked at me. He withdrew his hand and looked away from my eyes and downward as his eyebrows came together. He recovered somewhat, but not all the way, giving me another quick smile.

"You too."

"Have a seat," he said. "Coffee machine's broken. I can't offer you anything at all. No, not true. I have gum in my desk." He pulled open the top drawer and rummaged around nervously. "Would you like some gum?"

"No, thank you," Edwin said.

I said the same, but then I looked over at Edwin. His demeanor had changed. He now looked at Lyle suspiciously.

"Lyle," Edwin said. "We've come to ask you a question and it might seem an odd one, but we've heard something recently and I knew the only way to get the answer was to come right to a source who might know."

Lyle sighed and sat back in his chair. "I've been expecting you."

"You have?"

"Of course. I . . . in fact, I should have come to talk to you myself. I just . . . well, I've been so busy. Anyway, I'm sorry for what has happened."

Edwin and I shared a look. Clearly, this wasn't going as Edwin might have expected. Me either, but I didn't know what I'd expected.

"Lyle," Edwin said. "I need you to tell me exactly what you're talking about. I'm not sure if it's the same thing we're here about, but I need you to be as forthcoming as you can be. All right?"

Lyle's eyes grew wide. In that instant, we could see his surprise too. We'd all come together with different levels of knowledge about something that was somehow connected. It was important that we all get up to the same speed as quickly as possible. Lyle clearly thought it unfortunate that he was going to have to be the one to do the work. But there was no getting out of it now. I sensed that if he tried to leave the room, Edwin would block all exits, if he got to them before I did.

Lyle sighed. "I'm talking about the revocation of the bookshop's business license, because of the failed building inspection, of course, Edwin. I'm so sorry for the turn of events."

Edwin stared at Lyle as he fell into concentrated thought. He spoke soon enough though.

"Lyle, until I received a phone call about a week ago, I had no idea there were potential problems with the bookshop's buildings. Can you please shed some light on what has happened?"

Lyle's face fell. "Oh dear, this is all so dicey."

"Nevertheless, I need you to tell me everything."

I didn't know what Edwin had on Lyle, but the man on the other side of the desk didn't fight. In fact, he seemed momentarily ashamed.

Lyle sighed. "We sent out formal notice in letter form, Edwin."

"No letter was received," Edwin said. "Did you ask for a signature or serve me legal papers?"

"Well, I thought we did."

No one was more vigilant than Rosie. She oversaw the bookshop's mail and was the one there, attending to customers, more than the rest of us. She opened and read everything, and then shredded whatever didn't need her or someone else's attention. If a notice had come by mail, Rosie would have sounded alarm bells. Those bells would have rung even louder if she'd been served legal papers.

"Things get lost in . . . oh, I don't know what might have

happened but bottom line, we've had to crack down on rules and regulations already in place, Edwin. The bookshop—the stairs you put in between the two buildings to connect them, to be specific—is not in code, or something like that. The business license is to be revoked. The shop will have to close as of the end of next month."

The words had come out in a jumble, but they were easy to understand, and, frankly, it was good to have a tiny bit of clarification. Okay, it was the spot in between the buildings that was the problem. Maybe we could still work with that.

"Lyle, I will simply fix whatever is out of code. I would have done so a long time ago if someone had just talked to me," Edwin said.

Edwin didn't say the words, "you fools" but they rang in my mind. I clamped my mouth closed.

And then Lyle shook his head. "No, Edwin, there's no fixing it. An inspector, apparently, deemed it too dangerous to try to fix."

"This is not good, Lyle."

"No, I suppose it isn't."

"I did receive approval to build the walkway, the stairs. I went through the proper channels, years ago when I first did the remodel."

"Aye?"

"Aye, I did. This was a long time ago, Lyle, but I remember the process we had to go though. We received the approval. I would never have taken on the project without approvals."

Lyle's eyes lit and he sat forward, placing his arms on the desk. "Do you still have the paperwork? Was there paperwork?"

"I believe there was, but I'm not sure where it would be now. I will find it. I will find it if that's what's needed."

"Good, well, that might help."

"Might?"

"It has been deemed that the safety of your two buildings has been compromised. Even if you received approval, that was a long time ago and the inspection showed issues. Times, expectations change."

"Have you seen the inspection?" I interrupted. "Can we see it."

"Oh. No, I haven't seen it and I don't have a copy, but the council has, or we wouldn't be at this point."

"Lyle, nothing has so much as settled with the structures in between the buildings," Edwin said. "I made sure it was built well, and built to last forever. However, we can do whatever we need to do to come back up to code, or appease the inspector. Whatever might be needed."

"It's too late, Edwin, the process has been set in motion. Your buildings are set to be torn down. If the vote goes through, there's no stopping it."

"What? That's unheard of. We value our old buildings. We keep them, take care of them. None of them gets torn down on purpose!" Edwin exclaimed.

Lyle lifted his hands. "And this is why I should have come to talk to you. I thought you were more in the loop."

"More in the loop? I should have been *the* loop. This is ridiculous, Lyle, and I think you know that."

I cleared my throat. The two men looked at me. "Henry Stewart. The man who was killed in the bombing two days ago. He was the one who set this in motion," I said. Lyle nodded. "He's been killed. I think that if for no other reason than respect, this should all be moved further down the council's calendar." It was maybe a heartless move, unsympathetic to

Henry's murder, but I had to try, and I hoped to diffuse Edwin's anger for a moment.

"I don't disagree with you, lass, but I'm not the one to decide that. That's for the council." Lyle paused as he looked at Edwin. "I'm so sorry for all of this, and I really should have come to talk to you. I apologize."

"There are no other meetings until next week?" Edwin said, anger still lining his words, but at least it wasn't quite as heated.

"Not that I'm aware of," Lyle said with a shrug.

Round and round we go, I thought.

It took a moment for us all to gather ourselves. The air was rife with anger and confusion. Almost in unison, we took deep, cleansing breaths.

Lyle was the first one to speak. He looked at me. "You look so much like her, you know. I was momentarily confused. Why would Edwin be walking into my office with Mary Stewart, the woman married to the man who wants, wanted, to tear down his bookshop? You are younger."

"We do look alike," I said. "How do you know her? Through knowing Henry?"

"Oh. Many people know Mary. She's vocal about her past lives." Lyle laughed.

"What does she know about the bookshop buildings being torn down?" I asked.

"I have no idea," Lyle said.

I would have bet Tom's wedding kilt that Lyle Mercado was lying. His face reddened ever so slightly, and he closed his mouth tightly, as if he wanted to keep truthful words locked inside.

Edwin and I didn't even try to hide our shared doubtful glances.

"How well did you know Henry?" Edwin asked.

Lyle paused, tapped his finger on the edge of his desk. "Henry and I got on all right. Until all of this occurred at least. I wasn't in agreement with the decisions being made. But you have to understand how these things work. Though I have power in my office, I can't make policies or laws."

"Lyle, what if I tore down and then rebuilt everything? I would do that if it came to it. I would hate every second of it, but I would do it."

"I'm sure, but . . . I just don't know, Edwin. The council is making the decisions here."

"Lyle," Edwin admonished. "This isn't making sense, and you know it. You also know that I have friends in high places. I will contact all of them and get to the bottom of this. It would behoove you to tell me what's really going on."

The more we learned, the less any of it made sense. Until something came to me, maybe the obvious thing.

"Lyle, someone wants that land. They want that space specifically," I said. "This is bigger than just some building codes, isn't it?"

"Not that I'm aware of, lass."

I thought as quickly as I could. "Does that spot have any sort of historic significance to Mary, Queen of Scots?"

"I guess I don't know," Lyle said.

"Nothing recorded," Edwin said.

"You think Henry might have been doing this for his wife?" Lyle said, sounding truly unsure.

"I think it's a possibility. Until we have an answer, it's a thought at least," I said.

Lyle looked at me a long moment. "I . . . I don't think Henry and Mary are like that."

"Like what?" Edwin said.

"I don't think they would ruin someone's livelihood, take someone's life's work just because Mary, Queen of Scots, happened to be at that location at one time. No, they'd be more inclined to get to know you first and then turn it into a party or something. Then try to get you to give them what they want."

Isn't that what had been set into motion?

I looked at Edwin. He thought the same thing. There had been a chance meeting, there had been a party. Maybe we hadn't made it far enough. Maybe getting what they wanted would have come next if Henry hadn't been killed.

But Edwin didn't want to point that out to Lyle. He changed the course of the conversation. "Did Henry have enemies that you know of, Lyle? Anyone who might want him killed?"

"Goodness, with all of this and his grand ideas, he might have had some disagreements," Lyle said. "I'm not aware of any enemies, but I really didn't know him *that* well." He looked at Edwin and then back at me and then back at Edwin. He cleared his throat. "This might sound terribly unfair, Edwin, but when I first heard about Henry, I thought that maybe you had something to do with his death . . . well, you have connections and all. I'm sorry, but it is what I considered."

"I'm sure the police will consider it too," Edwin said.

"For whatever it's worth, I'd be happy to vouch for you. We've had good tidings over the years."

"Well, if they speak with you, I wouldn't want anything more than the truth to be told. A killer needs to be found."

"There's nothing you can do to help fix this?" I said to Lyle.

"The best I can do is look into it and let you know." Lyle worked hard not to sound defeated.

"That would be appreciated," Edwin said.

Lyle nodded sadly. "All right. I'm sorry you didn't know more. Something's gone wrong here, and any part my office played in that is regrettable. I'm sorry about Henry. No matter that I might have disagreed with him regarding some things, he didn't deserve to be killed. It's a sad thing."

I looked at Lyle over the desk. I wasn't sure which side he was on.

We didn't learn much more from him. In fact, Edwin became so distracted by his own thoughts I decided he wasn't really listening anymore, and we just needed to leave.

Making excuses that we had to go, I led us out of the offices, but just as we stepped outside, I had to regroup again.

FOURTEEN

"Dina?" I said as I opened an umbrella.

Her head was down looking at some papers she was holding. The rain was light but she didn't have an umbrella and I could see water spots on the papers. She looked up and moved her hair off her forehead. "Oh . . . Delaney, hello."

Her eyes were rimmed in red and her nose was swollen.

"This is my boss, Edwin, we're both so sorry about your uncle."

"Thank you." She sniffed. "It's so terribly awful."

"Lass, deepest condolences," Edwin said with a polite nod of his head.

Dina wiped her hand under her nose and sniffed again. "And life goes on." She looked around, but I couldn't tell if she was looking for something specific or if she just needed a second. We waited patiently. "I forgot to pay my yearly fee. I'm late. Just got this late notice today." She waved the papers but I couldn't make out any specific writing. "I had no choice but to hurry down and take care of it." She looked at me. "But I can't stop crying. I'm . . ."

I reached out to put my hand on her arm, but she pulled it away. She sniffed again and then walked around us.

"Please don't mind me," she said over her shoulder. "I'm embarrassed, but I'm all right."

Edwin and I watched her hurry inside.

"Should I go after her?" I said.

"I don't know," Edwin said.

"Wait for me a second?" I said and handed Edwin the umbrella.

I hurried back inside, speed-walked down the hallway, and pulled open the door we'd gone through. The room was much fuller now, customers were filed into two crowded lines. I didn't see Dina, and there wasn't a way to ask anyone if they'd seen an upset woman. I left and looked around the hallway, spying the loo a few doors away. I went to turn the knob, but the door was locked. I lifted my hand to knock, but I hesitated. Maybe she did just need a moment. I wasn't even sure she was inside, but I thought she probably was.

I opened my mouth to say something but we didn't know each other well enough for me to find the right words. Finally, I just placed my hand on the door and sighed. I wanted to see her antique shop anyway. I would track her down later and see if there was anything I could do for her. Sometimes people just need to break down a little without being held responsible for it.

With one last look down the hallway, I finally rejoined Edwin outside.

"How'd it go?" He moved the brollie so it was over me more than him.

I shook my head. "Didn't see her. I think she went into the loo, locked the door."

"Understandable."

"She has an antique shop. We probably have a lot in common. I might go see her later."

"Aye?" he said. "Where's the shop?"

"Cowgate."

"I knew she looked familiar. She and I and her husband, I believe, had some dealings some years back. They are a lovely couple."

But I blinked at his tone. "It sounds like you aren't sure about something. The dealings or if they're a lovely couple?"

"No, I'm sure about both, I just can't remember what the ultimate result of our time together was. I sense there was some contention. I'll think about it."

"Okay. Let me know."

"I will. All right, let's go talk to Rosie, see if she's forgotten to give me any mail, or if, by chance, she has that construction paperwork from all those years ago. I need to be armed with as much as I can, and she'll be good at helping with that. Any luck with the Burgess Ticket?"

"None, but I haven't given it my all yet. I will. I see why it might be good to have."

"Ta, lass."

I remembered that I still hadn't called Mary. But now I wanted to talk to Rosie first. Despite the tragedy Mary was living, I still didn't want to believe I had somehow been set up for something. Just like Edwin, I wanted more information.

I hoped Rosie could offer some certainty, but I didn't count on it.

"No! We have never, ever received such a notice. I'm certain of it," Rosie exclaimed.

"I didn't think so, Rosie love," Edwin said.

We were all in the front of the shop, Rosie sitting behind her desk. I was pacing. Hamlet had already sent me a couple of frowns, probably wishing I would stop moving so much. I'd tried, I really had, but I couldn't stop.

I'd heard Edwin use the term of endearment for Rosie only one other time since I'd been in Scotland. She'd been upset about something then too, though I didn't remember what it had been.

"And I will find the paperwork for the approval of the construction," she continued. "I don't know where it is offhand. It was ages ago. But I never throw anything away."

"I know," Edwin said.

"This is ridiculous," she said. "They simply cannae have the power tae do such a thing."

"It *is* bizarre," Hamlet added. "There must be some sort of law that will protect our rights to do business here, particularly if the buildings are out of code and you agree to fix them. I really don't get it. I will see if we've missed something from a legal perspective."

"Something's going on," I said. "Something we can't understand because we don't have all the pieces. Things have been kept from us, purposefully. We'll figure it out."

Though I was having a hard time standing still, I'd calmed down a bit on the walk back to the bookshop. The buildings that housed both sides, the dark and the light, were still standing. And while they were still there, there was a chance we could find a way to save them. But we needed to hurry.

Hope *was* coming back little bit by little bit. We *would* figure this out.

"Aye, Hamlet, research the laws, but we need an attorney. A good one. A mean one," Rosie said. "Ruthless."

"Aye," Edwin said. "I think I have just the man in mind. Excuse me while I make a couple phone calls."

Edwin stood and took the stairs up and over to the dark side. I watched him, watched the floor he walked on, the walls he walked next to. I'd never once felt like anything was unstable. Nothing was uneven, everything was straight, level. Nothing was wrong with any of the structures' integrity.

After he went through the door, I turned to Hamlet. "While you're researching, is there any way for you to find out if this place, this location once had anything to do with Mary, Queen of Scots? Did she like the view of the castle from here? Did she have tea here? Did she sneeze in the vicinity? Something, anything."

"I see where ye're going," Rosie said. "Mary Stewart wanted this place for something and her husband was going to get it."

"I can try," Hamlet said, "but it's highly unlikely that anything would be noted that way. We don't know as much about our historical figures as we claim to. But I'll scour whatever I can find."

"Thanks." I fell into thought.

Rosie stood. She picked up Hector and joined me at the front of the shop, bringing my pacing to a stop. She handed Hector to me. I held him close.

"It's going tae be all right," she said. She wasn't usually the one doing the comforting, but she took on the role well.

"If this doesn't work, Rosie, I'm going to try to convince

Edwin to open up somewhere else," I said. I thought I heard Hector harrumph.

Rosie's eyebrows lifted. "Aye? Well, I dinnae want tae disappoint ye, but he's auld, set in his ways, and he loves this place. There's not another for him."

I thought about the bookshop in some shiny new location with pristine walls and floors. That would be awful. Not for a new bookshop, one that hadn't yet lived its life, but for this one, it would. The blood, the vital organs of The Cracked Spine were inside these lathe-and-plaster walls, these old shelves, that ladder. The marble floor was in terrible shape, but it was also one of the most beautiful floors I'd ever seen. Tears came to my eyes as I remembered the first time I walked into the shop and saw those floors, how scared I'd been, how, when I'd seen the ladder that rolled up and down the shelves, I'd so quickly felt at home. The light was bad, the furniture old and worn. It was the most perfect place ever.

"I guess you're right," I said to Rosie. "This is the only place the bookshop could ever be."

"Aye, lass. Aye."

I pulled out my cell phone. A resolve had come over me. I dialed Mary's number.

"Hello?" a voice said, but I didn't think it was Mary's.

"Yes, I'm returning Mary's call. Delaney Nichols from The Cracked Spine."

"Aye? It's Eloise, Delaney. Mary's resting but I'm happy to let her know you called."

Sometimes reaching out and taking someone's hand is the beginning of a journey.

The bookish voice didn't come from the book about Queen Elizabeth. It came from Hamlet's inspirational calendar. I looked at the back table and saw him there, peering at something on his laptop. His tear-away calendar was behind him. I must have read the words recently.

"Yes, thanks. Eloise . . ." I said.

"Aye?"

Maybe I did need to get going on the journey of knowing Eloise; she and I seemed to find each other easily. "Any chance you have time for dinner tonight?"

"Well, I suppose I do. I don't think Mary will be up to attending. Should I invite Gretchen?"

"Yes, please. I'll invite Tom."

We solidified plans and I told her I'd see her in a couple hours. I wondered if Mary would wake up and want to join us. I wasn't sure if that would be a good or a bad idea.

"That should be interesting," Rosie said when I hung up.

"Want to come?"

"I need tae search for those approval forms and the Burgess Ticket. Not this time, but I'll expect tae hear aboot it."

"Of course."

It wasn't long before Tom came through the door. He saw the expression on my face and stopped in the entryway.

"Uh-oh, what happened?" he asked.

"I'll tell you all about it on the way," I said as I tried to look less terrified. "We're going to dinner."

FIFTEEN

On the way, Tom had asked me why I'd wanted to ask Eloise and Gretchen out to dinner. I hadn't gone into detail about my bookish voices with him yet, so I didn't mention that a calendar had told me to. I'd shrugged and said it was just a feeling I'd had. He thought that was a good enough reason. However, it was then I decided we needed to have a conversation about the bookish voices. It wasn't technically a lie that I hadn't shared that quirky part of me, but quirky things were supposed to be shared with significant others. I wished I'd told him already.

We'd met at a pizza place right at the top of Victoria Street. When I first arrived in Scotland, I thought a pizza place didn't quite fit with my idea of Scottish food choices, but I'd come to accept that it was okay for restaurants in Scotland to prepare and serve international fare.

Though still tinged with grief, Eloise and Gretchen seemed happy to be joining us; happy to have a distraction maybe. We were all quickly comfortable with each other too, Eloise greeting me with a hug and a quick, "See, I told you, once you meet someone through Mary, you're friends for life."

Once the pizza had been served, I asked Gretchen, "Did you see Mary too? How's she doing?"

Gretchen said, "I'm not as close with those weirdos as Eloise is."

"Oh."

She chewed a bite of pizza and quickly stuffed it into her cheek. "I mean the past-life people. They are a strange group, and since Henry is—was—with Mary, they weren't my favorite people to hang out with. Eloise had to drag me to dinner the other night. But you were all fine."

"I've been Mary's doctor for years," Eloise said. "I was the very first person she told about her past lives, many years ago. It's okay for me to share; she tells people that all the time."

"I didn't know until much later, after they became friends and we started socializing together. I took an immediate disliking to Mary as she did to me. We've become friendlier over the years, but she and Eloise are much closer," Gretchen said.

"Would you still be friends if you weren't her doctor?" Tom asked Eloise.

"I think so, but we probably would never have established a relationship. Gretchen and I have been together thirty years. I met Mary about twenty years ago, in a clothing shop in Glasgow. She fainted, and told me she didn't have a doctor. I've been her physician ever since, and once she started talking about her past lives, she felt like she could trust me with whatever she wanted to say, get it all off her chest maybe. It was a burden she carried for years."

"Meeting Eloise opened the gates for her," Gretchen said with a hand flourish.

I wondered if Gretchen and Mary truly had become friendlier toward each other or if Gretchen just pretended.

"What has she told you about her lives?" I asked.

"Can't tell you any more than I have. Doctor-patient privilege and all," Eloise said.

"Of course," I said. "Were you Henry's doctor too?"

"No. In fact, I don't think Henry had been to a doctor in years, until recently. Mary mentioned that he'd gone to see someone about his knees but we never talked about it much."

"Tell me about your art studio," Tom asked Gretchen.

"I have a shop and a studio together." Gretchen smiled and then continued, "I sculpt animals, smaller than actual size."

"Where's your place?" Tom asked.

Gretchen sat back in her chair and wiped the corner of her mouth with a napkin. "I wondered when you'd ask that."

There was nothing light or fun in her tone. Almost in tandem, Tom and I cocked our heads as we looked at her.

"That's why you asked us to dinner, right?" Gretchen said.

"I don't understand," I said.

"Gretch, I don't think they know. I think they were just being sociable."

"Really," I said as Tom and I shared a glance, "we don't understand. Have we offended?"

Gretchen's expression softened. "Perhaps I'm being sensitive. Never mind."

Eloise gave one stress-lined laugh. "I think it's okay to tell them, hun. The police will clear you."

"I think so too, but I don't want anyone to accuse me of anything. . . ."

"Tom and I aren't quick to accuse," I said.

"All right." Gretchen sat forward, pushed her plate back, and put her arms on the table. "I think Henry was trying to shut down my shop, my whole studio."

"Let me guess. Was there an upcoming vote? An alleged bad report from an inspector?" I said, anxiety zipping through me. Is this why my intuition wanted me to make friends with these women?

Gretchen shook her head. "No, nothing like that. I received notice that I was to present something called a Burgess Ticket. . . ."

"Yes, the things that were once delivered in miniature coffin-like boxes?" I asked.

"That's right," Eloise said, but she didn't look at me. I wondered if she remembered our conversation on the bus about Henry angering people.

"Anyway, I don't have anything like that," Gretchen continued. "My studio and shop are in an old building that has been home to many different businesses over the years. There's no way to track down the original business owner, or maybe even what the original business was."

"There aren't city records?" I said.

"Not going back that far, not that I could find. The tickets go back to the *eighteenth* century. I guess some people kept them, but I didn't even know about them to inquire when I purchased the building. Since I don't have one, I have to spend a fortune to bring the building up to today's standards. Who's ever heard of such a thing? We are all about our old buildings, our history. Anyway, I think Henry was behind all of it."

"What are you going to do?" I asked.

"I don't know. I thought I would see if the council switches gears now that Henry is dead." Gretchen shrugged again. "I have an alibi though, I need to make that clear. I haven't talked to the police or anything, but I have an alibi for the morning that Henry was killed. I mean, I would never kill anyone anyway, but I was setting up a presentation at a local school when the car bomb exploded."

I wasn't sure that made much of an alibi. Where was she when the bomb was planted? Where were any of us? Supposedly all of us were home in our beds asleep, but I didn't know when the police thought the device had been put on the car. No one had questioned any of us at the bookshop; Gretchen either, it sounded like.

"Where's your studio and shop?" I asked.

"In Cowgate, right next to Dina's antique shop."

I slid a napkin over to her. "Write down the address? I want to come look closely at the building."

She looked at the napkin and back at me. "I don't understand."

I looked at Tom. He nodded. "Let me share with you our situation. Then you might understand."

I explained everything, giving them every detail I possibly could. Even if one of them had killed Henry, we were on the same team, of sorts. What had been Henry's motivation for wanting to close any business?

"That's terrible," Gretchen said when I finished. "That bookshop has been around forever. I've been in a few times over the years. Maybe the vote won't happen now. I'm sorry if that sounds unsympathetic."

It wasn't just Gretchen, we all felt guilty about looking at any bright side to Henry being gone.

"I think it's set in stone," I said.

"Go to the meeting, fight," Gretchen said.

"Oh, I will. We will," I said.

"Have you talked to Mikey about all of this?" Eloise asked.

"No," I said. "Why?"

"He's a councilor too," Eloise added. "That wasn't mentioned at dinner?"

"What?" I said. "I had no idea."

"Me either," Tom said.

"He's the one who told Gretchen and me that it was Henry who had started the whole mess with the Burgess Tickets," Eloise said.

"He probably knows about The Cracked Spine too," I said.

Eloise shrugged. "You'll have to ask him. I remember wondering why Henry didn't mention he was a councilor. He's usually . . . well, he usually liked people to know that about him. Mikey doesn't talk much no matter what, so I'm not surprised he didn't say anything."

"Do you think Mary knows about all of this?" I asked.

Eloise thought a long moment. "I really don't. She hasn't brought it up to me, and she tells me everything. Besides, she would have been angry with Henry for doing anything to jeopardize Gretchen's business. We were going to talk to Mary, Henry, and Mikey about it the night of the dinner, but then you all showed and it didn't feel right to bring it up, and then Henry was killed."

"Is that why there was a strain in the air when we came upstairs?" I asked.

"Probably," Eloise said.

I thought about telling them the state I'd seen Dina in earlier, but I didn't. It suddenly occurred to me, though, that she might have been at the licensing office because of something similar to what The Cracked Spine and Gretchen were going through. Was there more to her emotions than a late payment? What had those papers really been? Was she upset because of her uncle's murder or those papers, or both? Surely, Henry hadn't been trying to shut down his niece's business too?

It was tumultuous to have bad feelings for someone who had been killed, someone who had recently hosted a lovely dinner where you'd had a good time and enjoyed delicious food. But I was now more convinced that my meeting Mary and us being invited to their castle was some sort of setup. What I wasn't so sure of was if Mary was a willing participant in the setup, or a convenient pawn.

"Eloise, when you left Mary today, was she still resting?" I asked.

"She was. I left a note that you'd called though. She'll get back to you."

"I'm sure," I said. She'd called me first after all. However, I suddenly wished I hadn't stalled in calling her back. If not to tell me Inspector Buchanan was going to ask me some questions, what did she want?

The front of the restaurant was a long row of windows. That was one of the features I liked so much about the place, the people watching. I looked out through them now and saw the same sorts of people I always saw; tourists, locals (those who didn't look around with awe, but simply made their way along), and the random man in a kilt. There weren't enough kilt-wearing men in Scotland anymore.

It had rained recently, and things glimmered. The light from the old-fashioned streetlights sparkled everywhere, off the brick buildings, the cobblestone road, the old shopfronts.

This part of Edinburgh wasn't about modern and new, but old and traditional. However, this part of Edinburgh was also built right on top of another version, an older version. There were probably even Burgess Tickets buried somewhere under the surface.

Time marched on. Things changed.

Was it time for the bookshop to close?

No! I thought as my dinner partners laughed about something I hadn't paid attention to. My eyes landed on someone who was walking past the window, looking at a book they carried. I didn't know the stranger, but I couldn't help but wonder what he was reading, and if he'd maybe picked the book up from the greatest bookshop on the planet.

Oh, it couldn't close. It just couldn't.

I turned back to the pizza and our new friends, grateful that we stopped talking about all the sad things, and moved the conversation to happier things, things new friends typically discussed.

But even as we enjoyed dinner, time continued to march on all around us.

SIXTEEN

I checked my phone again as Joshua walked toward me. Mary hadn't called yet, but it was still early in the morning.

It was rare that Joshua and I didn't meet inside the museum, but he'd asked to meet outside it today. His long legs moved swiftly my direction and I smiled at the Gryffindor scarf around his neck. I hadn't thought about it before, but with his dark hair and black framed glasses, he was only a lightning bolt to the forehead away from looking like a tall version of the beloved Harry Potter. I was surprised I hadn't seen it before.

Joshua was surely magical, in that he knew so much about so many things. I enjoyed our sibling-like friendship, and I dreaded the day one of his PhDs would take him someplace other than the National Museum of Scotland only a few blocks from the bookshop. Mostly, I cherished his friendship, but I also liked his brain too. I had some questions for it today; stuff about Mary, Queen of Scots, of course, including the papers I'd read about, the ones Mary had written herself and had been found in a box in the basement of the museum.

The café's outside seating area was covered by a wide canopy, but if I aimed my face in the right direction, I could feel the warm sun peeking around some puffy clouds.

"Hello, my friend," Joshua said as he joined me at the table. "Where have you been? Oh, that's right, on a honeymoon. Was it lovely?"

Joshua hadn't been able to attend the small wedding.

"It was." I stood.

We hugged and then sat across from each other. The café was humming pleasantly with other customers, but not too many. We shared quick personal updates that were peppered with the sorts of things we always talked about—old things we'd read about that might have been discovered at archeological sites throughout the world as well as inquiries on each other's circle of people. Joshua and Rosie had struck up a fast friendship and I was surprised that she'd already told him about our dinner with Mary and Henry and their friends. I was glad they'd found a grandmother-grandson relationship with each other.

"She has quite the obsession," Joshua said, speaking about Mary Stewart after I told him (retold him from my perspective instead of Rosie's) about my time with the woman with the past lives and her murdered husband.

"Even Lyle, the business license guy mentioned it that way, an obsession. Do you think you've ever met her?" I asked.

"Not that I recall. No, in fact, I would have remembered her, particularly if she looks as much like you as you and Rosie say."

"We could be sisters."

"Not mother and daughter?"

"She's twenty years older, so it's feasible, but sisters seems more appropriate. So, what about the recent Mary, Queen of Scots' papers that have been found?" I asked.

Joshua smiled. "They are extraordinary. Well, they are both ordinary and extraordinary. Notes, journals, lists about some of the things she had to do as queen, things such as having taxes collected and such. But still, even ordinary things are interesting if you know they were written by Mary."

"What shape were they in when you found them?"

"Surprisingly good. They weren't bothered for centuries maybe. They aren't overly fragile, though we're treating them as if they are. Do you want me to give you a secret look one of these days?"

"Only if it won't get you in trouble." I really hoped it wouldn't get him in trouble.

"I'll let you know," he said. But then he fell into thought.

"What?" I asked a long moment later. "What's on your mind?"

"Mary was young when Queen Elizabeth had her executed. Only forty-four."

"Okay."

"Well, and don't share this opinion with others because some Scottish people won't like it. Admittedly, my opinion is also jaded by time and how things have changed over the centuries, but . . . on one hand, Mary was a brilliant queen and did more than most would have when being born into her circumstances and position. She was strong where others might have weakened. She never let go of the idea that she was the rightful queen of England, well, not publicly at least. But there was one area where she wasn't the brightest of bulbs. If Mary had just given up her Catholicism and even *pretended* to be Protestant earlier than it seemed she was going to attempt to do, I do think there was a chance her life might have been easier, probably longer."

"She might have become the rightful queen of England too?"

Joshua shook his head. "I don't know if it would have gone that far, but she *might* have lived longer, perhaps not have been imprisoned for so much of her life. Ultimately and 'officially,' Mary was put to death because she was accused of conspiring to assassinate Queen Elizabeth. The letters used as evidence were probably forged."

"Letters?"

"Yes, the Casket Letters, they are called, because they were discovered in a box that looked like a casket."

"Like the Burgess Tickets?" I said, guessing that Joshua would know what I was talking about.

"Ah, you know about the Burgess Tickets." He smiled. "No, the Freedom Caskets were smaller, I believe. Casket-like things just make everything more interesting maybe. Anyway, the eight letters and sonnets were allegedly written by Mary to her third husband, the Earl of Bothwell. It was thought that Bothwell was responsible for the murder of Mary's second husband, Darnley. In them, Mary commits treason toward Elizabeth as well as encourages Bothwell to hurry up and kill Darnley. To the end, Mary denied writing them."

"Where are the letters?"

"Copies are reproduced online and such, but the originals

are lost to time, I'm afraid, probably destroyed by someone who didn't want it proven that Mary didn't write them."

"Many people conspired against her?"

"Yes, including many that she trusted."

"That's too bad."

"Mary was fierce. I wouldn't have wanted her to be less fierce, just maybe more . . . self-preserving."

I nodded. "I get what you're saying. If the letters were forged, back then there was no reliable way to validate or invalidate them other than by sight. Handwriting analysis didn't exist, at least in its current form." I thought about when Rosie and I, on the internet via my cell phone, found an old letter Mary had written. She'd signed her name "Marie" and the M had been noticeable. It had taken us only seconds.

"Oh, I'm sure it was an awful time to live, but not as awful for royalty, even for a queen who had to be locked in a castle or two."

"Do you think she killed her second husband? Mary, Queen of Scots, I mean? Conspired to at least?" I said.

Joshua fell into thought again, but I didn't think it was because he was searching for an answer, I suspected it was because he had to organize all the facts in his mind about the subject matter. His mind overflowed with all manner of things.

"Lord Darnley, Henry, was not a good man, but no, I don't think she played any part in his murder. You do know she was also, for a time, queen consort of France, don't you?"

"When she was younger?"

"Yes. Her father was the king of Scotland, but he died of some such thing I'm sure we could take care of easily nowadays, and she ascended to the throne when she was only six days old. A deal was made that she would marry a future king of France, and she was sent off to the land of truffles and baguettes when she was five or so. Her mother stayed in Scotland and served as one of her regent rulers. One of her father's illegitimate sons later acted as regent for Mary's son too. Moray." He paused and I heard the ominous tone when he said the name. "But Moray wasn't on Mary's side. I do think he and his Protestant leanings caused problems and hastened Mary's execution. He might have even been somehow involved in the Casket Letters. Anyway, regarding France, she married the Dauphin of France, Francis, when they were young, fifteen and sixteen, I believe. He was small and appeared unhealthy next to her beauty, unusual height, and robust health, but from what I've read they got along splendidly, enjoyed each other's company. Nevertheless, just over a year and a half or so into the marriage, the Dauphin died of a middle ear infection that turned ugly, leaving Mary grief stricken. Nine months later, she returned to Scotland. She'd been in France since she was a child, keep that in mind. France was all about Catholicism, so Mary was too. She spoke French most of the time, but she could also speak English and Scots. I think what I'm trying to say is that she was groomed and manipulated, but no matter how smart she was, she was never given the tools to fight fairly, or make many of her own decisions early on."

I nodded. "But some thought she was the rightful heir to the throne of England? How would that have worked?"

Joshua sighed. "Okay. Henry VIII was such a force. A giant pain in the arse for many, but a strong, strong leader. You are probably aware he had many wives?"

"Of course."

"Very good. Mary Tudor—this is a whole different Mary than the Marys we've been talking about. Mary Tudor was the only child of Henry's first wife, Catherine of Aragon, to survive until adulthood, and was the queen of England for five years after her younger half *brother* died. She was all for Catholicism, and tried to reverse her father's reformations, which were definitely more Protestant." Joshua sighed. "Mary Tudor only reigned for five years, though, before she died. Who was to be the next ruler? Her only surviving sibling at the time was Elizabeth I, who was, indeed, the daughter of Henry VIII, but also of his second wife, Anne Boleyn; a marriage that was annulled—and that's the sticking point, right there. Here also was Mary Stuart—Mary, Queen of Scots—she was a surviving legitimate descendant of Henry *VII*, the first monarch of the House of Tudor. It seemed to some that Mary should have been the queen because she was a *legitimate* descendant."

"The 'legitimacy' was used, and then it became a battle of two religions?"

"Well, in a way, yes. The Catholics thought Mary should be the queen of England, the Protestants thought Elizabeth I was right where she should be, on the throne. Much blood was shed because of the differences."

"Elizabeth I lived and ruled a long time, right?"

"Oh, yes, and she was quite the queen too. It's hard to know if she ever regretted what she did to Mary, but if she believed Mary was out to kill her, she did what she thought she should."

"You don't believe it though, that Elizabeth really thought Mary wanted to kill her? I can hear it in your voice."

Joshua shook his head. "Impossible to know, but, no, I think it was all a setup, and I'm on Mary's side of that one."

"It was all so different then. Different things were important."

"Correct," Joshua said.

Last night, after Tom and I had gotten home from dinner, I

looked closely at some of the online pictures of the queen, and the similarity was undeniable. Weirdly, though, I saw it more with Mary than with me. Mary and I looked alike but I'd created some sort of distance between the queen and me.

"Do you know anything about a crown-shaped birthmark?" I asked.

"What?" Joshua laughed.

"Did Mary, Queen of Scots, have one?"

"Gosh, not that I'm aware of. That's a wonderful idea though, that all royalty be marked with a special birthmark. I've read such fictional stories before."

"I think Mary has too. She has one and thinks that's proof that she'd reincarnated."

Joshua half-smiled, half-rolled his eyes.

I continued, "I wonder what *would* prove it though. Is there something she could know that would prove she was once Mary, Queen of Scots?"

"That sounds like an impossible thing."

"I suppose so."

"You are disappointed."

"Well, it would be kind of awesome, wouldn't it? To have her here with us? Not that she'd get a second chance to rule England or anything, but having insight into those days would be kind of cool. She might have *memories,* but right now I don't feel like I can believe a word she says. If I could know . . ."

"Our time-travel games!"

Joshua and I often wished we could travel back in time, to all times, and just stay for a few minutes. Both of us were too happy with the technology of the present day to want to stay away for long.

"Yes, something like that," I said.

"How else can I help find the proof? Can I break in somewhere, spy on someone?" Joshua asked. "I'm always up for an adventure."

"No, I'll never ask you to do something like that again." I still felt guilty about asking his help for something sneaky I'd had up my sleeve a while back.

"That's a shame."

We finished breakfast and made a plan for me to come over and see one of the museum's newest displays, as well as hopefully a time when he could sneak me a look at the queen's handwritten notes.

We said goodbye and I watched him walk away toward the museum. He'd grown up so much in the last year. A sense of sisterly pride washed over me. I hadn't learned anything that might help me with Mary Stewart, but it didn't hurt to be armed with the information, just in case. Just in case of what, I wasn't sure, but still . . . besides, time with Joshua was always fun.

I checked my phone again. No calls at all. I took off for another museum, one I hadn't been to yet, but one I'd been wanting to see since close to the first moment I'd arrived in Scotland.

SEVENTEEN

The Writers' Museum was located off the Royal Mile on Lady Stair's Close, an alleyway named after another Elizabeth, the Lady of Stair, the widow of John Dalrymple, the first Earl of Stair. A museum dedicated to Scotland's literary heroes: Robert Burns, Sir Walter Scott, and Robert Lewis Stevenson, I knew it would be a wonderful place.

Also, maybe, for me a noisy place. I'd read lots of Burns, Scott, and Stevenson. Their words were in my head and might all want to talk at once.

And not just *inside* the museum, but the courtyard outside it as well. Of course, I'd heard about Makers' Court, the place with paving stones inscribed with literary quotes. I'd managed to get my voices under control in the bookshop, but I fully expected them to pipe up once I entered the courtyard.

But when I did enter it, all was quiet. At least the bookish voices were quiet. I could hear the faint noises of traffic, both from vehicles and pedestrians' voices on the Royal Mile, but I was able to read some of the quotes, unbothered.

Violet Jacob had said, *There's muckle lyin yont the Tay that Mair to me nor life.*

I shook my head at the Scots. I'd need Elias, Aggie, Rosie, or maybe Hamlet for that one.

But Robert Henryson had also been quoted in Scots. I could understand his better, *Blissed be the sempill lyfe withoutin dreid.*

"True that, Robert," I said aloud. "True that."

I read as I made my way to the front door, pleased I'd been able to keep my intuition at bay. It had been talking to me about things I thought were associated with queens, but maybe there was nothing here to learn. That might be disappointing, after all.

I pulled the door and went through.

Once inside I closed my eyes and stood still. I listened so hard I could feel the strain. There were no voices. Until there was one.

"May I help you?" it said.

My eyes sprung open. "Oh, hello, yes, I'm . . . do I need to purchase a ticket?"

The woman reminded me of the current Queen of England, Queen Elizabeth II. Topped off with perfectly styled gray hair and eyes that twinkled happily behind proper glasses.

"You look so much like the current queen," I said.

"I get that a lot, though she wouldnae be caught deed with my accent." The woman winked. "Laila Brisem." She extended her hand.

"Delaney Nichols."

"Welcome. Ye've come a long way."

"A year ago, I did. I've lived here since then."

"Aye? A transplant. Come along and have a look around.

Ye've picked a quiet time. No tickets. Donations are always welcome. See what we're worth, leave what ye'd like."

I did want to see the museum, but I had come to ask questions about Mary Stewart. I didn't see how I could jump right in though. I'd look for the right moment.

Unfortunately, I was left to tour on my own, Laila telling me she'd meet up with me in a wee bit. I fell into my museum meander, but kept telling myself to step it up, move a little faster today.

I came upon a hand-carved chess set. It was as I stood there looking at it that I thought I might have finally heard a bookish voice.

Checkmate!

Or maybe that was a ghost. Probably just my imagination, I decided as I looked around.

I continued my meander to Robert Burns's writing desk. I smiled as I took in its simplicity. A small desk with a green felt covered and angled lift top, there were no drawers or file cabinets, but only a place where Mr. Burns could place quill to parchment and create magnificent works of art.

I thought about my desk in the warehouse, having seen the likes of kings and queens. Oh, it was a beautiful piece of old furniture. Without warning, I became overwhelmed by the fortuitous adventures my life had seen over the last year. I sniffed and blinked away the flood of emotions. I hadn't had one of those moments for a long time, but evidently they would still happen every once and a while.

I moved along as my attention was drawn to the wall above the desk. Inside a gold-rimmed frame, I'd finally come upon my first real Burgess Ticket, and it had belonged to Robert Burns.

"I'll be," I said quietly as I leaned forward for a closer look.

"What do ye think?" Laila came up behind me.

"Hello. This is a Burgess Ticket?"

"Aye. Do ye ken what that is?"

"I think so. It's kind of like a business license."

"Och. In a way. At one time, they meant verra much to the holder. A considerable asset. It allowed merchants and craftsmen to work in a burgh—this one is from 1787, Dumfries—but it also gave the holder certain rights, including the title of freeman and allowing their children to be educated in the local school or academy. They were a verra big deal."

"I see," I said.

It was a certificate covered in difficult to decipher calligraphy. It could have been mistaken for any sort of certificate I'd ever seen.

Laila continued, "This was an honorary ticket, but later Mr. Burns did reside in Dumfries."

"So interesting." I turned my attention back to Laila.

"Aye."

"I love museums so much," I said. "I have a friend at the history museum. He and I spend hours looking at exhibits there together."

"I ken what ye mean."

Seemed like a good enough time for some small lies. "I was just there last week and was approached by a woman who works here, maybe volunteers. That's why I'm here today. She reminded me about this place. Anyway, she looks like me." I looked at Laila.

"Aye, I thought I saw the resemblance, but I wasnae sure what tae say. Ye've met our Mary then? Mary Stewart. Did ye ken she thinks she was once Mary, Queen of Scots?"

"I do. Is she here today?"

"No," Laila said sadly. "She's had a tragedy."

"Oh, I'm sorry."

Laila sized me up, but only for a few seconds. "Did ye hear about the car being blown tae smithereens?"

"I did."

"Terrifying."

"Yes."

"T'was her husband who was kil't. Henry."

"Oh, no!" I put my fingers to my mouth and was slightly ashamed by my act, but not enough to stop. "That's terrible. I'm so sorry. Did you know him?"

Laila nodded. "I met him a time or two."

"What was he like?" I asked sympathetically, still slightly ashamed of myself.

She shook her head. "I'm not sure I ken. We only had brief hellos. One time he smiled, the other time he'd come tae pick her up, I think he was impatient for Mary tae finish her day. He wanted tae go home."

"I see."

"I know he worked for the city of Edinburgh and I know he took his job verra seriously. Mary recently told me she was worrit about him, that he'd become . . . what was the word she used? 'Obsessed,' I think. Aye, he'd become obsessed with a task. She thought he was working too hard."

"What was it?" There was that word again, "*obsession.*"

"I dinnae ken. I did try tae ask her, but she either ignored the question or didnae quite know what was happening. She was worrit though, I could tell. I wish I'd pushed more. Maybe that's the reason he was kil't. He was kil't, ye ken. The papers are saying it was murder."

"I'm sure the police will let us in on more as time goes on.

They'll figure it out," I said. "Also, Mary mentioned she'd gotten in some trouble here at the museum?"

That lie and question were based on a brief moment at the dinner party. Mary had mentioned that she had been welcomed back to the museum after Dina had seemed surprised that she'd been allowed to go back. The conversation had moved onto other things, but it was a moment that had stuck out to me then, and later too as I'd tried to contemplate what it had meant.

Laila's eyes opened wide. "Aye? She told ye that? I didnae think she'd tell a soul."

I'd been onto something, though I needed more. "She said it had all worked out, that she never really stole anything." That was the biggest lie of them all, but go big or go home.

"Och, not stole. No, she just shouldnae been exploring is all. She was looking in drawers and such." Laila looked at the desk next to us, but she didn't say anything about it being one of the pieces of furniture Mary had explored. "They're not to be touched. She was caught a few times, said she couldnae help herself, but *needed* tae ken what was inside them. We have given her no more chances. If she's caught again, we'll ask her tae leave permanently."

Well that had worked. "Oh, yes! That's right. She told me she was going to behave now."

Laila sent me a shameful bat of her eyes. "I called Mary and asked her not tae come in. I expressed my condolences, of course, but I told her not tae come in until things settle down or the killer is caught. Am I a terrible person? I just didn't know what tae do. Mary's such an odd creature, and Henry kil't—by a bomb! Gracious, I was worrit about the safety of everyone here. Is that reediculous?"

It was a little ridiculous, but I would never say that to her.

"Not at all. Safety first," I said.

"Aye. I suppose."

"Do you believe in reincarnation?" I asked.

She looked at me. "Sweet lass, I'm old enough tae believe in everything and nothing. You'll understand that when ye reach my age."

"Anything is possible?"

"*Everything* is possible, and nothing should surprise anyone, lass."

I nodded. "I think I understand."

More visitors came through the front door. Laila perked up and smiled to greet them. She turned back to me with another smile and told me she hoped to see me again someday soon.

I hadn't seen very much of the museum, not nearly enough in fact, but I told her goodbye and then left, happy to have seen the Burgess Ticket and the writing desk, and maybe heard someone playing chess. I left a sizable donation in the box before I walked out the door.

Why was Henry so *obsessed* with closing businesses? It all still seemed so random. None of the inscribed pavers were talking, even when I sent them my most stern look as I plopped my hands on my hips.

And then I had an idea. It came to me in a flash.

Sometimes, you just have to go back to the beginning.

I hurried back to where I'd come from.

Rosie and I helped three customers before we could talk. Over forty-five minutes, the weather outside the shop's windows went from cloudy to sunny to rainy. Customers liked it best when it was cloudy or rainy, and they would linger inside when storms hit. Usually, I enjoyed those who hung out with us. I liked learning their stories, where they'd come from, whatever their plans were. But today, I just wanted to talk to Rosie.

She sent me some side eyes and I noticed that my voice was clipped as I spoke to one of the customers. I cleared my throat and shaped up.

The customers didn't seem to notice and left on a happy note.

Once it was only Rosie, Hector, and me in the shop, Rosie said, "Did ye have something ye want tae discuss?"

"I do." I nodded toward the back table.

Rosie, holding Hector, followed me there. Once we sat, Hector squiggled from Rosie's lap and jumped into mine.

"What is it, lass?" Rosie asked.

"Two things. I never asked you again about the Mary, Queen of Scots' coins. Do you remember more?"

"I did check with Edwin but he's not sure what happened tae them, though he doesnae think they are in the warehouse. Do you think Henry or Mary heard about them and wanted them? Could that be what this is all aboot?"

"I have no idea but it's a possibility. Anything is. I'm just asking anything that comes to mind. Any idea what they might be worth?"

"Quite a bit, lass. Maybe priceless."

She hadn't said the word casually, but there was no infused awe either. Priceless items in the warehouse were not big surprises anymore. Although, there was something reckless about Edwin not knowing where they'd been put. Maybe he truly had forgotten, or he remembered but didn't want to share the details.

"I'll try to research them better," I said.

"What's the second thing?" Rosie asked.

"I know Edwin and the Lord Provost have clashed about some trees, but has he ever angered the council, or some of the members?"

"Oh, that's a fine question." She fell into thought again, her eyes coming out of focus as she looked toward the front window. "There *have* been moments over the years. Once, he singlehandedly rerouted a road."

"When?"

"Twenty years anon or so, I think,"

"Probably not that then. Anything else?"

"Aye, there was something . . . in Cowgate."

"Not far from here. Do you remember the details?"

"Zoning. Similar maybe tae what's going on now. There was a building. Someone wanted tae open a business there." Rosie tapped her lips with her fingers. "It wasnae all that long ago, but I cannae remember the details. I cannae even remember whose side Edwin fought for, but he went tae the meeting where there was a vote! Edwin's done this before." Rosie looked at me with surprised eyes. Then she sighed. "I suppose that doesnae mean anything at all though, does it?"

"Do you remember when?"

"Aboot ten years anon."

"Okay, well, that might be something. Rosie, any chance the business was either an art studio or an antique shop?"

"I simply dinnae ken, lass. I'm sorry." Rosie paused.

I grabbed a pen and piece of paper from Hamlet's stash in the drawer in the table. "Go on."

"There was also that time when one of the historical clocks stopped working. The council voted tae remove it and replace it. If I remember correctly, Edwin used his own money tae replace the antiquated parts inside the clock. Aye, that's exactly what happened. He had tae attend a council meeting on that one too, but he intervened before there was a vote."

"That seems like a good thing all the way around. No one would be upset. When?"

"That one was probably thirty years anon."

The floodgates had opened, and Rosie continued. Edwin had jumped in regarding the zoning for the zoo (I'd been and it's a wonderful zoo); some streetlight choices—older-looking was better in Old Town; castle hours—the Edinburgh castle wanted to be open longer hours, but the council fought against the plan. The castle won, with Edwin on their side.

There were many smaller things too. Book festival details that Edwin had been put in charge of; things like hosting an international author or perhaps introducing one. He'd worked with or argued with the council a number of times.

"My mind didnae even go tae all the other issues," Rosie said. "Edwin might have gotten off on a wrong foot with a number of the councilors."

"I don't know if any of it means anything or will give us any answers. It's more information though. I'll try to find and talk to some of them. Did you know Mikey is a councilor?"

"Mikey from dinner?"

"Yes. Neither he nor Henry mentioned their council positions that evening. I find that suspicious."

"Aye, I do too. Do ye think that any of this is tied to Henry's killer?"

"It's impossible to know at this point. I'm sad—and trying not to be too scared—about Henry's murder, but I don't want this bookshop shut down."

"Aye, but I *wouldnae* be surprised if the two answers are tied together."

"Why?"

Rosie shrugged and rubbed her arms. "I dinnae ken, lass. Just a feeling. Timing of everything meebe."

I looked at her. "Actually, I have one more thing to ask you about."

Rosie nodded and Hector panted along.

"Was what you said about the *Titanic* true or were you just playing along with Mary?"

"Oh, it was true, lass. I dinnae remember much of it anymore . . ."

I put my hand on her arm. "I'm sorry if my question bothered you."

"No, not at all. It's just. Well, I had a brief private conversation with our host, Mary, the other night too. A few years back, I wondered if there was any way for me tae recall any of those old memories. Back then, I found a place, no, it was a group, who gathered tae discuss their past lives. There was also hypnotism involved. When I went, I was gung-ho tae give it a try, but by the time I got there, I wasnae quite so interested. It was bothersome. I did observe a couple of times, but then moved on, not interested in remembering." Rosie blinked at me. "Mary is part of this group, she said. In fact, she said she was planning on attending this week, that it was royals' week and past royals are front and center, whatever that means."

"I'm sure she's decided not to go."

"I wouldnae be surprised if she does go. When she told me aboot it, she said they only do royals' week once a year and it's tae a full house. Everyone is interested in hearing some old royal blather."

Mary still hadn't returned my call. I was kicking myself for not calling her right back.

"When?" I said.

"Fridays. I guess that's tonight."

I pulled out my phone to search. "Do you remember what the group is called or where they meet?"

"Aye. At the Writers' Museum. It was called . . . Och, aye, Footsteps into the Past."

I was only surprised that it didn't have "ghost" in its title. I wasn't surprised that Mary volunteered at the place where the meetings occurred. "I was at that museum today, and met a woman named Laila. Do you know her?"

"No."

The information on my phone confirmed that the group did, indeed, meet tonight. "Should we go? We can leave if it's not interesting or if Mary isn't there."

Rosie laughed. "Ye'll not want tae leave, lass. Ye'll love every minute of it, unless it scares ye I suppose."

"Why would it scare me?"

"Well, if past lives are possible, then it stands to chance that all of us have lived them. If ye dinnae remember any, this sort of thing might cause ye tae remember. If I've learned anything at all, it's that not everyone wants tae remember."

I nodded, but I wasn't concerned.

"Delaney, I want tae make sure that ye ken that yer investigations, questions, just might lead you tae a killer," Rosie said.

"I'm aware," I said. "I'm not going to let The Cracked Spine close, Rosie. I'm just not. If it takes finding a killer, I'll be careful. I always am."

We frowned at each other. I *was* careful, but I heard what she wasn't saying aloud.

She nodded. "I'll go with ye then, but if it's bothersome, we have tae leave."

"Deal." I hugged her and kissed her cheek. And then scratched behind Hector's ears.

And they were only two of the reasons I didn't want the shop closed.

I looked out the window. "I need to run to Cowgate. That okay?"

"Aye. Call Edwin on the way, see if he remembers what trouble he ran into over there. Ask if he's found the coins."

"Will do."

"Dinnae forget a brollie," Rosie said.

"Right." I grabbed one from the collection on a front shelf and went back out into the rain.

EIGHTEEN

The art studio and the antique shop were, indeed, right next to each other. Two neighboring storefronts, different and yet similar in that they both gave off creative vibes. Gretchen's art studio was announced by a carved wood sign, simply stating Art Studio. Dina's awning was painted like a patchwork quilt behind letters that said Dina's Place, but both were welcoming.

I'd called Edwin on my way over, pulling him out of a meeting in Glasgow I didn't know he was attending. In an effort to make it a quick call, I said, "Edwin, three things. Do you remember what happened with the Mary, Queen of Scots' coins? How about something that happened in Cowgate, perhaps having to do with business zoning? What about any issues you might have had with Dina and Mikey Wooster?"

"I don't remember anything about zoning, lass, but the other two are one and same thing. Until you asked the question, I didn't remember."

"I don't understand."

"Some years back, I found Dina. She was young and had

just opened her shop. I thought I would see if she was interested in the coins. I like to meet up with new people, you know that. Anyway, I showed them to her and she wanted them, but she didn't have the money. She was upset that I wouldn't set up a payment plan for her. It's just not the way I work."

"What happened to the coins?"

Edwin laughed. "I saved them. I told her I would and she could find me when she had enough money. I think I remember where I put them now—they aren't in the bookshop, but I will track them down. I think they are in my house. This conversation has helped me remember."

"Did you give her a time limit?"

"I did not. But I never heard from her again. It wasn't contentious really, but she wasn't happy I wasn't willing to do business her way."

"Edwin, do you think there is a way that is tied to Henry wanting to shut down the bookshop?"

"Heavens, do I think Dina's uncle might have been offended enough by something that occurred years ago to shut down the bookshop? That would be quite the grudge."

"Some people hold them forever. Or maybe they just want the coins and this is, in their minds, a way to get them?"

"Lass, I simply don't know."

"I'm headed over there right now. If I don't make it back by dark, call the police," I said.

"Och, all right. Be careful, lass."

"Always."

I disconnected the call right after I disembarked the bus. For a long moment I stood across the street and watched the two buildings. No one went into or came out of the studio, but two customers entered and two others exited the antique shop.

I crossed the street and pulled on the door of the studio.

Soft background music played and pleasant floral scents filled the air.

"I'll be right there," Gretchen called from the back.

I zeroed in on a sculptured giraffe. Glazed to look like copper, it was an extraordinary work of art.

"Hello, Delaney," Gretchen said. "Good to see you again."

I'd decided that Gretchen just wasn't a smiler. She might seem unfriendly, but she really wasn't.

"Hi," I said.

"Here to have a look at the building?" she asked.

"Well, yes, I suppose so," I said. "And your sculptures too. They're extraordinary."

"Ta. Can I get you a cuppa or something?"

"No, thanks. I thought I'd stop by and see Dina too."

"Aye."

"Gretchen, may I ask you about Dina and Mikey?"

"What about them?"

"Do you really think Henry and Mikey are somehow involved in wanting a Burgess Ticket excuse to close your business, or do you think it's all something else? Do you think it's personal? Have you had any problems with them?" I cleared my throat. "That's a bunch of questions."

"I don't think I've had any problems with them," she said. "And I *have* wondered, but I can't think of a problem anywhere, other than I'm probably not being good at hiding how I feel about Mary. She's so strange. I don't know any of them all that well."

"Do you think Mary could have been involved in Henry's murder?"

She thought a moment. "No, I don't. They loved each other,

of course, but they were also a good partnership. Annoying with all that past-life stuff, but they were a team. I can't imagine either of them breaking it apart."

I nodded. "Okay, what about Eloise and Mary?"

"Have they had issues? Eloise not prescribing something Mary wanted so Henry sicced the Burgess Ticket police on me? Believe me, I've asked, and Eloise isn't aware of anything like that happening. I simply don't know. Look at this place though, Delaney, do you see any problems with it? Any reason I would have to reinforce the whole place? No, there isn't."

"It looks great to me. I don't know what's going on either and I'm no expert, but I can't see any reason you would have to do a thing here. Except keep sculpting." I smiled.

She didn't smile back, with her mouth at least. I thought I might have seen her eyes brighten some.

"Look around all you want," she said again. "I'll be in the back."

There wasn't much to look at regarding the building, but I did glance at corners, noting some cracks in the plaster walls, but thinking they were nothing dangerous. But again, I just didn't know what structurally unsound might look like, other than something obvious.

I loved every single one of Gretchen's sculptures and thought they would appeal to my new husband too. I wasn't in shopping mode, but I was genuine in telling her that Tom and I would come back in together soon. She walked back to the front to tell me it was good to see me as I left.

As I went into the antique shop, the two customers I'd observed walking in were leaving.

"Those desks! I can't believe how beautiful they are," one of them, with a distinctly American accent, said.

"I know," the other American said. "The shipping alone, let alone the cost of that one, would break the bank though."

"Yeah."

They nodded and smiled at me before they continued down the street.

The desk I'd most recently seen, Robert Burns's, was beautiful. I opened the door and looked forward to seeing something just as lovely.

"Welcome," Dina called from the back as the bell above the front door jingled. She looked up. "Oh." She cleared her throat. "Hello . . . Delaney."

She smoothed her jeans as she walked toward me. She kept her eyes down so I couldn't be sure how she felt about me being there, but it seemed she was working to normalize the tone of her voice. However, when she reached me and looked up, she smiled pleasantly as she extended her hand.

"I'm so sorry about my behavior at the business-licensing office. I'm still processing my uncle's murder, and that letter. I was distraught. I'm so sorry if I was rude."

"No, please, no need to even think twice about it. Did your license get fixed?"

"Oh, yes, it was easy in fact. I just had to pay a small late fee and I was good to go, back in business literally. I had infused it all with too much drama."

"That's great news! I really wanted to see your shop." I looked around. "It's extraordinary."

It was a more organized mess than the mess in the warehouse, but it still reminded me of the place where I did most of my work. Old things were everywhere—my eyes glanced over treasures such as swords, uniforms, dishes, and perfume bottles, but they landed on two desks next to each other in the middle and against a side wall.

Ornate, they reminded me of Marie Antoinette. So that we wouldn't linger on her uncle's murder, I pointed and said, "Those are French?"

"Aye. I mean *oui.*" Dina smiled. "One of them is. Come look."

I followed her as we wove our way around some end tables and an old straight-back chair, more utilitarian than comfortable, a trunk covered in faded travel stickers, and a fireplace grate, *the soot well baked on,* I thought.

The shop assaulted my senses, in a good way. It was just the type of place I liked to explore, but that wasn't why I was there today.

The desks were more similar to my desk than Robert Burns's simple writing desk. These each had a couple of drawers, and, like mine, were too old to have been originally fitted with any sort of hanging-file mechanisms. Dina, trying hard not to sound like she was selling me, pointed out the finely carved markings and the dove-tailed joints. They were undoubtedly old and well preserved.

"The two customers who were in here just before you loved them both, but the shipping to the States would be a fortune," she said with a sigh.

"How long have you had them in the shop?"

"This one," she nodded, "for about three months, but this other one for about a year. It's expensive." She displayed the price tag.

"Ten thousand pounds?" I said with lifted eyebrows. "Yes, that's expensive."

Dina laughed. "Yes, it's rumored to have been in The Tower of London during Queen Elizabeth I's reign."

"Really? It's in great shape!"

"It's surprising how furniture can make it over the centuries, particularly if it's not exposed to the elements."

"Is there any way to authenticate it?" I asked.

"Well, the maker's mark burned into the back of the side panel of it fits." She pointed and I knelt to look at the mark, "As well as the structural style. I have the provenance papers, but they don't go back all the way. At some point, it became a 'good possibility.'"

The mark was a simple tree with the letter E underneath.

"E is for Elizabeth?" I said.

"No, I don't think so. I think that belonged to the person who made the desk. I'm not exactly sure."

Edwin had told me about my desk, but he had never shown me any papers. I suddenly had an urge to search for and research furniture maker's marks.

"Fascinating," I said as I stood straight again.

"I know. I love all this stuff. I love history, and I particularly love a good story." Dina smiled.

There was a chance she and I could be friends. We were alike in some obvious ways. But I had some questions for her, and even risking our potential friendship wasn't going to stop me from asking them.

"Dina," I began. "Do you remember meeting with Edwin MacAlister about some years back when you first opened your shop?"

"The name isn't familiar," she said a moment later as her eyebrows came together. She kept eye contact with me.

She seemed to be telling the truth, but I had a hard time

believing she neither remembered him nor his name being brought up at the dinner Mary and Henry had hosted. Still, I saw nothing that made me think she was lying. Her expression remained engaged and thoughtful.

"He owns the bookshop where I work."

She nodded. "Okay."

"Anyway, back then, he brought in some coins for you to consider buying. They were Mary, Queen of Scots' coins."

Her mouth made a quick O and her eyes opened wide. "Yes, now of course I remember him! Those coins, oh, how I wish I could have afforded them. I didn't put all of that together. He's the man who owns your bookshop?"

"Yes." I paused. I didn't ask her about why she didn't contact Edwin again about the coins. Maybe she still couldn't afford them. Instead, I said, "Yes, it's the same bookshop that Henry was trying to shut down when he was killed."

Her expression changed quickly. "What?"

I nodded. "It seems the council wants to close the bookshop, allegedly because it didn't pass some sort of structural inspection."

"I'm so sorry." Dina cleared her throat. "Can't Mr. MacAlister do what needs to be done to bring the building back up to code?"

"He would, if . . . do you have a minute? I'd like to tell you about all of it."

"Of course. Come sit back by the counter. Pick any chair and I'll gather us some tea."

She turned before I could protest the tea. I didn't want her to have time to get her story straight in her head, whatever that story might be. But I needed her. I needed her connections—her husband, a councilor, might be able to help. If they'd all been in this together, all been conspiring to shut the shop, then maybe I could get some answers as to why if I shared my side of the story.

Over tea, and around a few other customers who came in, I told her what had happened. She seemed truly interested and truly perplexed by the circumstances, saying more than once that there must be some sort of misunderstanding, that she and Mikey never really discussed that part of his life, so she hadn't heard anything about it.

"Of course, I will talk to Mikey," she finally said. "There has to be a way to fix this. It seems so very unfair."

"It does." A tiny bit of hope bubbled inside me. "Thank you. I would appreciate any help you could give."

Dina looked at me and nodded and then shook her head. "So very unfair."

The bell above the front door jingled and a large group of customers walked in. Dina had expected them.

"Oh, I'm so sorry, Delaney, I've a meeting—these are some costume people. I'll have to excuse myself."

"Thank you for your time." I stood.

"Don't worry, Delaney, I will get on this."

Dina walked me all the way to the door. Once there, I decided to ask her one more question.

"What does Mary think about you having one of her past-life-foe's desks?" I smiled.

But Dina didn't smile back. She glanced toward the customers—they weren't in hearing range—and said, "Delaney, Mary is sure the desk came from Elizabeth's time, and place. She told me she's sure it's real. She touched it and could sense Elizabeth's presence."

"Really?" My smile stiffened. That sort of prediction went beyond past life stuff, didn't it?

"Yes, really. She's more fascinated than bothered about it though."

I couldn't be sure if she almost rolled her eyes or not before she excused herself again to help the costume people.

I stood outside the shop and looked up at the awning. Dina had been friendly, offered to help. That bubble of hope grew a little bigger. I listened hard for a bookish voice to tell me things were going to be okay. None were talking. Maybe my intuition was off.

Or maybe I still didn't have quite enough information yet.

NINETEEN

"Even if she's here, I'm not sure we'll be able to see her," I said as I kept my arm threaded through Rosie's. It was too crowded to let her go.

The museum, including the courtyard we were currently walking through, was much busier than during my first visit. A lot of people were interested in past lives.

"Maybe not," Rosie said as she looked around at all the people. She didn't like crowds, but I didn't realize until this moment that they actually made her uncomfortable and anxious.

"Are you okay?" I veered us out of the flow of people and stopped walking. "We don't have to do this."

I'd wished I hadn't asked her to go with me from the moment she'd opened her door. Her expression had been drawn and distracted. If she had lived past lives, I sensed she'd said goodbye to them a long time ago. She wasn't interested in getting reacquainted with any of her old, possible selves. And, the crowd made it even less worth it.

Rosie took a deep breath and let it out. "No, lass, I'm fine. I'm sorry if I seem like I'm not. I'm fine. I'm not a fan of so many people, but I can get past that. I can't find that paperwork and that's on my mind. I ken I will find it though."

I frowned. "Why don't we go back home. I'll help you search."

"No, lass, I need tae get out a bit, and I need tae search for it by myself, later. I would worry someone else would miss it and I'd end up searching everything anyway. I'm truly fine."

Her eyes weren't saying the same thing.

"All right," I said. "We'll just swoop through. If I don't see Mary right off, we'll get out of here."

The museum was much different at night, as most places in Edinburgh were. Night brought out the ghosts, if you believed in that sort of thing. Again, I didn't not believe.

Laila was nowhere to be seen. And this crowd had no interest in any of the artifacts inside. They might have interest in the writers being honored by the museum, but only if they thought they might have once *been* one of them.

We merged back into the crowd and were herded inside, through the main lobby and then back to a room I hadn't noticed before. Set up as a meeting room, the building itself wasn't very big so the meeting space felt cramped. Chairs were set up in tight rows, but by the time we made it in, most of them were taken. I ushered Rosie to an empty seat on the end of a row and stood next to her.

"I can see better if I stand," I told her.

"Aye."

Only a few seconds later, the doors were shut. I scanned, but didn't see Mary anywhere. It didn't make sense that she had come to this event so soon after Henry's murder. I should have thought it through better, but I hadn't predicted it would be such a big event. In my mind, I'd seen a group, seated in a circle, sharing the stories of their lives. I'd wondered if maybe Mary would have received support from the circle.

Hello, my name is Mary, and I used to be Mary, Queen of Scots.

Hello, Mary.

I rolled my eyes at myself. This was nothing like that.

A woman appeared at the front of the room and the crowd quickly fell into a whispering hush.

"Hello, everyone," the woman said. "Welcome, welcome, welcome. Do we have a treat for you all tonight." She smiled and clasped her hands together, causing the crowd to cheer and applaud. I obligingly clapped too as I looked at Rosie. She smiled, but she still looked uncomfortable. I was going to reach for her arm and tell her we should just go when the woman continued. I'd wait for more applause or cheers before I snuck us out of there.

"My name is Tia Zevon, and I am thrilled to be your host for another night of royalty. I look forward to this every year. And, I know all of you do too. It's good to see that the crowd only continues to grow. We are closing the doors on this evening's attendance. If you aren't here yet, you won't be allowed to enter. You may leave at any time, of course, but doors are closed the other direction. No one else is coming in, even by royal order!" She smiled.

The crowd laughed and clapped again.

Well, *maybe* we'd leave in a bit.

"I know you all know our guest this evening. She's one of our regulars and she's always ready to share a story or two. However, tonight is the first time she has agreed to be hypnotized." Tia then took a step closer to the crowd and pulled a serious expression. "Ladies and gentlemen, our special guest is here this evening after an unthinkable tragedy has happened this week. We shan't discuss that tragedy, even if we've heard about it. All right?" She looked out expectantly, like a teacher laying down the law. The crowd murmured their okays. "Very good then. Our own Mary Stewart, our Mary, Queen of Scots, is here tonight. Is everyone ready?"

The cheers and hollers came again. This was more like a revival than a support group. I understood Rosie's discomfort. It felt like we were going to end the evening being asked to fork out $19.99 for something. *And that's not all!*

I wasn't leaving yet. I did, however, angle myself so that I was mostly hidden by two people standing in front of me. I could peer around them, but I didn't want Mary to see me in the crowd. Rosie was just part of the sea of people sitting. Mary wouldn't notice her.

"First, I'm going to introduce our hypnosis expert. Ladies and gentlemen, let's give a warm welcome to Mr. Lyle Mercado."

As the applause came again, I blinked and then moved back to a spot I could better see.

Lyle Mercado was the name of the man in charge of the business-license office for the city of Edinburgh. Beyond the fact that the man's jobs or hobbies or whatever they all were made a strange combination of ingredients, it was just plain weird that I'd recently met him too.

It was only a moment later that it was confirmed. Definitely the same man.

"What the hell?" I muttered quietly. Only Rosie looked at me. I bent over and whispered in her ear. "Do you know him?"

"No."

"Edwin took me to meet him. He's in charge of the city's business licenses."

"Aye?"

I nodded and stood up straight again. Rosie sat up straighter and removed any hesitation from her face, replacing it with determination and question. I liked those much better than the worry and discomfort that were there before. She was now in the game.

Lyle stood front and center, commanding the space better than he commanded his small office. Of course, Edwin wasn't with us, so maybe he wasn't as intimidated.

"Thank you, ladies and gentlemen. Thank you, Tia, for welcoming me. I'm so very excited to be a part of the festivities this year," Lyle said.

From the sidelines where she'd removed herself to, Tia nodded and then bowed slightly toward him, her hands in a prayer.

"Oh, boy," I said.

One of the women in front of me turned and sent me a frown. I smiled apologetically and she turned around again.

"Now, without further ado, let us welcome our very own queen, Mary Stewart, once and forever held in our hearts, Mary, Queen of Scots."

Mary approached from behind the trifold that had been set up to signify "backstage." She did, indeed, look as if she hadn't slept for a few days. And I was pretty sure she looked thinner, as if she hadn't eaten either. But she was a trooper, with a forced smile, excellent posture, and a good layer of makeup to attempt to hide dark circles under her eyes.

Or was she just trying to look like a trooper? I was feeling so many levels of untruth that I was suspicious of everything, every single action, almost every person in the room.

When the applause died down again, Lyle continued, "Many of us know our very own Mary Stewart, but for those who aren't aware, she is a reincarnated soul, having once been the martyred Mary, Queen of Scots."

Lyle paused momentarily to let the information soak in. There were a few ooohs and ahs, but no one yelled out in shock. This wasn't news.

"All right. Mary has agreed to allow me to hypnotize her for the crowd. She's susceptible, both she and I know, meaning that hypnotism works on her. She and I have had a few private sessions."

I inspected them both. Was there some other meaning behind "private sessions"? I didn't see any expression or shared glances that made me think there was. Was this Mary's next husband, the one who might be accused of killing Henry? Or was that just the past life? I gritted my teeth and watched closely.

Lyle continued, "Are we ready?"

The crowd was ready. Briefly, I thought that Lyle and I made eye contact. He hesitated, but not for long.

"Do you have any words for the audience before we get to work?" Lyle asked Mary.

She frowned and then shook her head.

Rosie and I looked at each other. She signaled at me. I leaned over so she could whisper in my ear.

"What in the name of Jesus, Mary, and Joseph is going on?" she asked.

"It looks like we're going to see some hypnotism."

"Lass, this isnae right. Her husband was just kil't. I dinnae ken if the police suspect her or not, but I sense that this is being staged for something other than the entertainment of this crowd. We're all being set up for something, maybe to sway some suspicion or something. I would bet Edwin's money on it."

"I think that's possible."

Rosie thought a moment and then reached into her purse. She kept her hand hidden inside. "I'm going tae record. I know they said no recordings allowed. I dinnae care. Someone needs a record of this."

"I agree. Good idea."

I wondered if she knew how to work the recording app on the phone, but she didn't fumble or seem confused.

I stood back up and watched her. She sent me a pursed lip, confident nod.

"The only person susceptible to my words will be Mary Stewart." Lyle took a step toward the audience, keeping his hands clutched together in front of himself.

He cut quite the figure. Had I just walked in tonight, I would never have guessed his day job was in government. With more casual, carefree clothes, his scruffy appearance had transformed into artistic.

But it wasn't just that Lyle seemed to be two different people. It was everything combined. There was a weird mix of things and people happening. I just had to figure out how the bookshop and Edwin fit into the mix.

Lyle stepped back again and turned to face Mary. A person appeared with a chair and Mary sat, her hands on her knees, her attention up on Lyle.

The words he used were things I'd heard before. You are tired. You are sleepy. You will do as I say. The power of suggestion seemed to work quickly, and within only a minute or so Mary's chin was down toward her chest and her eyes were closed.

"Are you Mary?" Lyle asked.

"I am," she mumbled.

You could feel the tension in the room as everyone worked

hard to keep quiet. Except for the woman on Rosie's other side. She leaned forward and looked at me.

"Are you two related?" she whispered as she nodded toward Mary.

"No," I said just as quietly.

"Gracious." The woman stared for another moment.

I pulled up the collar on my jacket a little higher and wished I'd worn a hat. Fortunately, Lyle garnered everyone's attention again.

"Mary, I would like for you to take some steps back in time. Are you willing to do that?" Lyle asked.

"Yes."

"Very good. Here we go. Let's go all the way back to when you were a child. What can you tell me about that?"

"I can see the wash," Mary said with a happy tone. "Momma put the wash out on the line. It's pretty in the breeze."

"Okay, let's go back even further if that's okay. Is that okay?"

"Yes."

"I'd like for you to go back to a time before you were born into this life you are living as Mary Stewart. I'd like for you to travel far, all the way back to when you were living in castles. Can you do that?"

"I think so."

"Let's travel together. Tell me what you see as you look backward. I am right here with you and you are safe. These are only memories we are looking at and nothing in them can hurt you."

"I understand."

"Tell me what you see as you venture through your memories."

"I see horses. There's a bridge. Birds, beautiful birds."

"Keep going. Just stop when you see castle walls, maybe walls you didn't want to be locked behind. You might have been there against your will, but you aren't to worry. Just go there today and we'll remember together. You are safe."

Mary nodded, her chin tapping her chest. "Oh! There, yes, there's a castle."

She lifted her head then, though her eyes remained closed. Inside the room, there were a few tiny gasps, but still no one else spoke.

"Are you inside the castle?"

"No, no, it's there in the distance. I see it though. It's so lovely." Mary's face fell. "Lovely from this view. I've run away, you see, and I know I can't stay away long. But the freedom! Oh, the fresh air. It smells so sweet. The sky is blue today. It's not so blue very often, but today it is."

Her voice was younger, even younger than mine, like it came from someone in her early twenties. As if reading my mind, Lyle asked, "How old are you, dear?"

"I'm twenty and one," Mary said, though she still seemed bothered.

"Mary, please remember that you are safe. These are only memories. All right?"

"Oh. Aye. All right."

"I need to ask, Mary, are you the queen of Scotland?"

"Aye, *certainment,*" she said after a brief pause, now using a French word and accent.

"Thank you for speaking with us, your highness."

"Je suis heureux pour la distraction. L'homme m'a tellement dérange."

"En Anglais, s'il vous plaît."

"I'm happy for the distraction. The man has so bothered me," she said as, with eyes still closed, she turned her face toward the audience.

"The man?"

"*Oui,* the man who was under my bed on St. Valentine's Day. I forgave him the trespass then, but no longer. He was there in my bedchamber tonight as I was readying for bed. I told the earl to use his dagger on the villain, but he didn't obey. I was so angry and upset that I ran away."

"Do you know the identity of the man in your room?"

"*Bien sur,*" she said. *Of course.* "The poet! He thought his way with words would woo me. His book of poetry would wind its way into my heart. He was mistaken! He shall be hung, if I have my way. And I am the queen, I will have my way. I'm *désole* that my brother didn't do as I commanded. I shall have to deal with him too."

"Your brother?"

"The Earl of Moray, my bastard brother."

"Ah, aye, your closest advisor."

My eyebrows went up at the mention of the name, the same one Joshua had said in an ominous tone, the one who had potentially been involved in deceiving the queen.

"Well, yes, but I am angry, do not misunderstand," Mary said.

"I understand completely. Can you tell us the poet's name?"

"Pierre de Bocosel de Chastelard. His passion for me is untoward. I shall have him tried for treason in the morning. He will be found guilty."

"I have no doubt. Your highness, if you aren't in a hurry, may I ask you a question about something from a time ago?"

"If you must."

"I would like to ask you about your first husband."

"My first husband?"

"Aye. Your husband Francis. I want to know if you remember him."

"Oh, I loved him," she answered immediately. "No one thought I would. Everyone thought we wouldn't care for each other. We did. Perhaps we didn't have enough time to care for each other as we should have, as a husband and wife should have, but we got along so very well. I miss him. I miss my sweet friend."

"I'm sorry."

Mary nodded sadly. "I don't, however, miss his mother. I'm glad to be rid of her."

"The former queen of France, Catherine de' Medici?" Lyle looked out toward the audience.

"Oui."

"The two of you didn't get along."

"*Mais, non,* but she wouldn't have been kind to anyone who married her son, the future king. Between you and me, she's quite the wicked woman."

"I see. I'm sorry you had to put up with her."

Mary waved away the concern.

I was suddenly struck by the way she held her body, even as she sat in the chair. There was an unmistakable nobility to her posture.

Or this was all a bunch of parlor tricks and I was falling for them.

"I have struggled, I must admit," Mary said. "I lived in France for so long. This new world, this place where I am queen was foreign to me. I have had to learn much."

Lyle paused as if in thought and then nodded. "Mary, can we go forward in time now, to when you are a little older?"

I was hoping we'd get to the part where the queen's second husband was murdered; perhaps that's where Lyle was directing her to go.

"*Oui . . . non!* I must take leave. The constable has arrived. I must see to it that the poet is locked away."

"Are you sure we can't just move past this?"

"*Non, non, non!* I must go! Please, I'm afraid!"

"All right. Mary, when I count down from three, you will wake up, refreshed and unconcerned about these memories. They all took place long ago, in the past. Three, two, one." Lyle snapped his fingers.

Mary's eyes popped open and she smiled at Lyle and then at the audience.

"How do you feel?" Lyle asked.

"Fine."

"Do you remember what we discussed?"

"I do. I knew about the poet, but I've never had those memories before. You didn't ask me about the weather on the castle grounds. I was quite chilled. You should have offered me a wrap."

Mary and Lyle laughed lightly. The crowd, having become captivated, followed along a few seconds later with some laughs of their own.

"I apologize," Lyle said.

One person in the audience began clapping enthusiastically, the rest of us followed behind. Except for Rosie. She didn't clap. She kept her doubtful gaze forward.

Amid the applause, Tia walked back onto the stage and whispered something into Lyle's ear. He pulled back and sent her some tight eyebrows before he turned to look at Mary again. I looked too. Mary didn't look well, at all. She was pale now, and her cheeks seemed to have become even more sunken.

Lyle turned back to the crowd as Tia went and stood by Mary.

"Ladies and gentlemen, that's all for this evening. I wish we'd been able explore further, but when it's time to go, it's simply time to go," Lyle said.

No one was happy to hear this news. I didn't know what everyone expected, but they all wanted more of something. Weren't there more royals in the audience? Maybe not.

"I have a question!" a voice rose above the discontent.

Lyle looked doubtful for a moment. He looked at Mary who nodded at him.

"All right," Lyle said.

A woman stood from the middle of the crowd. I put my hand up to my mouth to quiet the gasp that traveled up my throat. I knew her. One of Tom's former girlfriend's, she was a reporter with one of the alternative Edinburgh newspapers.

Rosie looked up at me. "Is that Brigid?"

"I think so," I said.

"Mary, I'd like to know if you have any memories of killing your husband, either back in the 1500s or the one who was killed earlier this week."

Mary sighed as she stood. She didn't wobble at all as she put her hand on Lyle's arm before he could voice a protest.

"I'm prepared to answer," Mary said. "In fact, I should have begun the evening with a statement. It's only fair that it's asked, and it's only right that I say what I need to say."

She looked at Lyle. He wasn't happy but he nodded her on.

Mary stepped forward, and I sensed this still might be part of the script, that Mary had either hoped someone would ask her about her husband or had told someone to. Maybe she'd planted Brigid in the audience. I wouldn't put such collusion past the pretty blond who used to date my husband.

"The history has been scandalized over time. Like any good story, we only want to hear the juicy bits," Mary began dramatically.

I couldn't take my eyes off her, so I didn't look at Rosie, but I sensed she rolled her eyes.

"I did not participate in either murder of either husband. If you look closely you will see that the queen's life was on course to improve. She was about to receive a new treaty from Elizabeth. Things were going well, and killing Darnley would only harm the friendlier path that was being forged. I didn't participate in any way in killing him. Unfortunately, my sister queen didn't believe me, of course."

Many years later, Mary was ultimately tried for treason and executed. Darnley's murder was the beginning of the end, even though the end came almost twenty years later, I thought. Inwardly I kicked myself for not yet taking the time to study the history better. I should have at least read more Wikipedia by now.

"And of course I had no reason at all to kill this Henry." Mary's voice caught as she put her fist to her chest and seemed to steel herself. "I loved him. I loved him ever so desperately. I will miss him forever."

My throat tightened as she spoke. I cleared it and stole a look toward Rosie. Even she looked less suspicious and more sympathetic.

"That is all I have to say." She paused, but only briefly. "No, no it isn't. I'm here tonight because doing this was a commitment I made and being here helps me too. Helps me think less about myself. And . . ." She first looked pointedly at Brigid before she scanned the rest of the audience. "Think about it, I am certain I have lived other lives. Many of you here feel the same, so you should understand that there might someday be another way to have Henry in my life. Or at least the light of the spirit he carried with him."

With that, Mary turned and disappeared behind the trifold divider. Lyle frowned a nod at the audience and then followed her.

I kept my eyes on Brigid. I wanted to talk to both Mary and Lyle, but Brigid even more so. "I'm going to try to catch her," I said to Rosie. "I'll meet you out front, next to the lamppost on the corner."

"Aye," Rosie said as she shooed me away.

It wasn't too difficult to watch Brigid's blond curls as they wovc through the crowd and then out of the room.

"Brigid!" I said as I stepped outside and saw her walking hurriedly away.

She turned and spotted me. She tried not to look too put out, but her efforts were wasted. When I'd first come to know her, a part of me thought we might be friends if the circumstances had only been a little different.

"Hey," I said as I caught up to her. "How are you?"

"I am fine, and not surprised in the least to see you tonight. Are you and Mary Stewart related?"

"No, but the resemblance is uncanny, huh?" I said with a smile.

She didn't return the smile. "Yes, uncanny. So, I hear the deed is done. You married Tom."

"We got hitched, yes."

"Congratulations." She didn't sound like she meant it.

But I wasn't here to talk about that. "Thanks. Hey, I heard your question in there."

"Aye, that means you heard her answer too."

"I did, but I was wondering if there's more to it. Do you think she killed her husband?"

"Which one?"

"Fair question, I suppose. This one." I didn't much care about who killed Darnley, but I was going to research him at some point.

Brigid bit the inside of her cheek and fell into thought. "I really don't know. But someone killed him, and the spouse is usually suspected."

"So, that's all your question was based upon, the usual suspect? I was under the impression there was more."

"Sure, there's more. These past-lifers are a weird group and I wonder if some of them don't use their 'stories' to justify their actions of today. Mary, Queen of Scots, was ultimately beheaded because she was found guilty of treason, but suspicions about her involvement in his death stayed with her. Darnley was a complete louse by the way."

"The queen's husband was a bad guy?" I'd heard this from Joshua too.

"Sure. Opportunistic, mean, a narcissist who didn't like that Mary wouldn't crown him, even though she gave him equal power to reign in Scotland."

"What about the queen's lover? I heard he might have been the killer."

Brigid shook her head. "The queen claimed there was no other romance when Darnley was alive, though ultimately she did marry the suspect, Lord Bothwell. He was rotten too and probably did whatever he did at Queen Elizabeth's bidding. That's my interpretation."

"You think Mary should have been queen of England?"

"Yes. Elizabeth should never have ruled. Mary had the legitimate claim to the crown." Brigid took a deep breath. "Goodness, why anyone would let themselves get all worked up about something that happened four hundred years ago is ridiculous, but many of us do."

"Do you think that Henry's death has anything at all to do with Mary claiming to be a reincarnation of the queen? Do you suppose his job as a councilor to the Lord Provost might have had something to do with his murder?"

"I don't know. I haven't found anything substantial yet."

I did a quick, silent debate with myself. *Should I tell her?*

"What if I give you a lead?" I finally said.

"That would be quite rummy of you, Delaney, but why would you do that?"

"You'll understand once I tell you what it is. It's a bit self-serving, which might not be a surprise." She shook her head. I continued, "I'd like not to be named."

"An anonymous source?"

"Yes."

"I guess I can do that."

"Henry wanted some businesses to be shut down."

"What?" Even in the glow from the streetlights I could see Brigid's doubt.

"Yes. One of the businesses was The Cracked Spine."

Brigid looked at me a long moment and then laughed once. "I've heard about the Burgess Tickets, but I didn't pick up on using them to shut down any specific businesses. I sense you're telling me it might have been something deeper."

"I am. I think."

"So, you're telling me this why? You do realize that this makes you and everyone who works at The Cracked Spine possible suspects, right?"

"But I know we're all innocent."

"Hmm."

"Okay. Look, Brigid, I know what that looks and sounds like. You can either believe me or not. Even though I know that none of us at the shop killed Henry, the reason I'm telling you this is to give you another angle to explore. The Cracked Spine was not the only business on Henry's hoped-for chopping block. The Burgess Tickets were part of his plans, but there was more, even if I can't quite understand what all the more was."

"Ah, I now see the self-serving part."

I shrugged. "I'm being as up front with you as I can be."

"Aye."

"You can look into things better than I can, that's for sure."

"And you'd like me to let you know what I find."

"Actually, I'd like for you to also let the police know what you find."

"Well, it doesn't exactly work that way, but I hear what you're saying."

"If you found a killer, I'm sure you'd do the right thing." I wasn't. Not even close, but getting her on my side seemed like the way to go.

"Thanks for the info, Delaney. I'll be in touch."

Brigid turned and walked away, her curls bouncing haughtily. She turned around again. "It is definitely uncanny how much you look like her."

"I know," I said. I didn't want to tell her about my recent

meeting of Mary or the dinner party. It felt like too much information. The more I needed her, the more she might not want to help. I was keeping it as simple as possible.

"Talk to you later, Mrs. Shannon," she said before she turned one more time.

Very quietly, so she wouldn't hear, I said, "It's Delaney Nichols, but that's okay."

She kept walking and I hurried back to Rosie.

TWENTY

I searched in vain for Mary and Lyle, but the crowd cleared quickly. Rosie waited for me right by the streetlight; there weren't many others around by the time I made it to her. We walked to a bus stop, boarded, and then walked slowly to her flat after we disembarked.

"Do we need to look more closely at the queen's life to understand this Mary? Do you think history is repeating?" I asked as we meandered under clear skies.

"It is all odd, and the explosion is certainly suspicious, but Mary Stewart isnae a real queen, even if she was one at one time," Rosie said.

"Do you think she was?"

Rosie laughed. "Lass, I have no idea."

"Do you think the queen killed her second husband?"

"The proper question is do I think she *conspired* tae have her husband kil't. No, lass, I dinnae think that at all, but I'm Scottish, aye. I think she was treated horribly by almost everyone, including her second and third husbands. If we're trying tae see if there are similarities, think about something else too.

We met Henry. He cooked us dinner. I thought he was a lovely man. Didnae you?"

"I did. Until I heard he wanted to shut down the bookshop."

"Aye," she said, doubt lining the word.

"What?"

"I would bet more of Edwin's money that the answer as to why he wanted the bookshop closed and why he was killed are one and the same."

"Why do you think that?"

"I'm not sure, except that it's all happened at the same time. Find the connection, or let the police find the connection, and we'll know all the answers."

"Sounds simple." I smiled.

"If it were easy, everyone would do it, not just a redheaded lass in a Scottish bookshop."

I laughed. "I sensed your doubt tonight. Was is all just a bunch of bunk to you?"

"No, not all of it." She sent me a half smile. "I do think there's something tae past lives, but I dinnae ken what exactly. Maybe our spirits do travel from body to body, or maybe our memories, our experiences are just too strong tae die. I think it's more something like that. My 'memories' of being aboard the *Titanic* might have just been someone else's that the universe didnae want tae die, so the memories were then passed along. There's much we dinnae ken."

"That's a lovely idea."

We'd arrived at the door to her building. "We need to somehow stop the bookshop from closing. That needs to be our goal. The other answers will come from that."

"Ye think ye will find the killer that way?"

"I hope the police find the killer.The sooner the better. I do think I'm going to go to Mary's house again. She hasn't returned my call, and I want to talk to her. Want to come with me in the morning to talk to her?"

"No, lass. I'm afraid I wouldnae do ye much good. I'm too focused on finding that paperwork. Take Elias or Tom."

"Will do."

Rosie laughed once. "I ken ye wonder where my anger is. It's here." She put her fist to her gut. "Just as strong as yers. Like a rock in my stomach. I can barely stand it. I just don't want Edwin tae see it. If the shop closes, it will be worse for him because of the rest of us than for him personally."

I nodded. I wasn't going to be able to hide anything, so I didn't make any promises to such.

Rosie stepped up onto a stair. "Ye'll be late coming in tomorrow then?"

"I think I will."

Rosie took another step, but then stopped and turned to look at me again. "Maybe Mary did kill her husband. She might be dangerous."

"I think I can talk Tom into joining me."

"Aye. G'night, lass. Sleep well."

"I'll walk you in."

"No, no. I'm fine. And I'm tired. I'll see you tomorrow."

I hooked my arm through hers. "I won't stay. I just want to say goodnight to Hector."

"Aye." She gave me a weary smile as she pulled my arm closer to her.

I made sure she got inside. Hector took care of her from there. My friend Rosie was sad, maybe a little scared, definitely angry. I hadn't realized how much until this evening. That almost upset me more than anything else. I should know how to read these things by now.

I left her flat and sent one more glance up to her front window.

"I'll fix this, Rosie," I said. Even though she hadn't heard, I felt a wave of guilt wash through me. What if I couldn't?

What if no one could?

TWENTY-ONE

"Hang on," I said as I put my hand on Tom's arm.

He stopped the car just short of turning up and onto the driveway.

"You're having second thoughts?" he asked.

"More like twentieth thoughts," I said. "I've been wrestling with this all night. We really shouldn't bother her. It's too soon. It's almost cruel."

Tom steered the car to the side of the street. He turned and looked at me.

"Delaney, you are not even close to cruel. I understand why you might not want to do this, but I think we should. I think it's the only way for you to get any peace. Perhaps she can't help. She might not know about Henry's desire to close the shop, but this is the best way to find out. Apologize and tell her you won't interrupt her day for long. If she breaks down, we'll apologize again and leave her be. It's okay to do this, it really is."

I'd tossed and turned all night and had been distracted over breakfast. Had I thrown Tom for his marriage's first loop? His support was wonderful, but were his encouraging words for my sanity or his, or both? And did it matter anyway? As we both navigated this new thing called marriage, hopefully I would handle his first bump as supportively as he'd handled mine.

"Thanks," I said, letting it soak in again how lucky I was. I took a deep breath. "Okay, I'm ready."

"Good." Tom smiled and put the car back into gear.

Knocking on the castle replica's door during the daytime was different than at night. Oddly, the structure seemed more fortress-like under the diffused light from the cloudy sky. At night, the scene was theatrical and appealing. During the day, it was cold and foreboding. Nevertheless, I knocked before Tom could, only to prove I was up for the task. He sent me a knowing nod and another smile.

The door opened slowly. I didn't think I'd had any expectation as to who might be on the other side, but I was surprised that Mary herself was the one to greet us.

"Oh. Hello," she said as she pulled the door even wider.

"Hi, Mary," I said. "We're so sorry to bother you during this time. We're sorry about Henry."

"Thank you," she said with a distinct question to her voice. "You returned my call. Thank you. I'm sorry I haven't gotten back to you again."

She looked much worse than she had the night before; more tired and even thinner. But she'd had to put on a show last night, entertain. I looked at Tom who nodded me on.

"Mary, do you have a few minutes? I know this is a bad time, but could we talk inside?"

"Aye. Come in."

She pulled the door and we followed her toward the large round table. There were no fresh flowers on it today. There were no flowers anywhere, which I thought was strange.

Usually death brought flowers. There were no chairs on this level, and she didn't invite us up to the next. Instead, she seemed uncomfortable and looked at us expectantly.

"Why did you call me?" I asked. "Can I help you with something?"

"I imagine I called you for the same reason you called me back."

When she didn't continue, I said, "You know where I work, of course."

She nodded.

"Did you ever talk with Henry about his plans for The Cracked Spine?"

She deflated and leaned against the table. "Aye, Delaney, I did, but not until after you all left that night. Henry was stunned that I had met my doppelgänger, surprised by where you worked. He had no idea that his wife's lookalike worked at the bookshop he was responsible for planning to shut down."

"Oh, Mary, why did he want the bookshop closed?" I said.

She shrugged. "From what I could understand, it wasn't something he wanted, but something that had to happen."

I blinked and frowned. "Did the fact that you and I look alike change anything?"

"Well, building codes and all . . ."

"There's nothing wrong with the structure of the buildings that house the bookshop and its offices!" My raised voice echoed up the entryway all the way to the upper floor and probably down to the gallows too, if there were any.

"Of course, there is," Mary said. "Henry said an inspection had taken place."

"There's been no inspection," I said, working hard not to clench either my jaw or my fists. "Before that, do you remember if the bookshop ever came up in conversation? There must have been another reason."

She'd blinked when I'd yelled, gotten flustered when I mentioned the lack of an inspection. Now she fell into weary thought. "I don't think so. I don't remember if it did. I had no idea. I know you might think there was some sort of setup going on that night, but there wasn't, I promise."

"Why did you choose to bring your books to my bookshop?" I said.

She looked at me. "Well. Someone might have mentioned the bookshop to me, but I'm not exactly sure who, except that I'm one hundred percent positive that it wasn't Henry. Delaney," she looked back and forth between Tom and me, "let me finish. After you left that night Henry told me about the council's plans and the inspection—okay, so that's what he told me, I can't prove one way or another whether an inspection happened—but, what I'm saying is that we talked about it. And I really do think he was going to try to call off the vote. He liked you and Rosie and Tom so much that he was going to make a case for giving your boss a chance to make structural changes."

"Really?"

"Yes," she said. "And then he was killed."

She looked at me. Accusation both dulled and lit her eyes.

"Mary, none of us killed Henry. We didn't know the details of the council's plans until after he was killed."

I didn't like her insinuations. Neither did Tom; he crossed his arms in front of himself.

"No, no, I believe that neither of you knew. But . . ." She stood straighter. "Edwin MacAlister knew. And from what Henry said, he wasn't happy at all, threatening to sue, get Henry removed from the council, offering bribery."

I stalled mentally. *This was new information, right?* Edwin hadn't admitted that he'd done any of that, just that he'd had a phone call, a recorded one at that. And, he was out of town, allegedly in Glasgow. I hadn't pressed, but I had wondered what in the heck he was doing in Glasgow while our entire world was falling apart. Had he purposefully not told us about his threats?

"Edwin didn't kill Henry either," I finally said.

"Are you sure about that?" she said.

"Yes. Completely."

"Well, whoever did kill Henry stopped him from attempting to stop the vote. There's nothing to be done now."

"Nothing? What about Mikey?" I asked.

She shook her head. "Mikey doesn't see any reason it should be stopped. He thinks Henry was being too emotional about wanting to change directions. Henry met you all at dinner and enjoyed your company. In Mikey's mind, that's not enough to invalidate a valid inspection."

"There wasn't an inspection," I repeated.

Mary shrugged, but not unsympathetically.

"Maybe Mikey killed Henry," I said. It was a cruel, low blow.

She frowned and crossed her arms in front of herself, matching Tom's pose. "I only spoke with him about all of this after Henry was killed. He didn't know Henry was going to try to stop the vote. I was trying to help you too. Ultimately, that's why I wanted to talk to you, to tell you that I was sorry, and Henry was sorry too. But there was nothing to be done to save the bookshop now. I wanted you to know Henry was sorry." Her voice cracked.

I blinked at her. Okay, so she hadn't been calling to warn me about Inspector Buchanan. I was so, so angry, so frustrated, but she was trying to do the right thing, at least in her mind. I couldn't muster up any kind words, but I did manage a nod.

"Mary," Tom jumped in. "Thank you for that. Please, if you can think of any other way for us to save the bookshop, stop the vote, let us know. We'd be forever in your debt. We *are* sorry for your loss."

"Yes, we are," I said. I wished I sounded as sincere as she and Tom had.

Mary nodded too.

I tried to calm my insides before I reached out and put my hand on her arm. "Mary, do the police have any idea who killed Henry?"

"No," she said, her voice tightening with emotion now. "And, just so you know, I haven't said one word about Edwin MacAlister to the police. You can show yourselves out."

She turned and hurried up the stairs as we blinked at her back.

"Thank you for your time," Tom called after her. "Again, we are sorry."

I had so much more I wanted to talk to her about, but we had been dismissed. I wanted to ask about her friendship with Lyle Mercado. I wanted to tell her I'd been there last night. But I wasn't ready to chase her through her own house. Tom and I left, closing the castle door quickly but softly behind us.

"I think we need to talk to Edwin," Tom said quietly as we made our way to his car.

"Couldn't agree more."

We made it back to the bookshop in record time.

TWENTY-TWO

"Inspector Buchanan," I said as I came though the bookshop's door. Tom had dropped me off. I hadn't noticed a police car out front. I couldn't help but steal a glance out the window to see if I'd missed it.

"I walked," she said. "I like to walk. It's good for the mind and body."

"Yes," I said.

From behind the inspector, Rosie sent me a smirk. No one else was in the bookshop and I sensed that the inspector knew exactly the expression on Rosie's face. Rosie normalized before she could be caught though.

"Do you usually arrive at work at this time of the morning?" Inspector Buchanan asked as she worried her thumb over a piece of paper she held.

I bit down on what I really wanted to say—that it was none of her business—and just said, "Can I help you with something?"

"I'm going to be your favorite person today," she said.

"You are?"

"I am. You have quite the reputation at the police station at the bottom of the Royal Mile."

"Okay," I said.

"They all seem to know you, and believe it or not, many of them like you."

"I'm happy to hear that."

"I couldn't reach Inspector Winters, but I had some good discussions with the other officers at the station. They assured me that Inspector Winters would do everything he could to help you keep your bookshop open, that it would be a terrible shame to see it closed."

"Yes, that's true." I hoped, at least. I moved closer to her as Hector trotted to my feet. I picked him up and scratched behind his ears.

"There *is* a vote set to take place that will determine the fate of your fair bookshop, though. On Monday," Inspector Buchanan said.

"We've figured that out."

"I thought you might have. I didn't know how much more you could figure out on your own though." She looked at the piece of paper. "I brought you a few names."

"Names?"

"Councilors who were particularly adamant about voting to close the bookshop. You see, people have to tell me things because I'm investigating a murder, and I have learned some things, perhaps a sort of map even—a map that includes these names."

I wasn't following completely but I nodded her forward.

"Here's what I know so far—well, what I can share with you. Henry made a few phone calls to some fellow councilors the night after your dinner with him. I am speculating that he wanted to try to cancel the vote to close this bookshop. How about that?"

"What makes you think that?"

"Mary. His wife told me that he talked about it that night. I'm putting two and two together. It's what I do."

Hearing it from her made it much more real than hearing it from Mary, but the news coming at me two times in the last hour lifted my hopes to a level I wasn't previously sure they could ever reach. Those hope bubbles floated in my mind again.

"That's wonderful!" I said.

"Ah, right, so it is. That doesn't mean the vote's been canceled. Others seem to still want the vote to happen, think it's the right thing to do, considering the inspection and all."

"There was no inspection," I said.

"Well, I'm still working on that, but the councilors believe there was one and that the bookshop failed it. Now, I need something from you before I can help you more."

My hopes were dashed a little but I said, "Okay."

Hector barked once.

"I need you to tell me where you were overnight, after the dinner."

I shouldn't talk to her about this without an attorney, but her blackmail was working. I wanted that list of names, even though I still wasn't quite sure what I would do with it. "Home, with my husband. Sleeping mostly. We didn't know about the bookshop issue and it had been an enjoyable dinner. I was tired. I slept well."

"They're newlyweds," Rosie said cheerfully.

I smiled at her.

"Can anyone besides your husband confirm that?"

"No . . . I mean, yes, my landlord, Elias, came over to give us some rolls that his wife, Aggie, had made. He wakes up early. He woke us up as he put them right outside our door. I went out and grabbed the rolls before he got back into his cottage. The rolls are the best when they're warm. I stuck my head out and thanked him. He could confirm, but that's the best I can do."

Inspector Buchanan stuck the piece of paper she held into her pocket and pulled out a notebook and pen. "Name?"

After I gave her Elias's and Aggie's names and numbers, she reached back into her pocket for the piece of paper and handed it to me. "Henry called these people. They were part of the committee spearheading the shutting down of the bookshop. He told them he wanted to talk to them about the vote, but he was killed before he could. Based upon what Mary has told me, I do believe he wanted to cancel the vote, though for the life of me I can't understand how you made such an impression on him that he would change his mind."

"I look like his wife?" I said.

"That you do. Anyway, for the record, I've vetted the people on the list. I am sure they weren't responsible for Henry's murder. I wouldn't send you to talk to possible killers."

"Do you have any idea who killed Henry?"

"I'm afraid I do," she said.

"Who?" I figured it wouldn't hurt to ask.

Inspector Buchanan just sent us a sad smile before she said goodbye, turned, and left the bookshop.

Rosie, Hector, and I blinked at the door as it shut after her.

"Do ye think she really kens the killer?" Rosie asked.

"I have no idea." I looked at Rosie. "Where's Edwin?"

"Och, he's still in Glasgow."

"What is he doing in Glasgow?"

"Yer guess is as good as mine."

My guess was that he was removing himself from easy police access, but I didn't say that out loud.

"Did Inspector Buchanan ask about him?"

"No."

"That's good."

"Why?"

"I'm not sure yet," I said. "But I'd like to talk to Edwin."

"Aye, so . . . who's on the list?" Rosie asked.

I unfolded and looked at the paper.

"Three women," I said. "Bella Montrose, Simone Lazar, and Monika Hidasi."

"I dinnae ken any of them."

"I have addresses. That's good."

"How did it go with Mary?"

"She claimed she was trying to call me to let me know that Henry was going to try to cancel the vote. After he met us that night and liked us so much and I looked so much like Mary, he was going to try to call it off. I think Henry ended up liking all of us, and that was enough."

"That's a good thing isnae it? And it confirms what Inspector Buchanan just said."

"But then he was killed, and now there's probably nothing we can do to stop the vote." I looked at the piece of paper. "Unless, I can convince other councilors, I guess."

"I think that's what Inspector Buchanan was thinking." Rosie sighed. "I havenae found the paperwork. I havenae found the Burgess Ticket, but now I truly believe everything will be fine."

"I don't know." I shook my head. "Rosie, is there any

chance Edwin has the current queen's number? I'm beginning to think a royal decree is our only hope."

Rosie smiled. "I dinnae think it would be easy, but if anyone can do it, ye can, lass."

I tried to call Edwin but he didn't answer. I wasn't surprised. I tapped my finger on my mouth as I paced the front of the store. Hector let me hold him and scratch his ears as Rosie helped some customers. Once it was just us in the shop again she reached for Hector.

I gave him up reluctantly and the crook of my arm felt much lonelier without him.

"Go talk tae those women, lass. Ye're of no use tae me here. Hector can only do so much. I'll tell Edwin tae ring ye the second I hear from him."

I could take a bus. In fact, I might even be able to walk to see them with little problem. But, I needed some extra input and I knew exactly whom I wanted to talk to. I called Elias.

"I can't figure out what's going on," I said to Elias.

"Aye," Elias said thoughtfully. "These women might help."

"I might need you the rest of the day."

"That's what I'm here for." Elias smiled as he kept his attention forward, out the windshield, toward the traffic.

"Not really, but I do appreciate it."

In fact, there were actual days that Elias operated his taxi like a real taxi; driving people places and taking fare for such trips. I liked to keep that in mind and not bother him too much. In the past I'd offered him money for his time and fuel, but he'd made it clear that I was never to do that again.

"There. There it is," I said. "Montrose Photography."

"Do you want me tae come in with ye?"

"Yes, please."

"Will do." Elias puffed slightly. Though I hadn't meant to assign him the role of my protector, he'd taken it on himself and seemed to like it. His wife, Aggie, had told me he enjoyed the role, giving him something to do other than help her clean the "guesthooses" and drive the taxicab. I wasn't afraid of Bella Montrose, Edinburgh City Councilor, but since I was pretty sure she wasn't a killer, it would be okay to bring him along. Neither of us would be in harm's way.

He parked the taxi not far from the front door. No one greeted us as we went inside, but I was immediately stopped short by the stunning photographs adorning the walls and filling the two tables at the front of the small space. A wall separated the gallery from what I guessed were offices behind it.

The room was a tourist's to-do list, or maybe a wish list. There were so many places to see, and if you couldn't see them in person, these stunning photographs were almost as much fun.

"How does the light do that?" I said as I looked at one of the pictures on the wall, a shot of the Edinburgh castle. I'd seen many pictures of the castle and I worked right below it, but I'd never seen it captured so beautifully. "Is that real or photoshopped?"

"I have no idea what ye're talking about, lass, but that's a beautiful picture, I agree."

As I heard a door open somewhere in the back, I tried to glance over the rest of the pictures.

"Hi, can I help you?" The woman approached. She was dressed in jeans and a white T-shirt, her long hair pulled back in a messy ponytail.

"Might you be Bella Montrose?" I said.

"Yes," she said suspiciously. I wondered if she rarely got customers or if she knew I was coming to talk to her.

"I'm Delaney Nichols. I work at The Cracked Spine. This is my friend, Elias."

"Ah, I thought someone from there might come see me."

"Yer pictures are stunning," Elias said as they shook hands.

"Thank you." The ghost of a smile pulled at her lips but only briefly.

"Ms. Montrose, we're sorry to bother you, but a police inspector told me I should talk to you about the vote to close the bookshop, that you are a councilor and that Henry talked to you the night before he was killed."

She sighed. "He did."

I hesitated. I wasn't exactly sure where to go from there. I jumped in. "I'm trying to figure out how the bookshop was originally targeted? I'm trying to understand because there's never been an inspection. Can you tell me how all this happened?"

Her eyes widened and she shook her head. "Delaney, I've seen the inspection."

"You have? Do you have a copy?"

"No, I don't. But I have seen it and it is valid."

"Is there any way to get a copy?"

"Not at the moment." She frowned. "Delaney, Henry called me the night before he was killed. He said he wanted to meet for breakfast and discuss the vote regarding The Cracked Spine. When the police were here earlier, they told me they think he wanted to cancel the vote. He didn't come out and say that to me, but I could tell he was . . . concerned about something."

"Meet for breakfast?" I said.

"Aye, he was killed on the way."

Gut punch. "I'm so sorry."

She cleared her throat. "Thank you. Yes, there was something else he wanted to tell us, something else he wanted us to know. That's why we were having breakfast."

I pulled out the note from my pocket and looked at it. "Were Simone Lazar and Monika Hidasi invited too?"

"Yes, we were part of the original committee. The four of us and Henry's nephew-in-law, Mikey Wooster. Simone, Monika, and I felt the explosion but none of us could have guessed that Henry was the victim. We called him once he was late and he didn't answer his mobile, but even then we still didn't suspect he'd been blown up in a car bomb!"

I swallowed but forged ahead, hoping I wasn't treading too insensitively. "Was Mikey also invited to the breakfast?"

"I don't know. He wasn't there, with the three of us as we waited."

He'd been at the dinner the night before. Maybe Henry had talked to him after Rosie, Tom, and I left.

I said, "Ms. Montrose, can you remember when The Cracked Spine first came up in council discussions?"

She nodded. "I've been thinking about it, and, yes, I think I do remember. It wasn't Henry who brought it up first at all."

"Who was it then?" I fully expected her to say that it was Mikey Wooster, though I wasn't exactly sure why. It just seemed like that answer would somehow fit.

"It was someone from outside the council. He came to a meeting and made a small presentation. It wasn't scheduled, but he showed up and was given the floor. He talked about the city's building issues and he wanted us to pay attention to the problems. He used The Cracked Spine as an example. I don't know how Henry took it all over and made it his, but shortly after that, closing The Cracked Spine as well as asking for old Burgess Tickets became council discussions."

"What was his name?"

"His name is Lyle Mercado. He's the head of the business-licensing division of the city."

"I know who he is," I said. "Can you tell me any more about that?"

"I wish I could," she said. "I'm afraid I wasn't paying close attention. I've heard strange things about him and I didn't like the man. I didn't think anyone was really listening to him. I apologize. It's my job to pay attention, but I didn't give him much credence. I didn't think anything would come of his visit, but Henry trudged forward."

"Strange things?" I said.

"Yes, he's one of those past-lives people. He's also an amateur hypnotist. He's a weird combination of things I don't believe in."

"Do you know who Mr. Mercado thought he once was?" I asked, wondering if he and Mary had spent a different time together. "In a past life?"

"I'm afraid I don't. I'm sorry."

"Do you know Henry's wife?"

"Of course, I do, and I think she's weird too, though I never would have said that to Henry."

"Did it ever seem that Henry and Mary had a bad marriage?"

"No, not at all. Henry didn't talk about his wife much but when he did, it was with only loving words. He was loyal to her, as far as I could tell. I told as much to the police."

"Who would want Henry dead?" Yes, I wanted to make sure the bookshop didn't close, but even in my one-track mind, finding Henry's killer did seem important.

"Not everyone liked him, but none of us are universally liked. We have opinions, we have city issues we all want to, need to, get taken care of."

"Would Lyle Mercado be upset that Henry wanted the vote canceled?"

"I don't have any idea. Delaney, I think you're thinking Henry was killed because of the bookshop issue, but there were other things he was working on too. The police know."

"The Burgess Tickets?"

"Yes, I admitted to the police that it seemed Henry was trying to keep the bookshop issue on the down low, but everyone had heard about the Burgess Tickets. In fact, none of us had heard from anyone from The Cracked Spine, as far as I know. At one point I was concerned that the vote would happen almost secretly—there are ways to hide things like that—but I didn't give it much thought. I'm busy, like everyone else. I'm sorry. But there are lots of things we work on, government salaries, budgets. I never saw or heard of anyone angry at Henry, but it's more than feasible that someone was angry enough to . . . well, unreasonably angry, I guess."

"Will the vote regarding the bookshop still take place?"

"I think so, but I will vote against closing the bookshop because I am guessing that's what Henry wanted. At least it should be postponed until we understand more. Simone and Monika probably will vote the same way, but I can't speak for the rest of the council. I will try to make the case that Henry had potentially changed his mind. But, you have to understand, we all saw the inspection report. There are dangers with your buildings."

"Thank you," I said. "We will fix whatever needs fixing. I promise."

"I'll make sure I let everyone know. No promises, Delaney, but I think it's only right to try to slow everything down until we understand what's going on."

More hope bubbles. I wanted to cry in relief. She was on our team. I didn't cry though; instead, I thanked her again. I almost pulled her into a hug, but fortunately I caught myself. She might have been okay with it, but I'm glad I held back.

Finally, we expressed our condolences again and left Bella Montrose and her extraordinary photographs.

"What do you think?" Elias said when he got into the taxi.

"I think she's wrong. I think Henry Stewart was killed because he changed his mind and didn't want the bookshop closed," I said.

"Really? That's not what I expected you tac say, not really what I expected would get your attention."

I nodded. I felt oddly sure about this, even if I didn't know why. "But we're missing the real reason behind closing the bookshop, Elias. There's something else there. I don't know how I'm going to figure it out, but I'm going to, and when I do, not only will we remain open for business, I'll find a killer too. I promise you."

"Aye. Lead the way."

TWENTY-THREE

I couldn't let go of what Bella had told us. With the new information, Lyle seemed much shiftier than I'd first thought, and much more involved than he'd appeared. I asked Elias to make our next stop the business-licensing office.

"Is Lyle Mercado available?" I asked one of the people behind the counter. I didn't remember this woman being there when Edwin and I had visited. She was the only one there today.

"Who's asking?" she said.

"Delaney and Elias. I work with Edwin MacAlister."

Elias puffed up next to me.

"One minute."

I noticed her name tag said Susan. Slowly, Susan made her way through the doorway that led to Lyle's office. Elias and I watched her and then shared a frown.

"Goodness, she's not happy tae be working today," he said.

There were no other customers in the office. It was Saturday and I'd been surprised to find the office open.

"She's not fond of the Saturday shift, I guess."

Susan reappeared quickly. "He's not here. Must have left."

"Are you sure?" I said.

"Aye," she said flatly.

"Okay. Thank you." I turned to leave but changed my mind. An image of Dina being upset came to me, and I remembered I hadn't seen where she'd gone before I tried to follow her inside. I'd thought the loo, but now that I suspected she somehow knew Lyle Mercado, I wondered. I turned around again.

"Susan, are business licenses public information? I mean, if I were to ask you if a certain business had a valid license, could you tell me yes or no and how long before it expires?"

"Aye, it's public information."

"How about a place called Art Studio in Cowgate?" I said.

"One minute." She moved to a computer and defied the earlier impression she'd made. Her fingers moved quickly over the keyboard. "Aye, it's got five months before it expires."

"How about Dina's Place? It's in Cowgate too."

She typed more. "Aye, it's not set to expire for eight months."

"Do you make note of when fees are paid late?"

She squinted. "I can see if there are late fees included, but I'm not sure that's public information."

"Okay, well, I guess I'd just like to know if there are late fees attached to Dina's Place, maybe if she paid her fees recently, if you can tell me."

"Um. Well." she looked at the screen and then back up at me. "No late fees. The last payment was received on time."

"Do you ever just not mark the fees, let customers not pay

them?" I smiled. "You know, if they promise to never, ever do it again."

"No, there's no system set up to remove them. It's all done on the computer. We can't override anything."

"I see. Thank you."

"You're welcome."

As Elias and I left, I explained how I'd seen Dina upset allegedly about being late with her payment.

"She was lying but I don't know why," I said.

"Maybe it's something as simple as she was embarrassed about being upset. Her uncle had just been killed."

"Maybe. Or she was coming to talk to Lyle Mercado."

"About what?"

"I'm not sure yet." Was I onto something, a connection? If I was, it was a vague notion that left me feeling more like I was missing something than that I was onto something. But I felt like I needed to keep searching for that missing part.

We got back into the taxi.

"Ready for our next stop?" I said.

"Aye."

Brigid McBride wasn't happy to see me, but that was okay.

"Hello," she said succinctly as Elias and I came through the front door of the small newspaper office.

Last time I had been there, the place had been buzzing with activity. Today, it was just Brigid and a man with thick glasses peering at a computer screen. I didn't think he noticed that Elias and I had come in.

"Hey, Brigid, you have some time?" I asked.

"You have something good for me?"

"I think I might."

Doubt wrinkled her pretty mouth and the pretty places next to her pretty eyes.

"It's good," Elias added his endorsement.

"Well, I'll be the judge of that. Come on back." She swooped her arm for us to follow.

And we did.

I told her everything I knew. I was pretty sure Edwin hadn't killed Henry; at least I really hoped he hadn't. I put it all out there, hoping her journalistic mind could bring it together and make some sense of it.

"Something's up," Brigid said when I finished.

"I know!" I said with happy exclamation. "There has to be, doesn't there?"

"I need more answers," she said.

"Me too! That's what I was hoping for."

"No, Delaney, I mean I need more answers before I consider whether or not it's something I want to continue to follow up on. It's all over the place. A car bomb—the murder of a man who wants to shut down the bookshop and then allegedly changes his mind after he meets you all. The man in charge of business licenses. They're tied together, aren't they? A woman who thinks she's the reincarnation of Mary, Queen of Scots, and you and she could be related. That's bizarre, by the way. If I were the police, I'd still be suspicious of everyone at the bookshop. Mostly Edwin and you. Edwin because he's Edwin and he's a suspicious man, and you because you look like the dead man's wife. Spitting image."

Well, that hadn't totally gone as I'd hoped. "None of us killed Henry, Brigid, but no matter what you say, I think you know that already."

"I know nothing of the sort. You're all a suspicious bunch."

"But we're not killers." I kept my face as neutral as possible. That might not be entirely true, but what had happened between a university-aged Edwin, his friends, and the love of his young life on a boat occurred a long time ago. And, it was probably justified. Nevertheless. "You know we aren't killers."

She did that thing with her mouth and eyes again. "I don't know how I can put together a story in enough time to help you with the vote, Delaney. There's a lot to look at here."

"I know. What I was hoping for was that, yes, you get the story. I think it will prove to be a good one. But, what I hope for today is that you give me your contact in the Lord Provost's office. Surely, there's someone there you talk to, the press person. That's how it works, right?"

"You told me all that so I'd tell you my contact?"

"Well . . ."

"That wouldn't do me much good in keeping that contact if I gave up her name all the time."

"I won't tell her you told me."

She looked at me.

"Promise I won't," I said. "I'm desperate here, Brigid. Please. You'll have a story, I'm sure. There's something, or a number of somethings fishy going on here. I bet the answers will converge and make one good story."

"It's not enough. I'm sorry."

I couldn't hand over my husband (and I wouldn't if I could), so I had nothing else. Or so I thought.

"How about," she leaned forward and put her arms on the table. "You do something else for me."

Elias shifted in his chair as I said, "What?"

"Let me interview Edwin about the warehouse. Let me take pictures."

The warehouse had officially been deemed not so much a secret anymore, but we still didn't advertise it. We hadn't released pictures to the public.

"Why?" I asked.

"Because everyone wants to see it, wants to know it's real."

"Edwin's stopped denying it's real," I said.

"But he hasn't let anyone in. I haven't seen any pictures yet."

"I'll talk to Edwin, and I'll make a strong case. Cross my heart." I did just that. "But I need your contact's name today. Please. Time is running out."

Brigid sat back in her chair. "Give Edwin a call."

I looked at Elias.

I said, "I'm not trying to be coy, Brigid, but I really think this is a conversation to have in person. I promise I will do that."

The weight of negotiation filled the air between us.

"All right. Aye, I'll do some of your legwork, Delaney. I look forward to hearing back from you. Today," Brigid said a long moment later.

I nodded. "Absolutely."

From her desk, Brigid found a piece of paper and a pen and scribbled a name, along with an address. She handed it to me. "If she's not at work in an office down the hall from the Lord Provost's, here's her assistant's mobile. I won't give you hers, but she usually works on the weekends, so does her assistant. I know time's tight or I wouldn't give you so much."

I looked at the paper briefly wondering if I might recognize the name, Grace Graham. Didn't ring a bell.

"Thank you, Brigid."

"You're welcome. Talk to Edwin. Call me today."

"Will do."

Brigid walked us to the door of the newspaper office and told us goodbye. I could tell she was anxious to get to work. She'd said there was too much information, but she smelled a story, and I knew she'd wrestle to get to it, no matter what she'd said. I hoped her enthusiasm would help her find something that might help keep the bookshop safe.

And find a killer too, of course.

TWENTY-FOUR

Elias and I tried to find Simone Lazar and Monika Hidasi, but they weren't in the places Inspector Buchanan had noted as their offices. Simone worked out of her home, and Monika had a coffee shop listed as her office space. I hoped they felt the same way Bella did about the vote, and I decided I'd try to reach them later. I wondered if I should just try to talk to all the councilors, but I didn't know how I could accomplish that with the short time left before the vote.

By the time we made it to the government office that housed the Lord Provost's office as well as Brigid's media relations contact, Grace Graham, the entire building was locked tight. I tried the mobile number, but the call went directly to voice mail. I couldn't help but wonder if Brigid had warned Grace I might try to find her.

"No matter, lass," Elias said. "May I suggest ye talk tae Edwin first? Ye are correct in that he kens so many people. Maybe he and Grace are acquainted. Start there. I ken ye've only a wee bit of time left, but let's not bother Ms. Graham on the weekend if we dinnae have tae."

I agreed. He was correct, and, besides, that earlier fluttering of hope I'd felt was becoming stronger. The truth would win out, I was sure.

I just hoped my version of the truth was the correct one.

Elias dropped me off at the bookshop, and I watched his cab until it turned the corner.

When I stepped inside the bookshop with my phone at the ready to call Edwin, I heard his voice. I raced around to the back table though not because of any promise I'd made to Brigid. Even though I'd told her I would try to get her an exclusive regarding the warehouse, I was going to work on a way to get out of that one. I would chalk up my breaking the promise to desperate times.

"You're here," I said.

"I am, lass. I'm sorry I didnae return yer calls immediately, but I was looking for someone and," he glanced at a man sitting across the table from him, "once I found him, we hurried back."

"I was just going tae ring you," Rosie said with a confident smile. She and Hamlet sat next to each other at the table too.

Edwin stood and said, "This is our attorney, Jack McGinnis. He's here to help us."

"So good to meet you," I effused as I walked to him and shook his hand after he stood too.

"Good to meet you, lass," he said, much less effusively, but friendly enough.

"Have a seat, Delaney. Jack was just telling us what we might be able to do legally to save the bookshop," Edwin said.

"Oh, I am ready to hear this. So ready."

Jack McGinnis looked like someone out of *The Sopranos*. His light Scottish accent was difficult to get used to mostly because I thought he should sound like someone from New Jersey or New York, someone who stereotypically kept brass knuckles in his pocket and liked pasta.

He was firm in the fact that there was no way the vote to close the bookshop was in the realm of legal. Unfortunately, illegal and unethical things happened all the time. He was there to make sure that, ultimately, the bookshop wouldn't have to close its doors, at least not forever.

"I don't think I can stop the vote," he said. "But we can make our case at the meeting, and I can demand to see all the documentation. After that, there are other measures we can take, but nothing works exactly like we'd all want it to. Nothing is going to happen quickly, and it might take some convincing, but I'm confident that it will work out."

"Unless, the vote fails?" I said. "Then we won't have to worry about it."

"There is that possibility," Jack said.

"Let's call all the councilors," I said. "Between all of us, we can get it done."

"I don't think that's reasonable, Delaney. It wouldn't be easy to acquire all the numbers," Edwin said. "We'll make our case at the meeting."

"Edwin, did you ever talk to Henry? Tell him or anyone you would sue to make sure the bookshop doesn't close? Did you threaten to sue? Were you angry with him?"

"I haven't spoken forcefully to anyone other than Lyle, and you were with me," Edwin said. "That's why I tracked down Jack in Glasgow, so I don't have to make such threats. He can take care of that for me."

Jack nodded.

"Really?"

The bell above the door jingled. Rosie stood and walked toward the front.

"Lass, hello," we heard her say.

I stood to see who'd come in and was shocked to see it was the person who I was just thinking about. Why had Mary told me that Edwin had threatened Henry? Perhaps the better question was why had Henry told her that? I hoped the even more correct question *wasn't* why was Edwin lying about making such threats.

Rosie escorted Mary Stewart toward us.

"Oh. Hello. I'm sorry to interrupt," Mary said.

"Hello, Mary," I said.

"Edwin, Jack, this is one of our new friends, Mary Stewart. Mary, this is Edwin, Jack, and Hamlet," Rosie said. "What can we do for ye, lass?"

Mary frowned as she surveyed us. I didn't know if she'd come in just to see Rosie or me, but now she had us all.

"Lass, we're sorry for your loss," Edwin said.

Mary nodded.

"Wow," Hamlet said, "I heard about the resemblance, but it's . . ."

"Unbelievable," Jack said as he looked back and forth between Mary and me.

"Truly," Hamlet added. "Deepest condolences, Ms. Stewart."

"Thank you," Mary said with a sad smile. She gathered herself and continued, "I feel like now might be a bad time, but I have some important information to share. I might be able to help."

"We're listening," I said. "It's not a bad time, Mary."

"I . . . remembered something. I searched and found . . . I'm a wee bit afraid, though. It might be, I don't know. It might cause more trouble."

"Did you talk to the police about it?" Edwin asked as Jack continued to look curiously back and forth between Mary and me.

"No," she said. "I . . . feel responsible. May I explain from the beginning?"

"Aye," Edwin said. "One moment." He hurried to the door, locked it, and turned the sign to Closed.

As we all sat around the table, Edwin made it clear to Mary that Jack McGinnis was our attorney, that he was there specifically to help them fight the council, keep the bookshop open. No one tried to hide anything.

"I'm not going to ask him to leave," Edwin said.

Mary nodded. "I don't care. It's fine." She pursed her lips a moment. "I think this all began about two years ago. Henry and I were on holiday in France." She frowned at Jack as he, unashamedly, took notes. She didn't ask him to stop. "You all probably know that the queen spent much of her youth in France." We nodded. "On my holiday with Henry, we were enjoying Paris when a docent, a gentleman, in one of the museums there started talking to us. I'm afraid I don't remember his name—maybe Jean or Jacque, I'm not sure. He was just as intrigued by Mary, Queen of Scots, as I am. Though I didn't let him know about my past life as the queen, he mentioned that he thought I looked like her, and he wanted to tell us something when we said we were from Edinburgh." Mary looked at Edwin so pointedly that it was briefly uncomfortable. "And then he brought up the name of this bookshop. I just remembered this afternoon. Delaney must have jogged my memory. I don't think the man said your name, Edwin MacAlister; I would have remembered sooner if he had. But he mentioned The Cracked Spine, I'm sure of it."

She stopped talking and fell into thought.

"In what context was the bookshop brought up?" Edwin asked.

She looked at him again. "In his story, he said that the owner of this bookshop had some important documents, some so rare they might actually change the world."

"We have some rare documents, aye. Was he more specific?" Edwin said.

"He said that in your records, somewhere in your files, you have some notes, handwritten by Elizabeth I herself, regarding a letter aboot a sort of truce between her and Mary."

"Mary, Queen of Scots?" Jack asked, but I thought it was just for extra clarification. We all knew who she was talking about.

"Aye," she said.

Jack nodded.

"That's exactly what we were told," Mary continued. "I rang the museum just before I came over today and, based on my description of him, that man is no longer there. They couldn't or wouldn't give me a forwarding number or address, but I know it happened. I know what he said."

"Mary, you just remembered this?" I said. "Forgive me, but it was about the queen. I would think you would never forget anything said about her."

"Why? Because I should remember knowing everything about her, because I *was* her?"

"No," I said. "Because you *truly believe* you were her, I would guess you would remember everything that you learned about her. You would be interested in everything."

Mary laughed once. "Delaney, people tell me things about the queen every single day. I don't remember most. I don't pay attention most of the time, because I can sense what's real and what isn't. I know that sounds strange, but believe me—believe *in* me or not—for whatever reason, what that man said didn't stay with me. Maybe it didn't ring true at the time. Maybe it was more about Elizabeth than Mary. I don't know, but I finally did remember the conversation. Today."

"Fair enough," I said. "What else did he say?"

"The gentleman at the museum said that Elizabeth wrote down some thoughts right before Lord Darnley, Mary's husband, was killed. Her notes were being used as she drafted a letter to Mary. The man in the French museum said that Elizabeth had been considering ways to make the relationship between her and Mary—England and Scotland—better. This notion is backed up some by history, but not the notes or letter specifically. When Darnley was killed, the letter was either destroyed, hidden, or stolen. The docent speculated that perhaps, Moray, Mary's half brother, had taken the letter, maybe to use against someone at some point. Maybe he just didn't want it to come to light. Who knows what Moray was up to, but he certainly betrayed Mary."

Moray again, I thought. "Why did the docent think this letter existed? What proof did he have?"

Mary shook her head. "That's why I tried to find him today. I don't think Henry and I asked him for more details. I can't remember if we were interrupted, if we'd had too much wine, or if we thought the docent was a wee bit off in his head. I think I forgot about it all quickly. Until today."

"I'm not aware of anything of the sort," Edwin said. "Existing here in the bookshop or anywhere else for that matter."

Rosie, Hamlet, and I said we hadn't seen anything that might be a letter written by Elizabeth I. We all would have noticed something that significant.

"Mary, the likelihood that those documents, if they existed at all, could stand the test of time is . . . almost impossible," I said.

"Not necessarily," Mary said. "At dinner, you yourself mentioned Mary's recently discovered notes. The ones found in a box in the basement of the museum. It's very possible for documents to stand the test of time."

I nodded. "True."

"Edwin, what if you *do* have the letter or the notes? And," Mary paused and seemed to steel herself, "what if Henry *didn't* forget? I've forgotten much from that holiday, but I also remember this: I told him, in jest I thought, that we should buy the bookshop and all its contents. We shouldn't tell the owner—I didn't know your name at the time—what we'd learned but that we should just buy everything. We have plenty of money. I was just being silly. I was not serious. We were just having a good time."

"Oh, no," I said aloud.

Everyone looked at me.

"Edwin, you've said that you would give the shop to Rosie or Hamlet or even me, or you'd just shut it down, before you ever took a dime for it," I said.

"Aye."

"Did Henry approach you to purchase the shop?" I asked.

"I have no recollection of any such thing, but many people have approached me to buy the shop over the years."

"If he did approach you and you told him no, then closing the shop could have been Henry's revenge," I said. I looked at Mary. "Edwin says he never spoke with Henry about the vote, a bad inspection, about suing. Edwin just received a recorded call."

"That is the absolute truth," Edwin said.

"If Henry made that up, who knows what else he fabricated," I said.

"Delaney," Mary said. "Henry is the one who was killed."

"I'm sorry," I said to Mary. I looked at Edwin. "We need to search the shop again. If those papers are here, we need to find them."

Everyone agreed.

Edwin turned to Mary. "I know this was hard, this is a difficult time, but thank you. We will search and we'll let you know."

"I really hope . . ." Her eyes filled with tears but she blinked fast and furious. "That it will all be okay. I'm . . ."

"What?" I said.

"I'm trying understand what Henry was up to, what he was thinking, and what he did shortly before he died. I know that keeping the bookshop open is your priority, but I'd like his killer brought to justice, even if I'm afraid he was in the middle of doing something less than noble. I will tell the police all of this. I will tell the council. I will do what I can."

Rosie stood. "Lass, can we get ye a cuppa or some coffee? Perhaps a glass of water?"

"No, thank you. I've got to go. I need to talk to someone else today."

I couldn't help myself. "Who?"

Mary blinked at me. "Oh. Well, Henry's brother. I believe they spoke the day before Henry was killed. They shared secrets with each other, sometimes."

I didn't even for one second consider that I might be stepping over some line, butting into something that wasn't my business. I stood. "Want some company?"

TWENTY-FIVE

At first, Mary wasn't sure what to make of my offer. No one was. I sensed everyone's surprise or maybe it was embarrassment, but I didn't care. I didn't know what else I wanted from Mary, but I knew I wanted something. I wasn't ready to tell her goodbye for the day.

However, I thought she was somehow relieved to have someone with her. Henry's brother worked evenings at the castle on the hill. I'd been prepared to call Elias for a ride to wherever we needed to go, but it turned out we were only a short walk away. As we made our way, passing Tom's pub without stopping, I told Mary I'd seen the hypnotism.

"You were there?" she said, genuinely surprised.

"I was. It was interesting. Do you remember being . . . under?"

"I do. I remember it all."

"Are you and Lyle Mercado friends?" I asked.

"Oh, yes, Lyle and I have known each other for years. He remembers his past lives too."

"Who was he?"

"No one famous."

"No one associated with the queen?"

"No, I don't believe so."

"Mary, do you know he was the one who first planted the seed for not only closing the bookshop but the resurgence of the Burgess Tickets."

"I don't think so," Mary said.

"That's what Bella Montrose told me. Do you know her?"

"Of course I do."

"Would Henry and Lyle have been in on this together?" I asked again.

Mary sighed. "No, Delaney, but I could see Lyle doing Henry's bidding. Lyle is enamored with us, Henry and me. Lyle and I met through the past-lives group, but when we all became friends, it was clear that Lyle thought Henry and I were something special. It's a terribly vain thing to say, but it's the truth. If Henry didn't want to present a new idea that he wasn't sure he should present, Lyle would jump aboard and do it for him."

"Does he have any sort of romantic feelings for you?"

"No," she said after a long pause. "I'm sure of that."

No matter, I hoped the police were taking a good look at Lyle Mercado. Maybe I'd mentioned his name to Inspector Buchanan.

"You know, I blame Mary of Guise for the whole mess," Mary said.

"Hold on—who is Mary of Guise? And why do you blame her?" I said as we came upon the castle courtyard, thankfully stopping so I could catch my breath.

"There were a lot of other reasons, but she was Mary Stuart's mother. Mary of Guise ruled as regent for her infant daughter. And then she died when Mary was eighteen, still in France about to move to Scotland. Died!—right when Mary needed her the most. Mary never saw her mother again after she was sent to France as a child. Mary might have been able to fight those against her better if her mother hadn't left her. Her mother was trying to forge a better relationship with Elizabeth. She might have accomplished it and helped her daughter. But death was only a half a breath away back in 1560, one tiny scratch gone wrong."

"Did Mary of Guise die of an infection?"

"There was speculation she was poisoned, but it was never proved. The official cause was dropsy."

"Dropsy?"

"Too much fluid under the skin, around the organs."

"Tragic."

"The queen's life was one tragedy after another."

"No kidding," I said.

Mary's energetic march up to the castle had tired my calves. I was used to walking around the city, but whatever was fueling her energy felt more like a jog than a walk.

"Mary was young," I added. "She might not have had the sophistication to deal with Elizabeth."

"Exactly."

"How did their meetings go?"

Mary eyebrows came together. "Delaney, they never met, face-to-face."

"What?"

"No, never."

"I had no idea."

Mary turned and faced me. She reached up and held onto my arms. The moment was over the top, uncomfortable, though I didn't pull away.

"However, I have a distinct feeling that Elizabeth felt that we—she and Mary—would be queens *together*. I'm so sure of those words, that sentiment, but I can't understand why."

I swallowed hard. "Do you have a distinct memory of that? You can be straight with me. I won't tell either way. I'll be straight with you, I don't think the birthmark is much proof, though I'm not saying I disbelieve you."

"But you don't *believe* me?"

"Something like that."

She took her hands off my arms but still faced me. "Delaney, when I was four years old, I found some wild violets and brought a bouquet of them into my house. I told my mother I wanted to make some jelly or marmalade with them. She laughed and said that wasn't how those things were made."

"Seems reasonable."

"But at one time, it was exactly how marmalade was made—with the powder of violets into boiling quinces and sugar. To this day I remember being upset with my mother that she wouldn't let me into the kitchen. It was later when I started studying the queen that I learned that was one of her favorite pastimes. She liked to spend her time in the kitchen making cotignac, which is a marmalade-like creation made with the powder of violets. How else would a four-year-old know such a thing if she hadn't lived a past life doing it?"

"Maybe someone read it to you in a child's book."

"I don't think so, and I challenge anyone to find such a book. I've lost many of the memories, but they used to come at me all the time. Visions, colors, fabrics, smells, people's faces. When I was twelve, still before I started studying the queen, I started embroidery—and it not only was a passion, I was immediately good at it. Guess who else was?"

"The queen."

"Exactly. I'm not pulling anyone's leg. I'm not making anything up. I was Mary, Queen of Scots."

A tiny ray of sunshine peaked out from behind the clouds and seemed to illuminate Mary, and then it was gone, behind a cloud again. But, for that instant, I thought I was seeing a queen. I knew it could just be all the talk, and I knew she could still be making everything up. But, there's something different about a queen, and I thought I might have glimpsed that difference. Briefly.

I was still looking at her, processing her words when she emphatically added, "And guess what I was obsessed about embroidering? Just guess."

"I have no idea."

"Cats! That was one of Mary's first embroideries. Will you believe me now?"

"I don't think you're lying," I said, though I wasn't exactly sure. "But I don't want to lie to you either and tell you that I do believe you. I'm pretty open to anything, but this is a big leap to make. And I always feel like there's usually a believable explanation for everything, Mary. For now, I'm willing to just continue on not disbelieving. Is that okay?"

She looked at me with the same study I had made of her. "It's uncanny how we look alike."

"Yes, it is," I agreed. "But it's not because we're twins."

I hoped that made the point I was trying so hard not to offensively make.

She smiled a moment later and laughed once. "Fair enough. All right, come along. I need to see if Henry was at the castle the day before his death."

"Why?" I hurried to follow her resumed pace.

"He told his brother everything he couldn't tell me. They were close, and when he felt like he couldn't talk to me about something, he would talk to Clayton. He would always come up to the castle, where they were surrounded by mostly tourists, by people who probably wouldn't know he was a councilor. I always joked about Henry plotting battles at this castle just like was done in the olden days." A ghost of a smile rode over her mouth and then disappeared. "Maybe Henry said something to Clayton the day or days before he was killed that will help find the killer."

"Will he be here? I mean, he might be home, in mourning."

"No," she shook her head, "he'll be here. He'll mourn in his way, but it will include a stiff Scottish upper lip and a notion that he can't miss work for anything but his own death. Henry was the same way."

"Did you tell the police about Henry and Clayton's relationship?"

"Of course, but that woman who is heading up the investigation is not interested in what I have to say. She thinks I'm nutty in the head."

"I sensed she was a good officer though, thorough. Maybe she'll do okay."

She sent me another look. "I don't know, Delaney, the police didn't much like Henry either."

"Why?"

"They pay attention to which of the councilors vote to decrease things like police salaries and such."

"Oh dear. Did something like that just go through?'

"No, not recently, but Henry voted against an increase a while back. Though he only voted against it because he thought they should get more. He had to explain himself several times. People were angry."

"Angry enough to kill?"

"I don't know."

We reached the lines of tourists and Mary led us around, taking us directly to the ticket booth. We were none too popular for it, but once at the counter, Mary just waved at the woman in the booth.

"Och, Mary, what a surprise! So sorry about Henry, love."

"Ta," Mary said. "We're going in, Janice."

"Aye. G'on," Janice said before she signaled for the next person in line to step up to the window.

With swift feet I followed Mary as I sent a frown of apology back to the people in the line.

"It'll do you no good," Mary said. "We have business to do and we have to get on with it. We don't have time to wait in any lines."

"Okay," I said. "Do you have special privileges?"

"I do," she said.

She was behaving more like the Mary I'd first met. She'd struck me as confident and bossy then, and now too. In between, though, I'd seen sad, apologetic, and unsure.

However, she cleared her throat as if she'd heard herself. "It's not what you think. I have volunteered at all the museums. I love them, but you could probably already imagine that. Anyway, they all know me and they have all given me the freedom to come and go as I please."

A privilege fit for a queen.

"That's wonderful. I love museums too."

"I'm not surprised." She paused. "Do you think it's possible that Edwin has Elizabeth's notes?"

"I have no idea," I said, "but it's doubtful."

"Why is it doubtful?"

"It's hard to imagine that something like that would be overlooked."

"But it's possible?"

"Sure. I guess."

"Do you think you could take an extra look?"

"Absolutely. We all will."

"Thanks."

We'd crossed the courtyard and went through the wide entry doors.

"Mary!" A man in costume said as he walked toward us. "Hello!"

Mary hugged him. "Sammy."

I thought I saw tears in his eyes when he pulled back, "I heard about Henry. Everyone's heard about Henry. Do the police know what happened yet?"

"Not yet, I'm afraid."

"I'm so sorry, lass."

"Thank you, Sammy." She looked toward me the same time Sammy did.

"Is this . . . you don't have a sister or a daughter, do you?" Sammy said.

"I don't. This is a friend who happens to look like me."

"I'd say. Were ye the queen too?" he asked me sincerely.

"I don't think so," I said as we shook hands.

For a few beats, Sammy looked back and forth between the two of us. "Goodness."

"Yes," Mary said. "Sammy, is Clayton here?"

Sammy took two more quick looks back and forth and said, "Aye, I believe he is."

"Can we go on back?"

"Aye, certainly. He's going tae be as surprised as I am. Maybe more."

Mary nodded and they hugged quickly again before we turned and started walking deeper into the castle.

I'd been through it a time or two—maybe six or seven—over the last year. There was much to see, though I wasn't surprised when Mary led us in the direction of the Royal Apartments, which had at one time been home to the queen, and her husband—the one who was blown to smithereens, in fact.

"You do know that the queen gave birth to her only child here," she said to me over her shoulder.

"I didn't know that," I said.

"Bastard, he turned out to be. Well, not in the official definition. No, he was an arse to his mother," she said. "However, later, after the queen was cruelly beheaded, it must be pointed out that King James I turned out to be a pretty good king."

"How was he an ass?"

Mary slowed her footsteps as we entered the Laich Hall with its dark gold embossed wood paneling and magnificent fireplace. "Mary was not in control of her own life, even as she was queen. When Mary gave birth to James, who would be the heir to the British throne, both Mary and the baby had to be protected. They were separated. But it was toward the end of Mary's life, when she was close to execution that her son wouldn't come see her, wouldn't help make a case to save his mother."

"The end of her life was pretty terrible."

"You mean her assassination disguised as an execution?"

"Yes, I suppose."

"She was betrayed by everyone, her son included. Well, her servants were still on her side, her four Marys, all of her ladies were named Mary, did you know?"

"I think I heard that."

Mary stopped suddenly and looked at the walls. I knew that look—something deep that searched for clues to everything that had happened here. I'd had many of those moments in Scotland.

"Can you feel them?" she asked.

"Feel what?" I asked.

"The ghosts of the past."

I didn't feel them, though that didn't make the castle less impressive or less interesting to me. However, it was at that moment that I became one hundred percent certain that if I'd ever lived a past life, it hadn't been lived in this castle. I knew it, bone deep. Which made me wonder if Mary knew she *had*, bone deep.

No bookish voices were talking either.

"I feel the history," I said. "I don't feel the ghosts, I'm afraid. I have felt them at other times though, so I get what you're saying. That sensation is strong, isn't it?"

"Do you think everyone feels such things?"

"Oh, no," I said with a laugh.

She blinked at me. "See, it was destined that we were to meet."

I laughed again. "Maybe. But even though Edinburgh is a big city, we were either bound to run into each other someday, or someone would meet us both and let us know about the other."

She nodded, but then turned and resumed walking. We made our way through to the great hall. The only great hall I'd seen that compared in any way was Hogwarts. I'd seen a few castles while in Scotland, but this one was done up in its finest.

"Mary was crowned when she was nine months old," Mary said. "It was the solemnest of all events or ceremonies. And here," she stopped next to a display case, "the scepter, the crown, and the sword. They were carried behind her. We are not in a position to understand how important these were, but they were mightily important. Look at them. Do they look real to you?"

They were impressive, but . . . "They look like something that might be found in a costume shop."

"See," she said, "sometimes it's difficult to find the real stuff. Those notes could be in Edwin's things, right under your noses, looking like something from a costume shop, some forgeries, some scribbles."

"Point taken."

"Mary?" Another costumed gentleman came into the room.

"Clayton," Mary said.

This greeting was somewhat icier than Sammy's.

"I'm sorry about Henry," he said stiffly.

"Condolences to you too," Mary said.

They looked at each other for a long, silent moment. I sensed they were both sad, but trying hard not to be. The family dynamics were strained—Mary and Clayton didn't like each other, but that was psychology for another day.

"This is my friend, Delaney," Mary said.

Surprisingly, Clayton only shook my hand and said it was good to meet me. Either he didn't notice my resemblance to his sister-in-law or it didn't matter to him.

"Do you have time to steal away to a private room for a moment?" Mary asked.

"Right this way." Clayton turned and we followed him.

I was disappointed that the private room was nothing special, just something that had been walled off—not a secret castle cubbie or passageway, just a small, modern semiprivate space.

We sat in boring twenty-first-century office chairs around an even more boring small twentieth-century coffee table.

Briefly, I wondered if I could manage to get my phone out to record the conversation, but I dismissed the idea quickly enough. It wasn't a task I could handle subtly, and I didn't even know what was going to be discussed.

"How may I be of service?" Clayton asked Mary.

"Clayton, I need to know if Henry was here the day or few days before he was killed. I need to also know if he spoke to you, what you spoke about."

"Why? Are you investigating his murder?"

"The police are doing what they do, Clayton, but I need some peace and the only way I'm going to get that is to try to understand what my husband was up to. He talked to you about many things. He told you things he didn't tell me and I have a theory. I just need to know if my theory is correct."

Clayton frowned and nodded slowly.

"Henry *was* here the day before he was killed," Clayton said. "He came specifically to talk to me. He was upset about something he'd set into place."

"What?" Mary and I asked together.

"I'm not sure exactly," Clayton said.

Mary put her hand over his. "This is so very important, Clayton. Please tell me what you know."

Clayton sighed. "He was going to get you something, though he wouldn't tell me exactly what it was. He came to me upset that he'd set something in motion with the council that wasn't going to be reversible. It was going to cause harm to some people who probably didn't deserve it, people you'd recently met. He needed to work it out in his head, but he'd done it for you."

"What time was this?" Mary asked.

Clayton thought a moment. "I think it was around two in

the afternoon. I'd already had lunch, but that's as close as I can get."

"That's close enough," Mary said as she deflated.

"What?" I said.

"It was as I was finishing lunch that I rang him. I told him I'd found the most charming of bookshops and that someone there looked so much like me, he was going to be thrown for a loop. I told him the bookshop was called The Cracked Spine, and I'd invited you all over for dinner that night."

"That one call made him feel guilty?" I said.

"I can see that. He asked me if I liked the shop. He asked me about you, the woman who looked so much like me. And, he said something to the effect that it was some sort of sign or something. I asked him to clarify, but he just laughed off the statement and said he had to go. I wouldn't be surprised if he'd already been feeing badly about what he'd done, guilty, and that call with me was the tipping point."

I turned to Clayton, "What did you say to him?"

"All I said was that whatever he'd set into motion, if it wasn't already done, then he should be able to stop it."

"How did he react?" Mary asked.

"He said it was going to be dangerous to stop it, that he could be in trouble."

"Why dangerous?" Mary asked. I really wished I'd turned on the recorder app.

Clayton frowned and shook his head. "He said that 'they' were going to be upset. I asked if he meant you, but he said you had no idea what he'd been doing."

"Did you talk to the police?" I interrupted.

"No, what was I to say?"

"That he knew he might be in danger," I said.

"But that's all I knew. He didn't give me any further details."

"So when he began to change his mind about what he'd done, someone killed him?" I said.

"It seems that way," Mary said.

"Who in the world would that be?" I said.

"That's what the police need to figure out," Mary said.

Clayton sat forward and put his elbows on the table. "Mary, you need to tell me what's going on. I will go talk to the police if I feel I need to, but I need some missing puzzle pieces here."

In a scattered way, with my intermittent input, we told Clayton what had been going on.

By the end of the conversation, it didn't take much coaxing to get Clayton to say he would call the police.

Mary didn't walk with me back to the bookshop. She said goodbye as she hailed a taxi. She said she was going home, that it had been a tiring day, but that she hoped everyone at the bookshop would search for the notes and the letter.

"Do you really think they exist?" I asked her as she got into the cab.

She hesitated and looked at me a long moment. "I don't know if they're in the bookshop, Delaney, but, aye, I think they exist. A big part of me hopes so."

I didn't tell her as much, but it crossed my mind that maybe we'd find the Burgess Ticket, the old construction approvals, and the letter all together. It was just some more hope bubbling up.

If I were something that needed to hide inside the bookshop, where would I hide?

I have no idea, I thought as I watched the taxi drive away.

TWENTY-SIX

"What are you doing?" Tom asked in the dark. It was the middle of the night, and he hadn't been home from the pub long before I was up again, getting dressed.

"I can't sleep," I said quietly, even though there was no one else in our cottage.

"Where are you going?"

"I'm going into the bookshop. I need to search some more."

I'd stopped by the pub on the way back from the castle and updated Tom. Back at the bookshop, we all took on the search, except Jack. He'd left by the time I made it back. But our search had been interrupted by a tour group of twenty that had been caught out in the rain. We'd invited them inside until the storm passed. They'd been there a couple hours, ultimately buying many more books than they probably wanted. We'd left at five for the day, saying we'd resume searching again the next day. It was the next day, though earlier than the others had in mind.

"I'll come with you," Tom said as he swung his legs off the bed.

"No, you need sleep."

"I won't sleep now anyway. It's all right. It's my day off. I'll catch some rest later."

I hadn't meant for him to go, but it would be much better having him along.

I loved Edinburgh, during the daytime and at night. At night, particularly after it had rained though, when puddles glimmered and streetlights and dimmed shop lights shone differently. There was a sense of magic in the air, that sense of history that the older Scottish men in my life: Edwin, Elias, and Tom's father, Artair, held onto with a fierce stubbornness. They weren't stuck in the past, but they carried it with them, always. I understood them more at night.

Tom drove us through town and toward Grassmarket. The rain had only recently stopped, and steam came up from gutters as people moved along the streets. Like so many bigger cities, Edinburgh didn't really sleep, but it rested well. Still, night people, tourists, artists, and restless residents could always find something to do, and something to eat.

Plenty of takeaway restaurants stayed open. A couple of theaters played movies all night long, usually older American films. I'd even come upon one that hosted Rocky Horror interactive shows.

Early on in my time here, I'd spent a few nights making my way through the streets and back to the bookshop in order to work on a project that wouldn't let me rest.

The warehouse was mine now, no doubt. Mine slightly more than Edwin's. I thought he wanted it that way, but sometimes I wasn't sure. Sometimes I saw that look in his eyes, the one that glances back at the way things used to be. He never kept his gaze there long. He was also a firm believer in life going on.

"Delaney, after talking to Clayton, do you still want to talk to Grace Graham?" Tom asked as we made our way.

"First thing, when the sun comes up, I'm going to try to reach her," I said.

"Not confident that there's enough to cancel or postpone the vote yet?"

"Oh, no, not yet. I'm not going to stop until we know for sure."

"Did Mary think even for a minute that Clayton might be responsible for Henry's murder?" Tom asked.

"I don't think so. I admit it crossed my mind, but only because I'm suspicious of everyone. I'm still wondering about Mary," I said.

"An interesting couple. Interesting lives, a tragic death," Tom said.

"Do . . . did you like them?" I hadn't asked him that yet.

"Yes, particularly Henry, until I heard he wanted to shut down the bookshop."

Tom pulled to a stop in front of said bookshop. Over the last year, I'd come upon people and packages that had led to other surprises. Now, I took a good look at the shop and its surroundings before entering.

"All clear?" Tom asked me.

"Looks good."

It was unusually warm outside as we sidestepped the puddles along the cobblestone walkway. After I unlocked the door and we were inside, I relocked it behind us. All the while, Tom watched me and we nodded at each other, confirming we both saw the lock go into place.

Using the light on my phone, we made our way over to the dark side and down the stairs. It was colder on the dark side but not unbearable.

I turned the oversize blue skeleton key in the lock three times to the left before we pushed through the big red door, shutting and locking it behind us.

I flipped on the overhead fluorescents and Tom and I shared another nod and a smile. We were there, the place that even more than the city, more than McKenna's cottage, I'd lived in since moving to Scotland. More than Tom's blue house by the sea, this place was my home. Wherever Tom lived was my true home now, but if he wasn't part of the equation, this warehouse, this space was where my soul truly danced.

"Where do we begin?" Tom asked.

Tonight, the moon shone through one of the high windows, and I took in the rare sight. It would move behind a cloud or away from my view soon, but for an instant, it was lovely. Shelves lined the walls—and they were all packed with things, a wide variety. Need a Fabergé egg? Hang on, there was one here not long ago. How about some things that came from ancient Egyptian tombs? Right over there. Books filled some shelves but there were fewer books than one might think would be in storage in a bookshop. Mostly, the shelves overflowed with Edwin's collections, and the things he'd hired me to organize. I would never be done, there was no end to the project. For someone who liked to tick things off on their to-do list, it would be a surprise to most that I was thrilled I had a job I would never finish. But when it's the best job in the entire universe, who would want it to be over?

"There's a file cabinet under the bottom shelf on that wall. There are hundreds of documents inside it. I looked through it briefly twice today, but another pair of eyes wouldn't hurt."

"All right." Tom pushed up his sleeves.

The wood file cabinet wasn't valuable, but it was old, having seen its better days about a hundred scratches and dings ago. As I'd done earlier, we unwedged it from next to the wall.

I pulled open the top drawer. "There's so much in here. Lots of interesting notes, a couple of maps that would get my attention if I wasn't looking for something else, but I saw no letter that might have come from Elizabeth I, no notes hinting at a letter, no Burgess Tickets, and no construction paperwork."

We peered in at the packed drawer.

"No place to begin but the beginning." Tom reached into the drawer and carefully lifted out the top bits and pieces and carried them to the worktable.

I moved to the tapestries I'd been looking at a few days earlier. They were the real reason I couldn't sleep. I'd forgotten that I'd discovered what I thought was Queen Elizabeth's crest on one of them. I'd looked many places earlier today, but I hadn't taken a closer look at the tapestries. I didn't know what I might find, but it had suddenly seemed important that I investigate.

I lifted one over to my desk.

"You're more comfortable working on the desk than you used to be," Tom said.

The best we could date it was back to the seventeenth century. Edwin had said it had once resided in the castle I'd visited with Mary earlier today, maybe right next to the royal scepter and crown. At least, that's what I liked to think.

"I still cover it with paper, but I'm not as intimidated by it. Did I tell you about the desks at Dina's antique shop?"

"No."

I shared the details and added, "Edwin thinks this one is even more valuable. Yeah, I'm not *as* intimidated, but I'm aware."

"You're looking at a tapestry?" Tom asked.

I'd found a magnifying glass and held it over a corner. "Yes, I think Elizabeth I's crest is embroidered on it."

"You think it came from her time?"

"Possibly. I didn't double-check these earlier today."

"Are you looking for a hidden pocket or something?"

"I'm not really sure."

"Well, I have just come upon a receipt for some internal organs."

"I think I saw that receipt."

"It looks as if Edwin purchased a sarcophagus back in nineteen seventy-eight. The internal organs are listed as a separate line item."

"I've heard the stories about the sarcophagus. As you might imagine, it was quite a thing back then. Rosie wasn't happy because Edwin wanted to keep it in the front part of the shop."

"What?"

"I know. And she won. It was gotten rid of shortly thereafter."

I put on some gloves and ran my fingers along the tapestry. I *was* looking for a pocket or some place where the alleged notes or letter might be hidden. But I found nothing. I put that tapestry back and gathered another one; this one was a cat. I was reminded of Mary's comments about the queen enjoying tapestry and a cat being one of her first subjects. I hesitated. This wouldn't be Mary's tapestry, would it?

"What?" Tom said.

"I'm not sure." I slipped off the gloves and opened my laptop. "I need to look up something."

It didn't take long. In fact, it only took a few minutes, but that might have been because I knew my way around the internet.

I found exactly what I was looking for. Yes, Mary, Queen of

Scots, did like to embroider. It was easy to find a picture of a cat she had, indeed, created.

I sat back in my chair.

Tom joined me, crouching to see what I was looking at. "What's going on?"

"This was easy to find," I said.

Tom inspected the screen. "A wee cat?"

"A cat that Mary, Queen of Scots, embroidered. It's not the same one I have here."

"Aye?"

"I wonder if it's all this easy to find though. I mean, what if Mary, the one we know, is making it all up? I've thought it was a possibility this whole time, but what would that mean? That she's a liar or something more nefarious?"

"Or simply something else," Tom said. "Some people are compelled to lie, make up stories for attention. Sometimes it's not ill intended."

"You know those dreams where you're chasing something that just keeps getting farther away?" I said.

"Aye."

"That's what this feels like."

Tom stood and then leaned on the corner of the desk. "It's going to be fine, love, I know it. The truth is coming out little by little."

"I'm holding you to that."

"I would expect nothing less. It's going to be fine."

We continued searching but didn't find one note from Elizabeth I. We didn't even find anything that mentioned her. After we finished with the warehouse, we moved over to the other side to search Hamlet's files. We found nothing there either.

The sun had started to rise, but we'd kept working until we

heard the key in the front door and the bell jingle as someone came in.

"Hello?" Rosie called.

"It's me and Tom," I said back.

"What's going on?" Rosie asked as she joined us.

I told Rosie what we'd been up to.

"I havenae found the construction paperwork, and I'm sick aboot it. But, there's good news!"

I really wanted some good news.

"Jack says he can find the inspection paperwork if it exists. He said it had to be filed with the city and even if someone destroyed copies of it, he can track it down. Somehow, some way," Rosie said.

"When?"

"Soon, I hope."

"Oh, that *is* good news," I said, feeling another bubble of hope.

And then I started feeling guilty. If the bookshop hadn't been on the chopping block, I thought I would have thrown myself into trying to figure out who killed Henry. If he hadn't been the one to want the bookshop closed, he might have been a good friend. He *had* been delightful at dinner. We'd all liked all of them, and it had seemed mutual.

"Delaney?" Rosie asked.

I hadn't been listening to my bookish voices. I'd been listening to the sound of my priorities shifting, perhaps toward the direction they should have already settled. It was a deafening noise.

"Who killed Henry?" I said aloud.

"I dinnae ken, lass," Rosie said.

"Well, we need to figure it out," I said.

No one argued.

TWENTY-SEVEN

The answer wasn't going to be found in the next few minutes. In a brief moment of discomfort—that shouldn't have been because we were all grown-ups, for goodness' sake—Brigid walked into the bookshop just as Tom was leaving.

I sensed we all wanted to get past the fact that she was upset about Tom breaking up with her. It had been a long time ago, but some snark filled the air for a moment or two.

"Brigid," Tom said as he left. "Nice to see you."

She nodded and they did a quick awkward dance as he walked out and she moved in toward me.

"Delaney," she said.

"Hey, Brigid," I said.

"I wondered. Have you had a chance to talk to the person I told you about? Grace?"

"Not yet. I tried, but the offices were closed yesterday. I was going to track her down this morning."

Brigid smiled. "Good. Do you have time to come with me right now then?"

"Where?"

"A press conference. Grace will be there." Brigid smiled.

"On a Sunday?"

"The news doesn't take weekends off, Delaney."

Spoken like a true journalist.

"Okay," I said. "Do you think we can talk to her?"

"Maybe." Brigid shrugged.

I told Rosie what we were doing, and Hector gave us a bark of encouragement.

"Be careful, lass," Rosie said to me.

"We're not going anywhere dangerous," Brigid said. "It's a public place with many other reporters. It will be fine. But we have to get going."

I'd stashed my bag under the back table, and I went to retrieve it. Brigid, ever observant, stretched her neck to see if she was missing something in the corner.

"What do you have out?" she asked as she hurried next to me. Some of the documents that we'd found in our search were still spread out over the table. "Look at these. What are you doing with them?"

"Just organizing," I said.

"So interesting." She couldn't pull her eyes away, even though she'd just said we needed to get going.

"There are a million stories here," I said, giving her a little something. I picked up a letter kept inside a clear folder. "Here, here's a letter that talks specifically about William Wallace. The writer of the letter knew him, apparently."

"Really?" she said as she looked closer.

"Indeed."

"What's it say?"

The writing was next to impossible to decipher, but Hamlet

had done the work. Underneath the protected document was his modern version, his translation. In fact, there were three copies.

"Here." I gave her a copy. "Take this with you."

"Thank you." She blinked at me.

I still didn't think she and I would be friends, but we might get past the snarky moments. And, I wasn't going to talk to Edwin about an interview. Maybe the William Wallace letter would later help to diffuse some of her future anger.

She folded the piece of paper and put it in her bag. I sent Rosie a reassuring nod as we headed toward the door.

"Want to pop in for a quick one at Tom's pub?" Brigid asked.

"Only if you do," I said. "He's not going in today, and I'm just along for the ride."

She sent me a frown and then shook her head. "I was kidding. You know, I keep thinking he's going to show his true colors and you're going to end up terribly disappointed."

And the hopes for diffusing her anger were gone, just like that. "I know you do."

"I'm really beginning to wonder if I'm wrong. I might need to just accept that he didn't care for me enough."

Good feelings coming back. Brigid and my relationship was going to be rough, no matter what.

She glanced at me and laughed once. "I won't deny that I'm jealous, but not because it's Tom. I'm long over him. I guess I just admire you."

"For keeping a man around. That's not very feminist of you."

"No, that's not it. I admire your sense of self, your ability to see what's there even if everyone else is telling you differently."

"I think I've misrepresented myself to you. I have plenty of self-doubt, thank you very much." I paused. "But when you know, you know. I had no doubt about Tom. And, I'm glad to hear you're over him, because I admire you too. You're a very good journalist, an exceptional writer."

"You've been reading my stories?"

"I have, and they're very good."

"Prove it."

Boy, she was going to be a needy friend, but good feelings were still overriding the bad ones. I proceeded to list a few of the stories she'd covered in the last couple of months. I had been following her stuff. And she was good.

"I'm honored," she said.

I shrugged. "Like I said, you're very good."

"All right, that's enough of our mutual admiration society. It's time to get down to business. We are attending a press conference about Henry. Sort of."

"What's going on? Has someone been arrested for his murder?"

"I don't think so. The Lord Provost didn't express any condolences. Some folks thought that was wrong, tacky, and maybe even suspicious. The press conference should rectify the problem. That's why it's on a Sunday. They couldn't wait a day more."

"Maybe the police have someone though. I hope so."

"That would be good," Brigid said doubtfully.

I looked at her. "What?"

"I don't think the police have the killer yet. I would know."

"How?"

"You'll see. Come on."

We came upon Princes Street Gardens. A far corner I'd not visited yet. The garden was at the bottom of the other side of the castle than where the bookshop was located, and was once the place where the citizens of Edinburgh tossed their waste. And threw in accused witches, of course. If the accused drowned she was deemed not to be a witch. But if she didn't, she was pulled from the waste and marched to another, different horrific death, some taking place over in Grassmarket. It was a brutal history in more ways than that one, but I was particularly and morbidly fascinated by the witchcraft angles.

We were at least on time for the press conference, but if we'd wanted to be up front we should have been there earlier. Still, the weather was cooperating—some clouds but no rain. Yet.

We took up a spot at the back of the crowd.

"There are so many people here. On a Sunday," I said quietly.

There were probably about fifty people in attendance. A small area had been cordoned off for the press conference. At one end a podium with a microphone was up on a small riser and stood alone and unattended.

Brigid only gave me half her attention. She was stretching her neck, standing on her tiptoes, trying to see a way up closer. I looked too but there were no open routes.

"There she is," Brigid said.

"Grace Graham?" I asked.

"The one and only."

A woman appeared on the riser and made her way to the podium. The air about her was no-nonsense. She wore her clothes like a uniform and her hair like a bulletproof helmet. If she wore makeup, it wasn't visible from where we stood. She sent the crowd an impatient frown. I was immediately intimidated by her.

"Come on," Brigid said as she took my arm and pulled me with her.

I sent strained smiles and "excuse me's" as we made our

way. Brigid stopped in a small pocket close to the front, only two people back from the rail.

Brigid made eye contact with Grace, and I thought I saw them send each other a small nod, but it could have been my imagination.

"Thank you all for coming out today." Grace seemed solemn. "This will be quick. It has been brought to the Lord Provost's attention that his office has been remiss in expressing condolences for the friends and loved ones of our dear Henry Stewart. I shall read a statement directly from the Lord Provost." She looked down at the podium. "'We apologize sincerely for our oversight regarding esteemed councilor Henry Stewart. We, like so many of you, were shocked by the tragedy and haven't been able to get our heads around our loss. We should have said something sooner. We apologize and do, indeed, send our deepest condolences.'" Grace looked up. "That's it, ladies and gentlemen. Other than, thank you so much for giving me some of your Sunday."

A murmur spread through the crowd. Everyone wanted more, and hands shot up. Brigid's included.

Grace said, "I'm not here today to answer questions, but I'll take a couple. Yes, Mason," she nodded at a man in a blue shirt, "what's your question?"

"Are the police still sticking to their story that Stewart was the only person targeted in the bombing?"

"Yes," Grace said. She hesitated briefly "We have been assured that there is no further imminent threat to our city or to the citizens of Edinburgh."

"Grace, what evidence do the police have regarding Mr. Stewart's killer?" a woman in a green jacket asked without waiting to be called upon.

The press conference was exactly what Brigid thought it was going to be. So many people had attended because so little information had been released. Everyone was curious, everyone wanted answers.

"The police haven't shared with us any evidence they've discovered, but I know they are working diligently to find the killer." Grace leaned closer to the microphone. "Thank you all for coming out."

Just as Grace began to turn to leave, Brigid yelled, "Grace, Grace!"

Grace heard her, sent her a frown, but then faced forward again. "Yes, Brigid."

"What had Henry Stewart been working on right before he was killed?" Brigid asked.

A rumble went through the crowd.

"I don't know exactly," Grace said.

"I'd really like to get your statement on that, Ms. Graham," Brigid said.

"I just gave you the statement I came here to share today." She looked away from Brigid and back out at the crowd. "Thank you all."

This time Grace turned and walked away, ignoring any further questions.

"Don't worry," Brigid said to me. "She'll want to talk to me in person now. That's what we want, right?"

"Okay, whatever you say," I said.

Considering how Brigid had interrupted Grace's departure and the tone with which she had answered Brigid's question, I couldn't see how there was any way at all that Grace Graham would want to talk to either of us. Ever probably.

TWENTY-EIGHT

I was wrong, but I'd been tricked. Grace not only wanted to talk to Brigid, but she welcomed us, opening the door wide and signaling us in before she marched to her desk.

"She's my aunt," Brigid said quietly and with a satisfied smile as we made our way into a lovely office, much bigger than Lyle Mercado's, and furnished with modern lines and splashes of chrome.

"That's how you knew so much about the press conference," I said.

"Aye," Brigid said. "And that's why she's talking to us personally."

"Aye," Grace said as we came to two chairs and she turned to face us. "Brigid and I have been discussing many things lately. You must be Delaney." She extended her hand over the desk.

We shook. "I am. It's nice to meet you."

"Have a seat," Grace said. "I would have told you I was her aunt if you'd found me."

"I'm sorry," I said as I sat, but it was only in answer to her accusing tone. "I tried to call once, but I was worried about bothering you."

Grace laughed without humor. "If only my niece felt the same."

Brigid smiled again. "Thanks for seeing us, Auntie."

"I'm not sure I had much choice, but I'm happy you're both here." Grace leaned back in her chair and looked at me. "I've been researching everything Brigid told me. My first question is—is it true that none of you at the bookshop are aware of any inspection?"

"That's absolutely correct," I said.

"I've spoken with the Lord Provost, Delaney, and he is convinced the inspection is valid. I looked up the inspector. His name is Dwayne Stover. Do you know him?"

"I don't think so." The name didn't sound familiar at all. "It's not valid though!"

"However." Grace held up her hand. "The Lord Provost is going to make sure. He's contacting the inspector, Dwayne, himself and said he will investigate. He won't stop the vote because that would go against protocol, but he will make sure the council is fully informed."

"Well. That's good," I said, filing the inspector's name away in my mind.

"Yes, that's good," Grace said. "But, understand, if the buildings are dangerous, they'll have to come down."

I swallowed hard. "They aren't dangerous, I'm sure."

"Let's hope not," Grace said.

"Is the Lord Provost going to investigate Henry's actions?" Brigid said. "Aunt Grace, he was up to so many things, the Burgess Tickets, the bookshop. Maybe there were other things going on."

"Ah, now that would make a good story, wouldn't it? More secret stuff that government officials were trying to get done secretly and got Henry killed."

"Aye, that would be great."

"Brigid, the Lord Provost has looked, is looking, and will look at everything." Her eyebrows came together. "And I'm afraid this part is off the record, but perhaps some things *have* slipped through the cracks, but I promise you, many people are on the case now. The police are investigating, and we have many internal investigations going on too."

"Any idea who killed Henry?" Brigid asked.

Grace looked at me. "She's asked me every day. I still have the same answer. No, I don't have any idea."

"Okay, off the record still, who do you *think* killed Henry?" Brigid asked.

Grace sighed. "If I'd had my own children, maybe I wouldn't be wrapped around my niece's finger. Henry *was* respected, but he was sometimes a difficult man, may he rest in peace. He would become impassioned about something none of the rest of the council could rouse up any interest in. He was famous amongst council members for it. He would campaign, he would ask others to plant seeds of ideas because he knew people sometimes tired of hearing from him. But, I don't know of anyone who disliked him so much they would kill him."

"They would just vote against him?" Brigid said.

"Aye. Or just not listen to him." Grace looked at me again. "Are you aware that his nephew-in-law, Mikey Wooster, is also a council member? He was a part of the committee working on the things Henry had set in motion."

"Yes, I met Mikey," I said. "I talked to his wife recently. She didn't know anything about Mikey's actions on the committee, said she was going to talk to him, but I haven't double-checked to see what has happened."

Grace pursed her lips tightly as she inspected Brigid and me. "All right. Brigid, this is still off the record, but you might be able to use it for some background, okay?"

"Absolutely," Brigid said.

"I don't know the details, but Henry and Mikey argued the day before Henry was killed. Loudly. A couple of the councilors witnessed the argument."

"Who?" Brigid asked.

"We are still off the record."

"Aye," Brigid said.

I wondered why Grace shared information so easily with Brigid, even off the record. Was it because they were family, or did Grace have other motivations? Did she use Brigid to put information out to the public to help the Lord Provost behind the scenes?

"They were also on Henry's committee. Their names are Monika Hidasi and Simone Lazar."

I'd found Bella Montrose, but not Monika or Simone. They were the three names Inspector Buchanan had given me, the councilors she'd spoken to. She'd thought I might be able to convince them to at least postpone the vote. I wasn't going to tell Brigid and Grace about Inspector Buchanan's note. Brigid wrote down the names, but didn't ask more questions about them.

I sat forward on the chair. "Ms. Graham, if there really is a failed inspection, the results just can't be accurate. The building is sound, I'm sure." I hoped. "Could we hire an independent party to evaluate the building? Would that help?"

"I don't know. I can suggest that as an idea."

"I will do all the legwork, Ms. Graham," I said. "I'll take any direction you might give me."

"I hear you. Let me see what I can do."

"Thank you."

Grace nodded. "You are welcome. Now, I have other work to do. If the two of you will excuse me."

Brigid and I stood and moved toward the door, but Brigid stopped. "You'll be there for dinner this weekend, Auntie?"

"I wouldn't miss it." Grace smiled.

"Thank you," I said again.

"I'll be in touch," Grace said to me.

"Well, we know something more," Brigid said as we left the building and started walking back up the Royal Mile. "Let's track down Mikey Wooster."

"Because he argued with Henry? What about Monika and Simone? Or the inspector, Dwayne Stover?"

"Let's start with Mikey. Grace said that Monika and Simone didn't hear the exact words of the argument. Maybe later for Dwayne. Let's go directly to the source, see if the argument might have led to a murder."

"Okay." I shrugged.

"Delaney, there's a big story here, I can smell it."

"What if it turns out to be boring and something from a simple clerical error?" I said as we turned a corner I didn't remember exploring yet.

"It won't. There was murder. There's something big going on here."

"What if we find a killer?" I asked, thinking that perhaps that should have been an obvious concern.

"Isn't that the goal? I mean other than keeping the bookshop open," Brigid said with a smile. "Come on, I know where we can probably find Wooster, and it's a public place."

TWENTY-NINE

"Why do you think he's here?" I asked as we stood outside the restaurant.

"I looked him up already. When I heard he was married to Mary's niece, I thought he might be someone I should talk to. He eats here all the time, particularly on the weekends."

"Impressive," I said.

Tom had taken me to Makers Gourmet Mash Bar once before. It was a lively place with a variety of delicious food. Some American, some Scottish. Haggis, which was, of course, distinctly Scottish, was a big part of the menu and something I was sure I would never acquire a taste for, even when its reputation was talked about as lovingly as Makers' was.

The name of the restaurant jarred a memory loose. Or maybe it was the talk about Mikey and his wife in conjunction with the name of the restaurant that had done it.

After visiting Dina at her antique shop, I'd been gung-ho to check the maker's mark on my desk, but I'd forgotten to do so. Even when Tom and I had spent the night searching through files and noting that I was now more comfortable working on the valuable antique, I hadn't checked the mark. I still needed to do that, and I mentally filed the task away for later.

The restaurant was packed. *At least Mikey might not spot us right away,* I thought as we went through the door. Of course, we couldn't find him easily either.

"Let me know if you see him," Brigid said. "I'll either get him outside to talk to us or you can."

I stepped around her and to the side of two men blocking the way. I scanned the room and thought I saw Mikey in the back. It looked as if he was talking to someone, but I couldn't see the other person.

"He's in the back," I said to Brigid. I pulled her closer and pointed.

As we watched him, he leaned forward on the table, placing his arms on it. We could see him grasp other hands. We could see all four hands, but nothing else of the other person.

"Who is he with?" Brigid asked.

"We'll have to get closer. I can't tell."

It wasn't easy. First of all, we had to explain to the greeter that we were just there to meet someone. That didn't go over well with the other people waiting to be seated; they weren't happy to have anyone go around them. Brigid made no apologies, but I did. A few.

She led the way through the maze of tables, but a group of customers was suddenly leaving. We all dodged and darted and danced around each other, and Mikey Wooster was out of our sight for a long few moments.

And then, when we were only a couple of tables away, another customer stood up quickly from his chair. He and I collided.

"I'm so sorry," he said as he took my arms in his hands.

"No problem," I said.

But he'd inadvertently turned me a little so I was now facing the front of the restaurant more than the direction I'd intended to go. I still couldn't see Mikey, but I caught sight of a flash of red hair. Lots of people had red hair, in Scotland and everywhere else for that matter, but that flash I'd seen reminded me so much of me that I was at least ninety percent certain I'd seen Mary leaving the restaurant. I knew her hair because it was so much like mine. I blinked and did a double-take toward the front door. But the flash of familiarity was now gone, either out through the door or behind the waiting customers.

I'd thought Brigid's idea to find Mikey was potentially a waste of time. So what that he'd argued with a fellow councilor who happened to be his wife's uncle. Councilors argued, but Mikey wouldn't have done anything to hurt Henry. I still didn't want to think so, and even if him having lunch with his wife's aunt wasn't weird, there was something about the holding hands that struck me funny. Well, not funny so much as curious.

Was I working way too hard to try to find Mary, Queen of Scots' third husband, the one she allegedly had an affair with, the one who probably killed her second husband?

Eureka!

A bookish voice suddenly spoke up in my mind. It was Archimedes, talking about the amount of gold in a crown. He probably hadn't said the word, but many gave him credit for it. It all suddenly seemed so fitting.

"Damn," I said to the bookish voice. "Damn," I said to the whole entire mess.

"Are you okay?" the man said again.

I focused on him and smiled. "Fine, thanks."

He let go of my arms and turned to leave. I sent one more

glance toward the front of the restaurant, but whoever I'd seen was gone now.

"Excuse me," a server said as I continued to stand in the way.

I turned and made my way back to the table, where I joined Brigid and a clearly irritated Mikey. Whoever he'd been holding hands with was gone.

"Nice to see you again, Mikey," I said as I sat down.

"Likewise," Mikey said, his voice clipped.

I gestured toward Brigid. "This is my friend, Brigid."

"Yes, she introduced herself. Hello," Mikey said. "I'm afraid I was just leaving, but feel free to take the table."

As Mikey stood, I put my hand on his arm. "I swear I just saw Mary Stewart walk out of here. Was she here with you?"

"What? No."

He was a terrible liar, but more than being offended that he was lying, I wondered why he would do so. Why did it matter if he and his wife's aunt were having lunch? Unless that handhold did mean more than what should be between the two of them.

I wished my mind hadn't gone there, but it had.

"Okay," I said. "Mikey, I need to talk to you about something. Can you please stay a few minutes longer?"

He made a big display of looking at the expensive watch on his wrist. "I can't. I've got a meeting."

"We'll walk you out," Brigid said.

We were going to follow him no matter what he said, no matter how fast he hurried away. The crowd wasn't so bothersome when it was slowing him down too.

"Are you the councilor who originally wanted the bookshop closed?" I asked when we made it outside.

"Excuse me?" he said as he took quick, long steps toward a car.

"Did you argue with Henry the day before he was killed? Was it something about the bookshop?" I asked.

"What? No!" he said again.

"Okay, what about something else?" I said. Brigid looked at me with wide-eyed approval. She wanted me to keep talking. I didn't even know that what I was about to say was something I'd been thinking about, maybe processing. It was a shot in the dark, but I felt compelled to try. "You had a building inspector deem it unsafe, didn't you?"

He shrugged far too casually. "I would never ask an inspector to falsify documents."

"It's not unsafe," I said as I grabbed his arm, far too forcefully.

He stopped walking, frowned at my hand on his arm, and then pulled it gently away. "Ms. Nichols, I'm not sure what you are trying to say, but you'd better be careful."

"Just tell me why you wanted the bookshop closed? Or why Henry did. What do you want?"

"I don't want any business closed, but things have to be done correctly. There are rules to follow."

"Did Henry want the bookshop closed? Was he trying to get something for Mary?" I couldn't give up.

"Henry was also about doing things correctly. Nothing done has been done inappropriately."

I squinted and tried to think. "I know you from somewhere, I'm sure I do. It was in the rain. Where was it?" I'd all but forgotten that when I'd met him, I'd found him familiar, but as I looked into those blue eyes now, I remembered. Where had we met? "Did you come into the bookshop during a storm? Wait it out inside?"

"I have no idea what you're talking about."

"We have the name of the inspector," Brigid cut in. "We've already got an appointment with him."

Concern, maybe even fear, flitted briefly over his features. "Not that it would matter, but I don't believe you. Inspectors' names aren't shared with the public."

"I'm a reporter," Brigid said as she crossed her arms in front of herself. She didn't mention her aunt's name, but she did say, "Dwayne Stover."

He blinked again in surprise, but quickly regained his composure. "I wish you the best of luck, but I assure you—again—that everything has been done appropriately and within the letter of the law. And everything is set in motion. The vote is scheduled and cannot be unscheduled. Now, if you'll excuse me."

Mikey opened his car door and got inside. He shut the door too gently, trying to prove he wasn't ruffled by our questions, I thought.

"He's such a liar," Brigid said.

"About what?" I said. "Which part?"

"I wish I knew, but I just know he's not being truthful about *something*."

"But everything *is* set in motion," I said.

"The vote will not pass, Delaney. Grace will spread the word and it won't pass. I'll help. I'll write an article for tomorrow."

"The day of the vote."

"It's better than the day after."

I watched as Brigid stared toward where Mikey's car had turned.

"What are you thinking about?" I said.

She ignored the question. "Why did you ask if he was having lunch with Mary?"

"I thought I saw red hair that looked like mine."

"I didn't see that. I wish I had. Come on, let's go find Dwayne Stover."

"Do you really know where he is?"

"I have no idea, but I have people who can find anyone." She pulled out her phone. "I suspect Mikey will ring him and let him know we're coming. We need to move quickly."

"Let's go."

Dwayne Stover's office was hidden behind another building. In fact, we had to venture down a close to find the door. Painted on its front was simply: Dwayne Stover, City Building Inspector.

There were no windows, and neither of us was surprised that the door was locked. We knocked a few times, but also weren't surprised we didn't get an answer.

"Do you think he's out inspecting?" I said. "On a Sunday?"

"Anything is possible, but I'm more inclined to believe that Mikey Wooster told him not to be here when we got here. Damn, I shouldn't have played that card, but I couldn't stop myself. Mikey Wooster is an arrogant twit."

"It's okay, we'll track Dwayne down at some point. You have people."

"Sure." Brigid didn't sound as confident as I would have liked.

We called the number we found for his business, but no answer there either. The atmosphere in the close was a stark contrast with our moods. A park bench and some planter box trees made it a comfortable retreat. We knocked on the two other doors—one belonging to an artist, one a potter with some beautiful work we spied through the window, and the last one an accountant. None of them knew Dwayne well, but they saw him every now and then. He was described as a typical older guy with no distinguishing features.

"What about Monika and Simone? There are others we could try to talk to," I said.

Brigid looked at her phone. "I've got to head back to the newspaper office and get that article written. I'll keep working on this. I'll call you if I come up with anything else. I'd like to talk to Dwayne before the vote. I'll keep trying to find him. If he tells me more about why the bookshop's buildings aren't safe, I'll ring you right away. Maybe I'll send him over to you. You all should know—it's your right to know."

"We should have a copy of the inspection."

"Aye," she said doubtfully.

"What?"

"It's all so cagey," she said. "None of this is making sense. At first I thought you might just be using me to try to hide problems the bookshop was having, but I'm beginning to think you all were set up. I just wish I knew why."

"I do too."

We said goodbye and I watched her walk down the Royal Mile. I had a dinner date scheduled with Tom, but I was going to be late. I texted him that I was taking a quick detour first.

I couldn't stop thinking about the red hair I'd seen at the restaurant. I couldn't let go of the sense that Mikey was lying. *But about which part?* Mary had behaved like we might be friends. I'd gone along with her to talk to Clayton. Now, I needed something from her.

Tom texted back that he'd see me soon, and that I should be careful.

Always, I replied.

THIRTY

"That's her hoose?" Elias asked as the cab moved slowly up the driveway.

"Yes, it's something else, isn't it?"

"Aye."

Immediately after I'd texted Tom, I called Elias. He was close to dropping off a paying customer but could come get me after that. I only waited ten minutes, and when he arrived, I asked if he was up to being the Watson to my Sherlock again. He was willing and drove us to Mary's castle, parking the taxi in the same spot Tom had.

"Ye're not going into that hoose by yerself. I'm going with ye. That place is terreffeen," he said.

"Terrifying?"

"Aye."

With him by my side and as he puffed up some, I knocked and was surprised again when Mary opened the door. I wasn't sure who I kept expecting, but it seemed so ordinary that the person who lived in a castle be the one to answer the door. Didn't they have knights in shining armor for those sorts of things?

The first thing I noticed was that her red hair was pulled up into a ponytail. The second thing I noticed was that her eyes were rimmed in red. She'd been crying, though that was to be expected. I got no sense that she was being medicated, that Eloise had been here again today.

"Delaney," she said. "Hello?"

"Mary, this is my friend, Elias. Do you have a minute?"

Mary smiled tightly and nodded at Elias. "It's been a rough day, Delaney . . . but, sure, come in."

"Thanks," I said as Elias sent me some raised eyebrows before we followed her inside.

"What's going on?" Mary asked after she closed the door.

"I'm sorry it's been a rough day," I said.

She nodded impatiently. I needed to ask her what I'd come to ask her.

"Mary, did you have lunch today at Makers Gourmet Mash Bar?"

It was such a brief flash of surprise that I might not have caught it if I hadn't been looking so closely at her eyes.

"I did. Were you there?" she said.

"I was. I tried to say hello, but you seemed in a hurry to leave."

Ignoring my questioning tone, she said, "I had lunch with my niece's husband. Mikey—oh, you know him."

"I do. You seemed upset," I said. It was a guess. I hadn't seen her face.

"No, not at all. I just had another appointment I had to get to. I *was* in a hurry." She looked at her fingernails, and I wondered if she was pondering if she could say she'd had her nails done. "Just another appointment." She stopped looking at her nails and sent me a strained frown.

I put my hand on her arm, suddenly feeling more sympathy

for her than I'd expected to feel. "Mary, do you think Mikey had anything to do with Henry's murder?"

She blinked hard and fast, but didn't protest, didn't make a move to kick us out of there. "I don't think so."

"But ye dinnae ken for sure?" Elias said.

She shook her head and then looked me in the eye. "He said he didn't. I asked. I came out and asked him."

"Why? Why did you ask him?" I said.

"I'm just trying to figure it all out," she said. "Delaney, do you remember the night of the dinner?"

"Of course."

"I saw something between Henry and Mikey. There was some animosity."

"I think I saw that too."

I sensed Elias unpuffing a little with Mary's vulnerability. He was such a softy.

She looked at me. "I told you that Henry and I discussed the bookshop later that night, but I'm sure I sensed there was a problem between Mikey and Henry. Dina went home first, by herself. Mikey stayed and talked to Henry a while. I'm trying to put things together, and I wondered if maybe Henry told Mikey he was going to try to either cancel or postpone the vote about the bookshop and if that upset Mikey."

"Enough to kill?" I said.

"Enough to kill, aye, or enough to do something to get Henry killed. I don't know, but I just wanted some answers."

"What did Mikey say?"

"That he and Henry didn't discuss anything about the bookshop, that they spoke about all manner of council business that night except the bookshop."

"You don't believe him?"

"I don't know what to believe. Henry was so upset about what he'd done to get the bookshop shut down that I can't imagine him talking about anything else that night, and that contention I thought I sensed . . ."

"Did Mikey tell you any specifics about their conversation?"

"Mikey told me he would never do anything to hurt Henry. He couldn't understand why I would even ask him such things. That's all he would really say. I pressed him about the bookshop, the Burgess Tickets, anything I could think of, but he avoided answering specifically. He just kept saying he would never hurt Henry. Delaney, I'd insisted on meeting in a public place because it was that much of a concern, but maybe I'm not thinking clearly. He *sounded* sincere."

"But you still don't believe him, do you?" I said.

She shook her head slowly. "I wish I did."

"Did they have any problems in the past?" I said.

"No, and Delaney, I knew my husband. He could barely brush his teeth that night for thinking about the bookshop. I'm sure that if they had a disagreement, it must have been about the bookshop."

"Closing it or keeping it open?" I asked.

"I can't be sure, but Henry was bent on making sure he fixed what he'd set in motion, that it would stay open."

"Why would Mikey want to close the bookshop?" I said, but I had my own answer. The Mary, Queen of Scots' coins, even if parts of that idea weren't clear. I didn't say that aloud.

"I can't think of any reason at all," Mary said. "I didn't even ask him that. There didn't seem to be any point."

"Did you tell the police about your suspicions, lass?" Elias said.

Tears came to her eyes. "No, they'd probably think I'm crazier than they already do. Besides, he's my niece's husband."

"Are ye worriet about yer or yer niece's safety? If so, aye, ring the police immediately," Elias said.

"I rang the Lord Provost, left him a message that I needed to talk to him about what Henry had been working on. I will tell him he can't let a vote happen."

"I think the Lord Provost will be hearing that from a few people, but thank you."

Mary nodded and looked down, keeping her eyes away from my almost-matching ones.

"Do you want to come with us? Do you feel unsafe?" I asked. "You can stay with me if you'd like."

"That's lovely, Delaney, but no, I'm fine here. I can still talk to Henry here. Ta, though."

It was difficult to leave her in such a state, but she made it clear she wanted to be alone. I hadn't asked about anything lascivious between her and Mikey, but my mind had changed from that being a possibility. I hoped I wasn't letting my sympathy change my instincts or suspicions.

Mary walked us to the door. I heard locks being set, the noise sounding so much more modern than a castle's locks should sound.

As we got into the cab, Elias looked at me and said, "I hope it wasnae her. I hope she didnae kill Henry."

"Me too, but I didn't get a sense of that. Did you?"

"I dinnae ken what I got a sense of, but I dinnae trust her, or her niece's husband. Probably not her niece either if I think aboot it, and I've never even met her."

"I know. What a mess, huh?"

"Aye. Home?"

"Actually, back to the bookshop, if you don't mind."

"Not a t'all."

THIRTY-ONE

"She's sad, mourning," Tom said as he reached over to my paper boat for one of the chips I hadn't eaten. "She should probably let the police know about Mikey though, even if it leads to nothing."

We were at our favorite takeaway; a small shop in Grassmarket close to both our places of work.

"I agree," I said. "I know you didn't notice the same things I thought I saw that night, but what were your thoughts about Mikey and Dina?"

"Mikey was quiet, Dina was lovely. That's about all I got."

"Mikey didn't seem familiar to you?"

"Not even a little bit."

"I recognize him from somewhere, and the fuzzy memory has a yellow raincoat attached to it."

"It rains a lot here."

"Why can't I place him?"

"The councilors are in the news sometimes, maybe you saw his picture."

"Maybe."

We were sitting on stools at the small counter along the front window. It was rare that we managed to get a spot inside—simply because there were only three seats in the place. Sometimes we moved back outside to enjoy our fish and chips, sometimes we would walk around Grassmarket. Sometimes we'd take the food back to the pub. But atop a stool this evening, I enjoyed the break from the rest of the world. However, I could still see the bookshop at the end of the market, still open though Rosie and Hector would close in a few minutes. I tried to imagine something else in that spot. A convenience store, a souvenir shop, maybe even another takeaway. Tears came to my eyes, but I blinked them away. I didn't have time to cry. I truly believed things were going to be okay, but until the vote was either canceled or over, I didn't want to let down my guard.

"Lass," Tom said as he wiped his fingers on the paper napkin. "It's going tae be all right."

"I really do think so too, but I'm not ready to relax."

Tom's eyebrows came together. "What has Inspector Winters said?"

"He's on holiday. I called but didn't leave a message. I couldn't bring myself to bother him."

Tom sat up a little straighter. "I think you'd better bother him. Put in a call. Either he'll take it or he won't. I think he can help sew up the last pieces of this puzzle of the vote. Just in case you need someone else on your side."

I nodded and felt no need to argue. It suddenly seemed just fine to interrupt his vacation. "Makes sense."

I pulled out my phone.

Rosie and Hector didn't close on time because a storm hit. It was fierce and Rosie didn't want to get drenched on her way to the bus. Her staying open worked out just fine though. Edwin, Hamlet, Tom, and I joined them and sat around the table in the back as we told Inspector Winters everything.

He *had* been on holiday, but he'd been home for a full two hours when I called. He'd said he was surprised he hadn't heard from me earlier and that he and his family had very much enjoyed Ireland. His wife (I'd yet to meet her) had inquired a couple of times if I'd rung him.

As I'd tried to explain all the circumstances over the phone, he said, "Lass, I'll meet you at the bookshop. This is too much to digest on the phone and I've a wee'un who wants my attention. I'll be there shortly."

I'd never met his family, but I thought he probably made a great father. He did as he said and met us all at the bookshop. He hadn't shaved for a week and the beard slimmed his round face, reminding me of an artist's beard, though somewhat shorter. I knew it would be gone when he had to resume being a police inspector. But between the beard and his casual clothing, Rosie told him she might not have recognized him and he might want to consider some undercover work at some point.

I thought it curious that he didn't acknowledge the comment. Rosie and I shared a look. Maybe he'd already done undercover work.

"Have you received notices of the shop closing? There's due process," Inspector Winters asked Edwin. "Even beyond an inspection report, there are other procedures too."

"Not one word," Edwin said. "It makes no sense."

Inspector Winters looked at his notebook on the table in

front of him and then up at me. "You say the building inspector's name is Dwayne Stover?"

"Yes."

Back to Edwin. "Did you try to talk to the Lord Provost?"

"I did, left messages, but he's not returned my calls."

Back to me. "And you've spoken with his media relations person. Grace Graham?"

"Yes."

"I know her. She's good at what she does, but I'm not sure what power she holds," Inspector Winters said.

"She works directly with the Lord Provost?" I asked.

"Aye, but not in a policy advisor capacity, not really. She's his communications director. I'll figure it out."

"Do you know if the police have found anything pointing to Henry Stewart's killer?" I asked.

"I'll have to check, lass. Until you called, I had only heard a little about Henry. I didn't know the bookshop was somehow a part of it." He sent me a surprisingly friendly smile. "It looks like I'm going to have to stop taking vacations."

"I'm sorry to bother you," I said.

"Not at all. If the vote had taken place while I was gone, I would have been disappointed. I'm glad you rang."

You could feel the sense of relief fill the room. Yes, the vote was only one day away, but Inspector Winters was on the job. Everything was going to be fine.

The bell above the door jingled, but before anyone could move quickly enough to greet whoever was coming in, he hurried around to us, his bright yellow raincoat dripping all over the floor.

"Jack!" Edwin said as he stood. "Thank you for taking my late call, I'd like you to meet—"

"No time for that, Edwin, no time," Jack McGinnis said. "I'm afraid we've got a problem, a big one."

And just like that the sense of relief was washed clean away.

THIRTY-TWO

Jack McGinnis had been working hard. He'd pushed his way into every government official's home that he could find. He'd talked to councilors. He'd even managed to talk to the Minister for Local Government, Housing and Planning—a position I hadn't even been made aware of yet.

"There's no stopping the vote," Jack said. "There's no delaying it, but it's probably going to be okay."

"How can that be?" I said.

"Rules, regulations, procedures," Jack said. "It can't be taken off the docket."

"But there was no inspection!" I said.

That's when Jack reached into his back pocket. He'd rolled up some stapled pages so casually, as if they didn't mean the end of the world as we all knew it.

He placed the papers on the table, smoothing them even as the corners still battled back. "That's actually the bad news, and why it's only *probably* going to be okay."

Yes, the inspection was real, official, there was no doubt about it. We read it together and then we all took our turns inspecting it. And then, one by one, we marched up the stairs on this side of the shop, crouched at the top to look at the space where the wall had once been cut, a long time ago, to make way for the connection to the neighboring building. There was absolutely no sense that the connection was going to fail. Nothing was sinking, nothing crumbling. I even jumped up and down on it. It didn't move.

However, there was a crack in the plaster. One, tiny, five-inch-long crack—that, by the way, seemed to get longer every time I looked at it.

The failure of the building was based upon this crack. There was a picture and everything! Someone had come in and done an inspection, even taken this picture, and no one had noticed.

Or maybe remembered.

"Edwin, I'm sure this didnae happen," Rosie said several times, becoming less emphatic and more distraught each time she said it.

There came a point when we transitioned from being worried about the building to worrying about Rosie, mostly when Hector, atop her lap, barked at us to get our priorities straight.

"Rosie, it's going to be fine," Edwin said. "This isn't your fault, love."

She held her fist to her chin and nodded sadly. I'd never known her to have any sort of memory problems. In fact, she was the one who seemed to remember everything.

We'd all come back to the table and I grabbed the report. I'd memorized the part that Jack had highlighted, the part that had been stamped with a big red "fail" over it. There were other pages too, all with small print; legal stuff that reinforced the validity of this inspection.

Until the very last page, at the bottom. Because there was so much black print on the page, I hadn't noticed the small, handwritten note, also in black.

"Hey," I said aloud. "What's this?"

Everyone looked at me.

"What?" Jack asked.

"There's a handwritten note. The writing is so small, it almost just looks like a continuation of the typed print on the page."

Either not noticing or not caring that it was rude, Jack grabbed the inspection from my hands. I had to restrain myself from grabbing it back.

"This is a copy. They wouldn't give me the original, of course. Damn, I need a magnifying glass," Jack said.

Hamlet reached to a drawer against the wall. He had a few magnifying glasses.

"Ta," Jack said as he grabbed a glass from Hamlet.

Hamlet and I shared a shrug. At least Jack had said thanks to him.

"Huh."

"For heavens' sake, Jack, what?" Edwin said.

"It says, and I quote: 'The young woman tending the shop wouldn't let me go to the other side. She looks so much like Mary. I'll have to come back.'"

We all exclaimed something along the lines of "What?"

I grabbed the report and glass from Jack.

"I was here when the inspector came by?" I said as I repeatedly read the small print. "I . . . I don't remember it at all. No! I would remember it. I wouldn't have allowed it."

"No, I don't think you would have," Edwin said.

"No," Hamlet said.

"I think there's something more important here," Tom

added. "Whoever came into the bookshop and allegedly conducted the inspection knew Mary Stewart, well enough to just say 'Mary.' "

"And they thought it was important to communicate the fact that Delaney looked like her," Hamlet added.

"Unbelievable," I said.

"Well," Edwin said as he looked at Jack. "I don't understand everything going on here, but I think this was just a note to someone, and the inspector was an imposter, just someone who wanted to see the other side of this bookshop." He looked at the inspection. "And somehow had access to official paperwork."

"The warehouse is not a secret anymore, Edwin. If someone asks about it, we tell them. But not many people ask. I remember each and every one . . ."

Jack had taken off the raincoat and placed it over the back of a chair. He lifted it from the chair, noticing it was still wet, and moved it over to a small table we weren't using. He sat down in the chair and looked at me intently.

"What, Delaney?" Rosie prompted.

No bookish voices had been talking, but pictures of memories had suddenly started flooding my mind.

Hector, again sensing who needed him the most, hopped onto my lap.

"Oh, no," I said a moment later. The memories weren't fuzzy this time. "About three months ago, there was a man dressed in a bright yellow raincoat, just like the one Jack wore tonight. It was just me and Hector that day, and it wasn't raining. At first the man kept his gaze averted when I tried to talk to him. I just let him look around, tried not to bother him—and he definitely seemed bothered. He seemed to need to move closer to the shelves to read the books' spines, he hummed to himself. I thought about offering him one of the magnifying glasses. I thought briefly about seeing if Hamlet was on his way in, but then I decided that the man wasn't dangerous. Just odd. He climbed the stairs to look at the books up there. I let him be, but then he got quiet. I came around and didn't see him. I wondered if he'd left and I didn't notice. I just asked if he was okay. He popped upright, as if he'd been sitting in the corner—or now I think taking pictures probably—and he said he was fine. He asked if there were books on the other side of the door up there. I told him there weren't. He asked what was there. I said there were just offices." I looked at Edwin. "He didn't ask specifically about the warehouse or I would have told him. I don't just offer it up, I wouldn't have given him a tour, but I would have told him."

"Makes sense," Edwin said. "What happened next?"

"He left."

"What was the inspector's name?" Hamlet asked Jack.

"No, no it doesn't matter. Or maybe it matters, but . . ." I said. "The man who was here was Mikey Wooster. I have no doubt. He had dirt smudged on his face, but those eyes. I saw them and I remembered thinking how lovely they were. I remember him so clearly now. I don't understand the act he was putting on, but there must be a reason he took the picture and forged the inspection. Was it just because I wouldn't tell him what was on the other side?"

"No," Tom said. "If he'd come in as Mikey Wooster, you would have given him more information, more details, as you would to any councilor who asked you questions. He wanted the bookshop, or to harm it in some way. I have no doubt."

"The coins?" I said. "Did he want to try to find the Mary, Queen of Scots' coins Edwin wouldn't sell to Dina ten years ago?"

"Oh, lass," Edwin said. "I found them. They were at my house, but I didn't think they had anything at all to do with what we're going through. No idea at all. I didn't even think to let you know I found them. I'm sorry."

"Why would ye?" Rosie said.

"You thought he looked familiar from the moment you met him," Tom said.

"Hang on," Inspector Winters said. "We need to get Inspector Buchanan here too."

We watched as he moved to the front of the bookshop to make a call.

"If Mikey was posing as an inspector, this will of course change everything," Jack said. "But an investigation will have to happen. The vote can't be stopped, but we will ultimately win, no matter the tally."

"I've something I need to attend to," Edwin said, surprising us all.

"What?" Rosie asked.

"What are you up to, Edwin?" Jack asked. "You can't leave until Buchanan gets here."

"I've an idea," he said. "I'll be in my office on the other side."

"Edwin?" Rosie said. "What's going on?"

Edwin stepped to Rosie. He took her hand and held it. "It's going to be fine, love, but I've an idea. I think I know how to seal the deal, if that's the proper expression."

"All right. Let me know." Tears came to Rosie's eyes.

Hector jumped off my lap and back to Rosie.

"It's going to be fine," Edwin said as he hurried over to the dark side.

The rest of us looked at each other for a long moment. Hector couldn't decide whose lap needed him the most.

THIRTY-THREE

It was a very late night. I hadn't slept much the last few days, but I was so revved with adrenaline, I didn't notice. Well, not much.

Inspector Buchanan showed up and we rehashed everything. Unfortunately, there was no proof that the inspector had been Mikey Wooster. There were no pictures of the man in the raincoat who had come in, just my word to go on. At least Inspector Buchanan had found Mr. Stover earlier that day. He was, indeed, an older man with no distinguishing features. From his front porch as he peered out his front door, she'd asked him if he had inspected The Cracked Spine. She shared with us how the conversation had gone:

"Is my name on the paperwork? Then, aye, I did the deed. You can't expect me to remember every detail of every building I inspect, including the names of the businesses inside."

"Any chance you could check your records?" Inspector Buchanan had asked him. "Did you keep a copy of the paperwork?"

"No, there is no chance I will check my paperwork. Not

today. If my name's on it, then it was me. I'm not going into my office on a weekend. Not without a warrant of some sort. Next time I'm there, I'll look."

"Any chance your name could be forged?"

"Who in the name of the queen herself would do that?"

Who indeed?

Mikey Wooster, I thought.

Now that there might be more to go on, Inspector Buchanan could be more forceful in requesting a copy of Dwayne Stover's records, but that wasn't a huge priority.

Once all the information was shared, the police inspectors quit caring about the bookshop. They wanted to catch a killer, and they were trying to figure out if there was any evidence that Mikey had killed Henry. Did the murder have something to do with the coins? Were the coins as valuable as Edwin had thought? He assured the police they were. He told them he would gather them if they wanted. He wanted me to see them too. I wasn't prepared to figure out their value, but a look wouldn't hurt. However, the police weren't ready to see the coins, wanted them to stay safe for the time being.

When Edwin had rejoined us, he'd had a mischievous sparkle to his eyes, but he wouldn't tell us what he'd been up to. He assured the police his activities in no way interfered with the police's murder investigation.

At around two in the morning, I spied a van pulling up to a newspaper machine halfway up Grassmarket. I knew it was Brigid's paper being delivered; that was the machine where I'd picked up other copies of her articles, though never so soon after they'd been delivered.

The rain had stopped, and I excused myself to go get a paper. Tom came with me.

"Brigid said she was going to write an article. She didn't have any of the new information we've discovered tonight. I need to see what she wrote," I said.

"Aye?"

I laughed once. It was the middle of the night and the air smelled like rain. For the first time ever, I didn't see any other people in Grassmarket. Of all the magic I'd felt over the last year, this moment with Tom, the relief I felt over the answers we seemed to have, the concern over the continuing questions, might have been one of the most magical. I was either under Edinburgh's or Tom's spell. Maybe both. Even the doubt I heard in his tone couldn't ruin the sensations I felt, the electric giddiness.

"I think it will be a good article," I said.

"I hope so."

It was.

It was also on the front page, headlined with: "The Fate of a Beloved Bookshop Hangs in the Balance. Vote Today."

Brigid turned the facts as she knew them into a favorable article for the bookshop. She used the space to further condemn the council and some of their secretive ways. But I only skimmed that part, glad that, bottom line, she made it clear that it seemed the bookshop had been wrongly put on a potential chopping block, and the council should consider taking a step back until the facts were given another look.

The other interesting part was about Henry Stewart and his murder. A killer was still on the loose, but it seemed obvious to "this reporter" that Mr. Stewart was killed because of something nefarious he'd been involved in via his councilor capacity. It only made sense, after all. Get to work, police.

"Oh dear," Edwin said when we all finished the article.

"What?" I said. "It's great."

"It is, but I might have put something in motion that will prove to be an overkill, in the grandest of ways."

"To save the bookshop? I'm all about overkill until the vote is over, killed," I said with a weary smile.

"Aye," he said doubtfully.

Inspectors Buchanan and Winters discussed the best way to approach Mikey Wooster. Buchanan wanted to knock on his door right then and ask him a few questions. Winters suggested that she wait until the vote, not because Mikey's vote was important, but because all the councilors would be together for the vote. Maybe there was a way to gather some strong evidence against Mikey. Or not, if he was innocent.

No one thought he was innocent though. But it would take evidence for an arrest.

With only a few hours of night left, we all went home, with the plan to meet again at the vote. None of us were going to miss it.

I looked at myself in the mirror and sighed. Oh, boy, did I look tired, but today just had to go well.

"You look perfect," Tom said. "Beautiful, aye, but also fierce, like you won't put up with any crap anyone wants to try to give you."

I'd pulled my hair back, though there were some frizzy flyaways. I wore a white shirt and a black skirt and black pumps. It wasn't a fancy outfit, but it was fancier than I usually sported. In fact, other than our wedding day, I couldn't remember the last time I'd given much thought to my clothes. I hadn't worn heels even that day.

"Thank you, sir, and you look . . . well, Tom, if you don't know what I think about how you look then I need to work on my communication skills. Also, keep an eye out for me falling down. I'm not sure I've retained any muscle memory regarding how to wear these shoes."

He laughed and pulled me in for a hug. It would have been wonderful to stay that way for the rest of the day, but we had a vote to attend.

The City Chambers building of Edinburgh looked just like a building one would expect in this beautiful old city. A cobblestoned courtyard decorated with flowerpots and the statue of a man and a horse greeted us as we walked under a stone arch. The U-shaped building extended up three floors. The old brown stones of the building were blackened around the edges. The only splashes of color came from flags and some circular crests attached to the turrets right outside the courtyard. I scanned the crests, looking for the one I'd recently become acquainted with: Elizabeth I's, but it wasn't there. Of course, it wasn't. This was Scotland, not England. I shook my head at myself and wished I'd looked up Mary, Queen of Scots' crest.

I'd walked past the chambers many times, but I'd never seen such a crowd as was gathering today. And, I'd never seen so many kilts.

"Is this normal?" I asked Tom about the crowd.

"I don't know. Maybe Brigid's article got some attention."

"Lass," a voice said behind me.

"Rosie! We would have come to get you," I said as I saw her walking toward us. When we'd left her last night, she wasn't going to attend, but sleep in.

"Look what I found!" She waved some papers.

"The construction approvals?" I said.

"Aye." She smiled. "Guess where they were?"

"I have no idea."

"I'd slipped them inside a book. The first book that Edwin gave me, poems by Robert Burns. Last night, just as I was aboot tae fall asleep, I remembered putting them in the book. Edwin had told me how important they were, how he was so excited about receiving approval. I slipped them in the book I cherished, the first book he gave me. I should have remembered sooner."

"That's perfect," I said as I pulled her into a hug.

"I dinnae even think we'll need them, but I'm ready if we do."

"Aye," Tom said with a smile.

"Hamlet will be here too. I called him an hour ago. I saw Inspector Winters already. He's over by the front of the courtyard."

"That's good news," I said. "What about Edwin?"

"I dinnae ken, lass. He's not answering his mobile. But he'll be here."

"He's not answering?"

"No, I've been trying tae ring him all morning."

"He'll be here," Tom said. "Come on, let's go find some seats."

"Rosie!"

We turned to see Jack hurrying toward us. "Good morning, everyone." Once he made it to us, he wiped his forehead with a handkerchief and continued, "Has anyone talked to Edwin? I've been trying to reach him since last night."

A thread of concern tightened my stomach. Had something happened to him? What had he been up to the night before that might lead to overkill in the grandest of ways? Why wasn't he answering his phone?

"Should I run by his house?" I asked.

"No, no. He's up tae something is all. He'll be here," Rosie said unsurely.

I blinked at her.

"Edwin is always up tae something. Come on," she said.

We walked toward the building, toward a door decorated with a sign above that said: City Chambers.

"Here we go," I muttered as we went inside.

There were sixty-three councilors, the council having added six to the count during the 2017 election. Each councilor represented a different part of the city designated as a ward. Council members worked together but they were also broken out into committees to work on specific issues.

The Council Chamber hall oozed history. Historical king and queen scenes were painted on the wood paneled walls. Diffused light set a respectful tone as it came through the domed stained-glass ceiling. The roomed buzzed and hummed with the growing crowd. As we found some seats along the perimeter, I realized that though many of the people in the room were councilors, many weren't. And many observers held Brigid's newspaper. She had hit a nerve.

Just as I sat down in a cushioned chair, I noticed Mary. She walked in, her arm looped through Lyle Mercado's. I locked gazes with them both. Mary sent me a weak smile and wave as Lyle frowned and nodded. Oh dear, he wasn't playing the part of the third husband, was he? I shook my head. No, enough of that. They were friends, and maybe Mary just wanted someone there with her.

Hamlet slid into an empty seat behind me and touched my shoulder. "Where's Edwin?"

"Hello! No one knows," I said quietly.

"Okay."

"All right," Jack said. "Technically we must get permission to speak a week or so before the meeting, but I managed to get ahold of someone last night who said we could have the floor for a few minutes. But I really, really hope Edwin joins us. It will all mean so much more coming from him. And, from what I'm seeing, the public is going to want to have their say too. Your friend's article might have done some good."

Tom and I shared a knowing smile. Brigid wasn't necessarily a friend, but maybe she would be.

"We *all* hope Edwin shows up," I said.

"Did you see the bust?" Hamlet asked me.

"What?" I turned to look at him.

He pointed. I would have known her even if there hadn't been a small metal tag on the base. Mary, Queen of Scots.

"Wow," Hamlet said. "You do look like her."

I did. Or at least I sort of looked like the bust. It was made of white porcelain, so the hair wasn't red, but there was a similarity to our chins and our cheekbones as well as the set of our eyes. The red hair might have sealed the deal. A morbid thought regarding Mary's beheading crossed my mind.

I still hadn't taken the time to do any extra research, but I knew that one of the biggest surprises the queen had sprung on the people who witnessed her execution was the fact that she wore a wig. Yes, she'd had red hair, but at some point, probably during the time of her last castle imprisonment, it thinned, fell out probably. She'd only been forty-four when she'd been beheaded, but her final imprisonment had been more seriously imposed than the others. She'd been confined inside. A woman who'd loved to ride horses, she'd been trim and healthy most of her life, able to exercise even during other imprisonments. But being stuck inside with no exercise, no fresh air, had taken its toll. She'd gained weight, her legs becoming so puffy that she struggled to walk to her own execution.

I had no thought that I'd lived a past life, the queen's included, but my heart suddenly went out to her. For whatever reason, I suddenly sensed that on some strange level, I finally understood her. She'd only wanted what she deemed best. She was a kind ruler, at least from everything I knew. She'd had her beliefs and she'd been born into circumstances that she wasn't able to become victorious over. She'd become a victim of her circumstances.

"I do look like her. Sort of," I said.

But I wasn't her. Never had been, I was sure.

As I turned to face front again, my eyes landed on Dina Wooster. She was walking purposefully toward someone. I craned my neck to watch as she handed a piece of paper to someone. Mikey. If Inspector Buchanan had visited Mikey in the middle of the night, no arrest had occurred. He looked at the note his wife had given him and then directly at me. Dina seemed irritated that he'd been so obvious, but after she rolled her eyes at him, she turned and made her way back to another chair on the perimeter. She wasn't sitting close to Mary and Lyle. She didn't smile at me. In fact, there was nothing friendly in her glance.

Hadn't she said she was bothered by what the council had done regarding the bookshop? Hadn't she said she was going to talk to Mikey? I saw no reason for her to be bothered to see me.

Maybe I hadn't read her expression correctly. Or, maybe she'd known what her husband was up to all along.

Something about that idea niggled at me. What had Dina known? Had she even tried to do anything about it?

"The gang's all here," Hamlet said quietly, pulling me out of my thoughts about Dina.

"Everyone but Edwin," Tom said just as quietly.

"And Inspector Buchanan, but we just might not be able to see her," I said.

"Aye," Tom agreed.

Someone pounded a gavel somewhere but just as I tried to figure out where it was coming from, sirens interrupted the proceedings. The buzz of noise in the room ramped up as we all noticed the siren noises coming closer.

"What's happening?" Rosie asked.

"I don't know."

More noises came from outside the chambers. We were all looking toward the door we'd come through as a slew of men paraded in. Dressed in black suits, they moved purposefully and then seemed to make some sort of planned formation.

"MI6?" Tom said.

"Really?" I said. I craned my neck even more.

"Ladies and gentlemen, excuse me," a voice said through the sound system. "Please, may I have your attention."

The room fell into a hushed silence and I saw the podium where the voice had come from. Grace Graham stood at the microphone. Brigid was behind her a bit. Brigid's eyes caught mine and she smiled and nodded. Then she winked.

What the hell did that mean?

"Thank you," Grace said. "Thank you. Well, it seems we have a very special guest today. It's a surprise and a wee bit unreal, but I assure you, it's very real. We are breaking protocol, but I think you'll all understand why. Without further ado, ladies and gentlemen, please may I present Her Royal Highness, Her Majesty, the Queen of England."

Gasps and murmurs filled the chamber as we looked toward the door again. A moment later, along with none other than Edwin MacAlister following behind her, the Queen of England walked into the chamber. Everyone stood then and bows and curtsies moved like a wave as the Queen made her way to the podium.

"You have got to be kidding me," I said as I laughed. I didn't realize I was crying too until Tom wiped a tear from my cheek.

"It's going to be okay," he said.

"That's the freaking Queen of England," I said, almost too loudly.

"Aye," Tom said with a crooked smile.

She was adorable, just like she was on TV. She wore a yellow suit and carried a piece of paper and an off-white purse. I wondered for a moment if, perhaps, she was an actress playing the part. But she wasn't; she was the real Queen.

With Edwin still in tow, she made her way to the podium and tapped on the microphone.

"Hello," she said with a smile. "Thank you for giving me a few moments. I'll be brief. The Cracked Spine is one of Scotland's, of Britain's beloved bookshops, and Britains don't take any bookshop lightly. We cherish them, one and all. But this one might be a little more special than some. This is a place I have visited myself, a place where I met Rosie, a lovely woman who knew exactly what book would be fit for a queen."

I smiled at Rosie as she wiped a tear away as well. She'd never told me she helped the Queen shop for a book.

"If there are any sort of safety concerns regarding the buildings the bookshop is housed in, Mr. Edwin MacAlister will take care of the problems." She waved the piece of paper she'd brought with her. "In case it is necessary, I have The Cracked

Spine's Burgess Ticket here with me. It seems Mr. MacAlister still holds every right afforded him by this ticket, which includes operating the business of selling books. Surely, the council sees that today is not a good day to vote to close the shop. Perhaps more inspections need to take place before such drastic measures are taken. Please consider the circumstances. Thank you all for your time."

By the end of the lovely speech, even Jack McGinnis had to sniff and wipe away a stray tear.

"That did not just happen," I said.

"Aye, it did," Tom said. "Only Edwin."

"Where did he find the Burgess Ticket?" Rosie asked me.

"Somewhere on the dark side last night, I suppose," I said.

Where would it have been?

Without further ado, the MI6 men led the Queen out of the building. Once she was gone and after a stunned silence filled the air for a few minutes, cheers broke out and soon cries of "Vote! Vote! Vote!" rang through the hall.

THIRTY-FOUR

"Ladies and gentlemen," another voice came from the podium. I didn't know the woman speaking and pounding the gavel. "I'm going to call for the vote. Item number 425, regarding The Cracked Spine. Shall the failed building inspection be considered appropriate to invalidate the business license? Those in favor, say aye."

Not one "aye." Not even from Mikey Wooster. I craned my neck again to try to watch him, but I couldn't see him. Nevertheless, not one "aye" broke the silence.

"Those against, nay," the woman on the podium said.

"Nay!" rang through the chamber.

And then more cheers.

"The nays have it!"

"It's over," Rosie said. "It's over."

I felt the same relief as I hugged her, but it wasn't over, not for Mary. A killer still needed to be found.

"Come on, let's go find Edwin," I said when we disengaged.

Edwin wasn't far away, just outside the chambers, in the courtyard and waiting for the rest of us.

"Overkill?" he said to me as we approached him.

"Maybe a little." I laughed. "But it was the best overkill ever. Where was the Burgess Ticket?"

"In the box with the coins," Edwin said. "I have no recollection of keeping them together, but I must have. When I went to gather the coins this morning, I looked through the box. And, there it was. Finding it this morning seemed fortuitous. The Queen was lovely to do the favor she did. The ticket was the icing on the cake, I suppose."

Tom, Rosie, Hamlet, and Jack and I gathered around him.

"How do you know her?" I said.

"She's stopped by the bookshop a few times, but it's not me she knows. It's Rosie." Edwin pulled Rosie close as he put his arm around her. "Rosie has helped her find some of the best books. Rosie's skills and ways with people brought the Queen. It wasn't me, truly it wasn't."

"Och, on with ye then." Rosie waved away the compliment.

"Rosie found the construction papers too," I said.

"Aye?" Edwin said. "Everything's been found then! That's lovely."

But everything hadn't been found, I thought as I saw Mary and Lyle walking toward us. No, there was still something missing.

"Hello," Mary said to us all. "I'm shocked by the Queen's visit, but I'm thrilled the bookshop was saved. I apologize for whatever Henry did, and whoever he recruited to help him do it. Please accept our apologies." She looked toward Lyle who nodded.

"Aye. Me too," Lyle said.

"Lyle, did you present the idea of closing down the bookshop to the council?" I asked.

"Aye, I'm afraid I was requested to do so and I did. I'm so sorry."

"Henry requested you do it?" I said.

Lyle blinked at me. "No, Mikey Wooster asked me."

"What?" Mary said.

"Aye. You thought it was Henry?" he said. "No, Henry led the way later because he was the senior member of the council, but all of this was set in motion by Mikey. Henry was helping him."

"Helping him do what?" Mary said.

"He wanted the bookshop," I said as I looked at Lyle.

"I don't know. I was never told why, I was just asked to be a part of setting things in motion," Lyle said.

"Did Dina come talk to you right after Edwin and I did, in your office?" I asked.

"Oh, aye, I was told she stopped by, but I'd left by then. I was upset by the conversation with you and Edwin. Later, I tried to ring her, but she didn't return my call. My staff told me she demanded to see for herself that my office was empty, so they showed her."

"Why would they do that? Why did you set things in motion?" Mary said.

"Because Mikey is married to Dina, your niece, Mary. I'd do anything for your family, you know that. My staff knows that."

I pulled out my phone and called Inspector Winters.

"Delaney? I'm in the chambers. Where are you?" Inspector Winter said.

"In the courtyard. Where's Inspector Buchanan?"

"Talking to Mikey Wooster, I think."

"Hang on a second," I said as I pulled the phone away and held it so he could hear.

I looked around the courtyard. The crowd was dispersing. If the council was voting on anything else, we hadn't stayed to see it. Neither had the wonderful people who it seemed had come out to support the bookshop.

"Mary, you were in trouble for looking inside drawers and such at the museum. That's why they asked you to leave, right?" I said.

"Well, I suppose," she said, embarrassed.

"I'm sorry. I don't mean to make you uncomfortable, but I need to know something, and this is more important than anything else because it's about Henry's murder. I need you to be one hundred percent honest with me."

"Okay."

"The letter, Queen Elizabeth I's letter that talked about a truce with Mary, Queen of Scots."

"Aye," she said. Her cheeks reddened. I knew the look. My cheeks reddened the same way.

"You came into the bookshop to tell us you just remembered the trip to Paris, the alleged letter, but, and tell me the truth, you didn't just remember it that day, did you? You and Henry talked about it after the dinner party, didn't you? You told other people about that time in Paris too. Of course you did. A letter like that would be too important to Mary, Queen of Scots, and extremely valuable. Dina and Mikey knew."

"Delaney," she said.

"Didn't they!"

She blinked at me. "She's my niece."

"She might have killed your husband."

"No, I can't believe that." Tears started to fall down Mary's cheeks. "Mikey said she didn't, that he must have been killed for something else. No!"

"You were looking in drawers because Dina asked you to. You were searching desks and drawers for some sign of that letter. Dina had desks in her shop—she'd bought them because she thought it was a possibility that the letter was inside them? You were all searching, weren't you?"

After a long pause, Mary nodded once.

"When did you think the letter might be in The Cracked Spine?" I asked.

"A few months ago." Mary deflated. "The first time we met the docent in Paris about five years ago, he told us about the alleged letter being stolen by the queen's bastard brother, Moray, and then hidden inside a desk in a castle. He didn't know which castle. We found him again a few months ago, and he said he had it on good authority that Edwin MacAlister at The Cracked Spine had the letter."

"And you don't think Mikey or Dina killed Henry?" Tom said to her.

"Henry was going to come forward with everything, wasn't he?" Jack asked.

"I don't. I . . . I didn't want the bookshop closed. Henry didn't either. I didn't know . . . I tried to help."

I put the phone back up to my ear. "Did you get all that?"

"I did," Inspector Winters said. "I'll find Buchanan."

"I have an idea," I said.

"I'm listening," Inspector Winters said.

I stepped away from the group and told him my idea.

THIRTY-FIVE

Edwin relocked the bookshop's front door after we'd all entered.

"Follow me, everyone," I said.

Edwin, Rosie, Hamlet, Tom, Mary, Lyle, Inspectors Buchanan and Winters, and Mikey and Dina Wooster were all there. Jack had headed back to Glasgow. It was going to be very crowded, but we'd make it work.

The inspectors had been put on alert. Mikey, Dina, Mary, and Lyle were being watched closely. In fact, Inspector Winters hadn't liked my idea, but I thought it was probably the only way to find the killer. My plan was to push the suspects to the brink of their obsession, and hope the killer would crack.

It might not have been the best, but it was all I had.

I led the way over to the dark side. I was the pied piper of a sort. We snaked over the stairs and then down the dark hallway on the other side. I put the key into the door and turned three times to the left.

"What in the world?" Inspector Buchanan said as she followed me directly inside.

"I'll explain it to you later," I said as I started removing things from the desk, including the paper I'd spread over the top of it. "Come in, everyone. Edwin, help me."

He made his way around everyone else to join me. The space was too small for three people, let alone eleven, but we crowded in.

"First of all, is there a maker's mark anywhere on this desk?" I asked Edwin.

"Aye, I've seen one," he said as he walked to one side and crouched. "Right here."

I crouched too. A tree with an E underneath. It looked just like the mark on one of the desks at Dina's.

I looked at her as she put her hand to her mouth.

I looked back at Edwin. "Do you know where any secret compartment might be?"

"False drawers? Backs? I don't know," Edwin said. "Let's look."

There were five drawers on the desk. Once by one, Edwin and I pulled them out and looked at each one closely. Then we passed them around for everyone else to look at too. Inspector Winters and I shared a glance as we both noticed that our suspect guests were particularly focused on the task, but I went back to the desk with Edwin.

There were no false fronts, no false backs, nothing that seemed like a secret hidey-hole.

"May I see the maker's mark?" Dina asked.

"Sure," I said as I moved to the side.

Inspector Buchanan stayed right next to her as she inspected. Dina looked at the mark and nodded at Mikey.

"This is the desk you wanted?" I said to Dina. "You and

Mikey were willing to ruin the bookshop just so you could have it."

"They didn't know what else to do," Mary said. "They tried to figure out a way to break in. They knew they couldn't just talk to Edwin. They didn't know what to do."

"Mary," Mikey said.

"Don't . . ," she said to him. "Henry changed his mind. He knew better."

Mikey shook his head, but no one admitted to murder. Yet.

We continued searching but to no avail. A thread of disappointment mixed with panic inside my gut. My plan was falling apart.

But someone else didn't think so.

You're too focused on where you've been to pay attention to where you're going.

I laughed. It was Mary. But not any of the Marys we'd become acquainted with lately. It was Mary Poppins. Close enough.

"What?" Tom said.

"We've got to turn it over! I mean, we need to be really, really careful, but we have to turn it upside down. See it from another angle."

Three people had to leave the room—Rosie, Hamlet, and Lyle—to open the space enough to turn the desk as gently as we needed to turn it. Tom, Edwin, and I managed it quickly though and the three who'd left returned.

At first glance, there was nothing unusual about the bottom of the desk. It looked like the bottom of any desk, except maybe this one was made with real wood. Hamlet started knocking on the bottom—the areas where there were drawer spaces on the other side as well as the area where there was just desk.

And suddenly, something sounded different.

"Wait! What was that?" I asked.

Hamlet knocked again. "Aye, it sounds as if there's something missing there."

I tried to look at the piece he was knocking on from different angles. "Do we have to cut it open to get inside?"

"We can't do that," Inspector Winters said. "It's too valuable."

"I'll do it," Edwin said. "I'll need a knife or something."

A second later, I handed him a letter open, one with a pearl handle that I'd found on a shelf.

Edwin placed the blade of the letter opener into a seam.

He looked up at the rest of us. "Here we go."

He pried the wood—once, twice, and then three times. And on the third and most exuberant try, it sprang free. Well, a piece of it came off easily, hopefully intact, but none of us double-checked right away.

We were too interested in what was there. There was a secret space where secret things not only could be hidden, but had been.

Parchment with writing.

"Nobody touch it," I said as I reached for some gloves.

Maybe it should have fallen apart, crumbled to dust. But it didn't, it hadn't. With tweezers and my gloved hands, I pulled out a single sheet of parchment and took it to the worktable, where I unfolded it and we all stared.

The parchment might have stayed together, but the ink had faded. There was still some of it there, but it was difficult to read. I would need to use a special light as well as take other precautions to save it, but for now, we all looked closely at the final few words that had been written on the page and were still legible.

We shall be queens together. Elizabeth.

Mary cried out once and then turned to Mikey. "Did you kill Henry for this?"

"No!"

"He did!" Dina said. "He killed Henry for this letter, this bookshop. Our future."

"I didn't!" Mikey exclaimed as both he and Dina were being handcuffed by the inspectors.

"It wasn't ever about the coins, was it?" I asked.

Mikey and Dina wouldn't look at me.

"I can't believe this!" Mary said.

But I wasn't sure what she couldn't believe. Was she overcome by the letter, surprised about the coins, did she still think Mikey killed Henry?

Both inspectors were informing their suspects that they were being arrested for the murder of Henry Stewart.

I looked at Mikey. "The thing is, if you'd just talked to Edwin, he would have worked with you in searching for this. You killed Henry and you didn't have to."

Mikey looked at me with a long, evil glare. He finally said, "I didn't kill Henry."

"Yes, you did!" Dina exclaimed.

"No, I didn't." He looked at his wife. "You did, and I have the proof."

Dina's glare at her husband was even more evil than Mikey's. We all waited, hoping one of them would say more, keep spilling the beans. Even the inspectors seemed to pause a beat. The suspects had been read their rights. Was there more they wanted to share?

But there wasn't. Mikey stopped talking and Dina stopped speaking real words; strange mewling sounds came around some tears, but no more words came.

The inspectors, with Rosie leading the way, took the suspects away.

My plan had worked. I wasn't sure how it was going to play out, but I knew that if we'd found a letter, the strange obsessions these people had would take over, and the killer would somehow be uncovered. I was glad it had worked. At least we knew the killer was one of the Woosters. I had faith the police would sort it out from there.

I was really glad that Mary wasn't a killer. I liked her. Lyle wasn't a killer either. I couldn't envision him and Mary becoming a couple, but who knew. Hamlet escorted them out of the bookshop, and soon it was only Tom, Edwin, and me.

As Tom and Edwin looked at the letter and pondered its validity, I became lost in something else. I didn't know yet if the note had anything to do with Mary, Queen of Scots. I might never know because I might not be able to save the letter completely. But I knew one thing without a doubt—the woman I'd recently met, the one who'd just left with Hamlet, the one who claimed she was once a martyred queen of Scotland, had spoken the same words I'd just read to me as she and I had visited the Edinburgh Castle.

We shall be queens together.

Maybe that was proof enough.

THIRTY-SIX

I held the paper on my lap and read aloud to Tom:

Edinburgh resident Dina Wooster has been arrested for the murder of her uncle, Henry Stewart. A city councilman, Stewart had been working with his niece and her husband, fellow councilman Mikey Wooster, attempting to steal a priceless letter hidden inside a desk at a Grassmarket bookshop, The Cracked Spine. When their efforts to take the letter were unsuccessful, they planned to use government procedures to shut down the bookshop so they might attempt to take possession of its full inventory. Their plan went awry when Mr. Stewart told his niece that he was not going to follow through with their nefarious activities. In a fit of rage, Ms. Wooster attached an explosive device to Mr. Stewart's automobile, using instructions on the internet to build the bomb. He was killed in the explosion; there were no other casualties. Ms. Wooster had hoped to prevent Mr. Stewart from reversing the decision to vote on the bookshop's demise. As it happened, the bookshop was saved by none other than the Queen of England herself.

Full story to be printed in this weekend's special edition, "When Queens Collide," by Brigid McBride.

"She's a good writer," I said. "I can't wait to read this weekend's version."

Tom sat next to me on the couch and kept a doubtful expression on his face. "She's not bad."

I laughed. "I'm not that insecure. You may fully admit that she's good at her job."

Tom smiled. "So, what now, my bride? Now that you've solved another murder."

"It just all came together."

Tom laughed. "Aye, with your help."

"Well . . ."

"That was one of the craziest things I've ever seen. I'm sad about the murder, but you are one adventure after another, Delaney."

"I still can't believe it." I laughed. "The real Queen!"

"Aye." Tom shook his head. "How about the other queen? Do you think you and Mary will be friends?"

"Well, we've been invited to another dinner. Eloise and Gretchen are hosting. Along with voting in favor of keeping the bookshop open, the council is no longer pushing for the revival of the Burgess Tickets. Gretchen is relieved and thankful. It's a celebratory dinner, but also something to honor Henry. Mary should be there too. Tomorrow night? Are you available?"

"I am."

"There will be more details in the article, but Brigid told me that Dina decided to use an explosive because that's how Mary, Queen of Scots' second husband was killed. She thought it would throw the police off track, make them think Mary was having an affair. No one would guess that Dina Wooster would attach an explosive to a car. Bridgid also learned that Dina had forgotten about the coins until I mentioned them. They weren't nearly as important as the letter."

"She's wicked."

"And we fell for it a little. I mean, the affair idea seemed feasible to me, until it didn't. Inspector Buchanan said she never considered it, but maybe she's just saying that."

Mikey had done a good job preserving evidence. He thought his wife would try to throw him under the bus if it came down to it. Dina's fingerprints were on the bomb-making materials still at their house. Her fingerprints only. When he told the police what he'd saved, Dina cracked and said she should have killed him too.

Tom said, "Mikey got lucky."

"I think he was trying to protect her but, in the end, he just couldn't any longer. He was smart to save the evidence, but he should have spoken up sooner. He's in some trouble."

"Any word on the letter?" Tom asked.

Reluctantly, and after the Scottish authorities had become involved, I had to hand over the letter.

It was going to be a *very* big deal. And I had an in with the person who would be in charge of transcribing and preserving it. Joshua had been chosen to do the job. He'd already told me I'd get to be the first one to read his transcription. I couldn't wait. I'd take Mary with me, but I hadn't told her that yet.

"Joshua will let me know the second it's ready. Maybe the second before." I smiled.

Tom's phone rang and I watched as he seemed pleased by what the caller was telling him.

"Aye, that's wonderful. All right. We'll be there." He disconnected the call.

"What?" I asked.

"The house is ready, love. The electrical is fixed. It's ready to move into. What about you? I don't want to rush you, but are you ready?"

I looked around my wonderful cottage and at my wonderful husband. Elias, Aggie, and I were going to be friends, family, forever. But it was time. There was a blue cottage by the sea waiting for Tom and me and our life together.

"I'm so ready," I said.

It was time for our next chapter.

ACKNOWLEDGMENTS

As always, thank you to my agent Jessica Faust, editor Hannah Braaten, assistant editor Nettie Finn, and everyone at Minotaur. It's so cool that you all aren't tired of me yet. An extra shout-out to cover designer, Mary Ann Lasher. I love this cover so much! Thank you. As I was finishing up this book, a box of letters written by Mary, Queen of Scots, was found in a museum storage facility in Scotland. Since Mary plays a role in this story, I couldn't help but feel the timing was somehow fortuitous. I love it when stuff like that happens. If you're interested in reading the real letters, the Smithsonian Mag online has a great article on it.

As far as I know, the Robert Burns's Burgess Ticket is real, but not housed in the Writers' Museum. It would be a good place to put it though.

Mary, Queen of Scots, is a completely fascinating historical figure. I loved researching her life. In fact, I ended up reading much more about her than I would ever use in this book. If you have interest in knowing more about the martyred queen, I fully recommend you begin with *Queen of Scots: The True*

Life of Mary Stuart, by John Guy. It was captivating, and is on my reread list.

Any mistakes regarding Edinburgh government are not only mine, but purposeful for the benefit of the story. Apologies.

Thanks always to Charlie and Tyler. Love you both so much.

June -- 2020